LOVE KILLS

A REDCLIFFE NOVEL

First Published in Great Britain 2012 by Mirador Publishing

Copyright © 2012 by Catherine Green

All right reserved. No part of this publication may be reproduced or transmitted, in any form or by any means, without permission of the publishers or author. Excepting brief quotes used in reviews.

First edition: 2012

Any reference to real names and places are purely fictional and are constructs of the author. Any offence the references produce is unintentional and in no way reflect the reality of any locations or people involved.

A copy of this work is available though the British Library.

ISBN: 978-1-908200-78-5

Mirador Publishing
Mirador
Wearne Lane
Langport
Somerset
TA10 9HB

Love Kills

By

Catherine Green

C Green

MIRADOR PUBLISHING
www.miradorpublishing.com

To my Mum, Karen.
Thank you for all those childhood visits to the library!

www.catherinegreencrafts.moonfruit.com

1

I was running through the forest on the outskirts of the Cornish town of Redcliffe. It was evening and the sky was growing dark with that smooth, silky blackness that descends gradually as night progresses. There was an eerie feel to my surroundings, where tall trees shadowed me with their heavy green branches, but I saw only light and colour. The air was clear and fresh, late summer, and I paused and breathed in the delicious scents of plant life and nature. Here, deep in the forest, I could still taste sea salt on my tongue, and I relished the sensation. It was beautiful, and I was blissfully happy.

My long, auburn hair hung loose around my shoulders, cascading down my back like a silk sheet. It brushed against my white skin, which appeared translucent in the strange light of dusk, where I was hidden beneath a rich, green canopy of trees. Dressed only in a summer vest top and denim shorts, I was warm and alive. My vision was sharp, and I saw every movement, and heard every sound with my youthful, alert body. Even my scars seemed to have healed, and I touched a hand to my neck, feeling only smooth, healthy skin where once it had been puckered and red after a werewolf attack. Smiling, I continued on my journey, feeling the power in my legs propelling me forward, excited about the prospect of seeing my lover again.

Suddenly a man burst through the trees into the clearing where I stood, making me jump with surprise. My fright quickly turned to welcome when I recognized my boyfriend Jack Mason standing before me. My gaze rose from the ground up, taking in the delicious definition of muscle that showed through the grey t-shirt he wore with black jeans. His skin was glowing with health, he was smiling, and his deep blue eyes were sparkling with a promise of delight and excitement. He stood for a moment as I stared at him, and he ruffled a hand through his short dark hair in a gesture that melted my heart. As he strode towards me I stood still, waiting for his embrace. He put a hand on the back of my head, drawing me close, and touched his soft lips to mine.

The kiss started out gentle but quickly escalated and I knew this wasn't Jack; it was his identical twin brother Danny. I pulled away, gasping.

"Danny, what are you doing?" I said breathlessly, my heart pounding, "We can't do this!"

He laughed and spoke in a low, deep voice, with a hint of growl betraying his werewolf lineage. The sound rumbled through my body, setting off shivers of excitement that I tried to suppress.

"You know Jack will not mind, Jessica." he said, "After all that we have been through I am sure you understand."

He advanced upon me again but now I backed away, shivering at the delightful menace in his voice. I was both frightened and excited, and my body was unsure of how to react.

"Danny, we cannot do this." I said firmly, "I can't cheat on Jack with his own brother. It's not right."

I started to walk past Danny, back out of the darkening woods towards his house, remembering that I was staying with the brothers tonight. Jack would be waiting for me, wondering what took me so long. For a fleeting moment I wondered why I had chosen to walk through the forest on my way back from work. Usually I would follow the main roads and footpaths, or even drive if I was feeling tired.

Danny suddenly grabbed me and pushed me against a large tree trunk, pinning me with his body, leaning in for another kiss. My body reacted to him with a mixture of fear and excitement. He was so much stronger than me. I could not refuse him. I didn't want to refuse him. I wanted him so badly, and it was only my own sense of right and wrong that held me back. But the fear won over and I struggled.

"Danny, please," I gasped, writhing beneath him, "Leave me alone, stop doing this!"

He just laughed and moved his hands over my body, intensifying the shivers of excitement and desire that shot through me. His voice was husky, deep and sensual, with an Irish lilt that sent thrills down my spine.

"I know you want this, Jessica," he growled, "I can give you life and heat where my brother cannot. Just relax, enjoy it. I will show you great pleasure."

I closed my eyes in anticipation as he moved closer to me, while the voice in my head screamed at me not to do this, that it was wrong, that I could not hurt Jack in this way.

I woke with a start, sitting straight up in bed. There was a man asleep beside me and for one terrifying moment I thought it was Danny, and I stifled a gasp. But of course it was Jack; my boyfriend, my lover. He was lying on his front with his head turned away from me. The duvet had moved down his body when I sat up, and I saw that he was naked as usual. I had already been asleep when he came home. Jack was working late on a police case, and I guessed there had been some physical action, because now he was literally dead to the world. As a vampire he should have woken the second I sat up, but he was obviously drained and in need of rest. In fact his skin looked deathly pale in the moonlight that shone round the edge of the curtains. Usually Jack's skin was tanned like his brother because he used magical abilities to blend in with humans. Now he was white and wasn't breathing, which told me he had lost blood somehow and would need to feed when he woke. I was struck by the importance of his trust in me, that he could willingly fall asleep next to me, knowing that I was a human who knew his secret. I could quite easily stake him through the heart and put an end to his existence. Well obviously I couldn't because I'm not a murderer, but the fact remained that Jack was vulnerable in this state.

Breathing deeply in and out, a hand on my stomach in a comforting gesture, I thought about my latest crazy vision. Why was I dreaming about Danny? Well that's a long story, but not really a mystery. Danny is Jack's identical twin brother and I met both men several months ago. I met Jack first, while Danny was finishing a police investigation in Scotland. When Danny returned home to Redcliffe he made no secret of his attraction to me, but he had to play human for my benefit. Everything changed about a month ago, when I discovered the truth about my boyfriend and his brother. I almost died after being attacked by a werewolf who was trying to kill Danny. This werewolf wanted control of Danny's pack, and he used me as a hostage after realizing the depth of Danny's feelings for me.

The strange thing is that Jack is actually a vampire, while Danny is the werewolf. I was still learning all of their history, but basically two separate monsters attacked the brothers, at around the same time during the First World War. They survived their attacks and became very strong metaphysical creatures as a result of their genetic bond, blood sharing rituals that they attempted, and their individual abilities. I was still adjusting to the fact that such creatures could actually exist in modern society, but I think I was getting the hang of it.

I let out another deep, soothing breath, and raked a hand through my auburn hair, tossing it back over my shoulder and enjoying the comforting weight of it down my back. Looking round the darkened bedroom, I smiled. Everything was normal. It was just a dream. I lay back down in bed, my heart still racing from the intensity of my dream. The room was warm since it was summer, and we didn't really need the duvet. I was using it more as a comforter, something familiar to snuggle into. We were staying at my house tonight, and I had finally given Jack his own key. After I almost died, Jack had saved me with his blood, and now that I was still recovering from my injuries, it seemed silly not to give him a key really. After all, I couldn't leave him now. I was in too deep.

Thinking about my injuries sent a twinge of pain through the right side of my neck. That was where Seamus Tully had tried to tear my throat out. The doctors thought I had been stabbed, and that was my official story to all of the humans who weren't personally involved. I couldn't betray the secret of the Redcliffe werewolf pack, and besides, how could I even begin to tell my human doctors that fictional creatures actually exist in our world? They would have admitted me to a psychiatric hospital. I could still barely believe it myself.

I had been bitten, and it was only because Jack had fed me his vampire blood while I was dying that I hadn't turned into a werewolf. Well, that and the fact that apparently I was a witch. This was another revelation that had happened in recent months. I was an orphan who had been raised by foster parents from the age of six. Just before I met Jack, my mother had appeared in my dreams, and she had warned me about my new friends. She had also told me that she was a witch, and that subsequently I was, but that my powers had lain dormant all these years because there had been no one to guide me, and no need for me to use them. Of course I thought I was going crazy. But gradually as my life descended into chaos with vampires and werewolves appearing everywhere, it actually began to seem like a good thing. At least I wasn't completely helpless amongst all of these supernatural creatures. Actually, it seemed that I belonged with them but I was still learning, and I wasn't ready to give up my life as a human yet.

Anyway, my mother had appeared in several dreams and had given the proof I needed that she was real and not just a figment of my imagination. She uses some form of metaphysical energy to communicate with me, and now that I am healing from my injuries she is slowly starting to reappear in my dreams. Actually when I have a night of sleep without dreaming it seems strange. But this dream, with Danny and me almost having sex together, was new, and it frightened me. Knowing that my dreams often reflect a version of reality, I couldn't be sure that Danny wasn't already aware, or that he hadn't engineered it in some way. He had already made it clear to me about his feelings, and Jack also knew. After I discovered their secret Danny seemed to think he shouldn't hold back, and was bombarding me with non-human actions and behaviours. I was doing my best to adjust and get used to these strange creatures that just happened to be my friends.

I was tired, it was very early in the morning, and I needed to go back to sleep. I could think about what this dream meant during the day. I carefully turned my head enough to see the bedside clock, careful not to stretch the thick scar on my neck. It felt like a collar, almost choking me sometimes, but it was healing and I was getting used to it. The deep emotional scars would take longer to soothe, but I hadn't the energy to focus on those right now. The time was 03:24. I didn't need to get up for work until 07:30. So I could go back to sleep. But it was never that easy. My body was tired, but my mind had woken up.

Jack never stirred, and I could vaguely see that his clothes were strewn across the floor near the bedroom door. I wondered if he carried a gun tonight. I would be careful not to move his clothes if I was up before him. The last thing I wanted was another vampire attack. The first time I discovered Jack's gun hidden in his pocket he leaped out of bed and almost strangled me before he came to his senses. I shivered violently at the memory, and a wave of nausea washed over me. Breathing deeply once again, I forced the panic out of my mind. My body slowly calmed down again.

I looked at Jack where he lay beside me. He was perfectly still since his heart didn't beat. Apparently when I thought he was human he had simulated it beating for my benefit. Now he didn't need to waste his energy. His skin was cold to the touch, and he was pale. I could see a faint translucent glow to his skin in the darkness. My bedroom wasn't completely dark because there were streetlights out at the back of my terrace, and they sent an orange glow around the edges of my curtains. I tentatively reached out, and touched his cold skin with my fingertips. I imagined he felt like marble, although I had never really been close to a sculpture of that kind before. Jack was just so beautiful that he had to resemble something of mythical splendor. Suddenly I felt a wave of tiredness wash over me, and I welcomed it. I fell back to sleep, dreamless this time, and I didn't wake until my alarm went off later that morning.

2

The day passed slowly and without any drama. It was my first day back at work properly after the 'incident' as I had decided to refer to it. My best friend and business partner Elizabeth Gormond kept an anxious watch over me all day, and barely allowed me to leave the safety of the desk. She wouldn't let me move any stock around for fear of aggravating my injuries, even though I assured her I was healing well and she needn't fuss. Besides, she was almost nine months' pregnant and she needed more rest than me. It was a strange sort of day; very flat after all the excitement I had experienced. I did some paperwork to pass time, and watched anxiously as Liz insisted on carrying books around the shop, distributing them to the appropriate shelves. She had spent two days in hospital when she was twenty-two weeks pregnant, and I did not want her to aggravate her situation any more. But she was as stubborn as me, maybe more so, and she refused to listen to my tentative protests.

I idly watched her moving slowly around the square space that was our shop. It was a good size, really, and we had dropped on well with the sale. There were two windows at the front with a door between, which led out into the cobbled main high street of Redcliffe. At the end of the street was the promenade, and beyond that the beach and ocean. There was a constant smell of sea salt inside, and we both thrived on it. Returning my gaze to Liz, I watched her manoeuvre carefully round the central table where we exhibited our special offers. Her short, black hair was cut in a pixie style and was neatly styled and glossy with good health. Her plump features had grown only slightly rounder with the addition of her baby, but her stomach was rather large now, and she had a hand across the bump in a protective gesture. She was surveying one of the floor-to-ceiling pine bookshelves that covered three walls of our shop.

"Liz," I said.

Love Kills

She turned her head, smiling distractedly.

"Yes?" she replied.

I looked pointedly at my watch.

"Come on, I think it's time for some food." I said.

Liz and me shared lunch together, which consisted of our favourite cheese ploughman's sandwiches purchased from the café two doors away, washed down with a large mocha for me, and a decaffeinated coffee for Liz. We made plans for Liz's maternity leave. We had a couple of students who worked for us when their schedules allowed, and besides, once summer was over the shop would be quieter anyway, so I should be able to manage it alone. Jack had even offered to help, saying that he was owed some time off from work and might as well take advantage of it. Somehow I couldn't envision him working in a boring little bookshop when he was used to such an active and dramatic lifestyle as a supernatural police detective. In truth I didn't want him working at such close quarters. I needed some space and time to myself again. I had always been a solitary person, only socializing with Liz and her husband, and my other close friend Simon Bunce. Having so many people around me recently made me feel claustrophobic and even a little anxious.

Liz still worried about me despite our discussion, but it was now starting to get a little annoying. Finally, I lashed out in exasperation.

"Liz, please, I'm fine now," I said tersely, "I am healed, all I have is scars. You need to rest. This baby is the important thing and you know that. If I need any help with the shop there are plenty of people I can ask."

Shocked into silence, Liz's face fell, and I felt a rush of remorse at upsetting my best friend. But then she smiled and laughed.

"Sorry Jess," she said, "You can't blame me for worrying when you nearly died a month ago." She took a deep, exaggerated breath, "Alright, fine, you win. If you say you are healed then I believe you."

We relaxed back into general conversation, and were eventually distracted by a string of customers who gave a welcome break to the fairly dull day. Some were local people who had heard about my accident, and who came to express concern and delight that I was healing so well. It felt nice to see that people cared, even if I didn't know them very well personally. I laughed and chatted, listening to their tales of life in Redcliffe. We heard about a recent engagement between a woman who worked in the hairdressing salon we used, and her long-term boyfriend who was a chef. There was a scandal between a local doctor and his receptionist, to which Liz and I expressed our disgust at his actions towards his wife and family. In truth I wasn't really listening to their stories. Liz was the people person. I was usually in a dream world, although now I began to wonder about its true reality.

Later in the afternoon my mind wandered back to the dream I had about Danny. I felt embarrassed, and was convinced that he and Jack knew about it somehow. I still didn't know the extent of their abilities, and had to believe that it was private, at least for now. But what was I going to do about Danny? It wasn't just that I knew he was attracted to me. I felt the same for him, how could I not? He was after all an identical twin for Jack, the man who I was in love with. And both men had been there for me when I needed them. Admittedly it was their fault I had ended up in that situation, but I reasoned that something had led us all to our destinations. It was some form of fate or karma, I was sure.

Then I was assaulted by another guilty secret. My heart leaped into my throat when the shop door opened and Marcus Scott walked in, smiling politely as he approached the counter.

"Good afternoon Jessica, Elizabeth," he said warmly, nodding to each of us in turn, "How are you both today?"

My throat was suddenly dry and I coughed before answering.

"Marcus," I said in surprise, "what are you doing here? I mean, hi!"

He laughed, and I caught Elizabeth's suspicious glance. She said a polite 'hello' to Marcus, but she wasn't sure about him. He was an old friend of Jack and Danny's, and a vampire. On our first meeting he had attempted to seduce me with the intention of drinking my blood, but I had been slightly drunk and thought he was trying to rape me. When I told Liz she had wanted me to have him arrested, but in my confusion at the time Danny had talked me out of it. Liz didn't know anything about the vampires or werewolves, and I could never tell her because it would put her in danger. She was surprised that I had apparently changed my mind about Marcus, but she was still wary of him.

Love Kills

The reason I had changed my mind and my attitude was that Marcus had saved me from Jack when he almost attacked me in a vampiric rage. Jack had been badly beaten and had simply seen me as food, and Marcus had appeared on the scene to stop him and bring him to his senses. It had been Marcus who told me the truth about what they were, and he had offered comfort and support when my world fell apart. One thing led to another, and somehow I had ended up in bed with him, cheating on Jack, and the memories came flooding back. Jack insisted that it didn't bother him, because vampires weren't so uptight about sex. But it bothered me. I was supposed to be faithful and a good person, not someone who could sleep around.

I stood up, asking Marcus again what he wanted. He was dressed in his customary black pinstripe business suit, very expensive and tailor-made. His short blond hair was neatly styled with gel, and his blue eyes sparkled in a face that was young and mischievous, yet showed intelligence beyond his years. Or so it seemed. Although Marcus appeared to the world as a young man in his early twenties, he was in fact older than Jack and Danny. He spoke to me now in a quiet, pleasant voice.

"I simply came by to see how you were managing your first day back at work, Jessica," he said in a polite Southern accent, "And there is a particular title I would like to order please." I think Marcus was originally from Hampshire, but he hadn't yet told me his history.

Another shared interest for Marcus and me was our love of reading. He had an extensive personal library at his large home on the outskirts of Redcliffe, and he had invited me to enjoy it whenever I liked. So far I hadn't had the courage or the energy to return to his house, since that was where all the revelations took place the night Jack and Danny almost died. But I had glimpsed the library through an open door and it was in the back of my mind now. Perhaps I could go there, borrow some books, maybe speak to Marcus about the vampires and werewolves. I knew he would tell me what I needed to know. The question was whether I could behave normally around him, and quash my schoolgirl reaction to his attentions.

We spent some time in polite conversation, and I placed the order for Marcus while Liz busied herself in the stock room. Marcus knew that she disliked him but he pretended not to notice, understanding that she only remembered our first meeting and that she was just being protective for her friend. I had asked him not to interfere and he respected that. Marcus also asked if I had returned to the Ship recently. That was my local pub, owned by Danny and managed by Simon Bunce. I had received one hell of a shock to find out that Simon was also a werewolf and second-in-command to Danny's pack. It had been in the cellars beneath the pub, in the wolves' lair, where I had almost died from my injuries.

When I said that I had avoided the pub, Marcus nodded.

"Perhaps you should return there, Jessica," he said, "It is after all your local haunt. Surely Elizabeth will become suspicious soon?"

I nodded and sighed, my shoulders heaving with the effort.

"I know, I know. I can't avoid it," I said, "But it all still feels so strange, Marcus. I mean Simon kept that secret from me for three years! And now the place just won't feel the same."

Marcus nodded.

"Well if you wish to attempt a return, I will accompany you if it helps." he said.

I knew he meant well but I still felt awkward. He was so damned attractive still, and my body kept instinctively tensing up around him. I was relieved when he left. When did sex become such an issue? It must be something to do with the supernatural element of these men. And I suppose the fact that they are all incredibly handsome anyway just adds to it. Maybe it was just me. Maybe I am really some wanton, sex-obsessed female who needed an excuse to be promiscuous. I sat behind the counter deep in thought as Elizabeth walked in carrying two mugs of coffee and a packet of biscuits. She had finished her tidying in the stock room and had been in my kitchen at the back of the building waiting for Marcus to leave.

"I really don't like that man, Jessica," she said with a shiver, "There's something creepy about him."

I looked up sharply. She knew! Liz must know that something was different. Her own husband even knew about the vampires and werewolves; it was only a matter of time before Liz found out.

"What do you mean, creepy?" I asked tentatively.

Liz laughed.

"Oh, you know, he's weird Jess," she said lightly, "I'm still not convinced about what happened that night at the Ship when he attacked you, no matter what you say." She shrugged and sighed, "I just don't like him, sorry. It's an instinct, and you know I always trust my instincts."

Phew! She didn't suspect anything. I was being paranoid. I stared at her clear, brown eyes and smiled.

"He is a little strange, yes, but I think he's just misunderstood, Liz." I said slowly, "He was very supportive after my attack, and he has become my friend over the last few weeks."

"Fair enough," she replied, "But I still don't like him and that's all I can say."

With that she dunked a biscuit in her coffee and nibbled at it, a hand on her belly and her eyes watching the ripples as her baby kicked and rolled. I followed her gaze and my heart lifted. This baby was going to be such a breath of fresh air for us all.

"Are you nervous about the birth now, Liz?" I asked after a short silence.

"No." She replied, "I have to go through it in order to bring our child into the world, and that's all there is to it. It will be fine."

Her practical attitude was just so normal that my heart warmed, and for the next hour or so I managed not to think about all of the scary creatures I was living with. I was simply a normal human being with a wonderful best friend.

3

That night I decided to stay home again. The dream was still haunting me, and I worried that if I stayed at Jack's house something might happen. Not that I would actually sleep with Danny, but that I would embarrass myself somehow with him. Since I discovered the truth I felt like an awkward teenager, and that made me angry and irritable. I considered visiting Simon at the Ship, but the minute I turned my attention to the pub all I saw was the black corridor of the wolves' lair and the horrors that lay beyond. My body became weak, feverish, and I felt dizzy just thinking about what had happened. The doctors had offered me counselling for the trauma my body received. It would have been ideal if I could talk about the supernatural creatures. But since I couldn't talk to humans about my experiences, it was pointless. Jack suggested I see a non-human counsellor. The thought filled me with dread. I just couldn't trust anyone that I didn't personally know at the moment. I was struggling to trust the ones I did know.

Instead I soaked in the bath and tried to relax, enjoying some time alone. I had phoned Jack during the afternoon and told him not to hurry home after work. He would be here soon enough, and maybe we could snuggle on the sofa together and watch TV like a normal couple. I hadn't eaten anything for my dinner but my stomach didn't feel empty. My appetite had been greatly reduced over recent weeks and Liz was getting worried. She said it was a symptom of post-traumatic stress, but she didn't try to persuade me to get help for fear of upsetting me further. I hated deceiving her to the point where she was treading on eggshells in my presence, but I felt helpless for any other action. As long as she was safe I would find a way to deal with our now altered friendship.

I sighed, closed my eyes, and sank lower in the lavender scented bath water. Bubbles tickled my nose and I scrunched my face up but didn't bother to move. The water was soothing and warm, easing my tense muscles and lapping around my scars. The healed wounds protested only slightly, sending faint shooting pains up my neck. I knew it was largely psychological and did my best to ignore it. I listened to the soft music playing on my stereo. It was a relaxation CD I had found in a local holistic health shop, and I had bought it with the intention of calming my turbulent mind. It was helping, and I drifted aimlessly to the tune of panpipes and rolling waves on a soft beach.

As my mind wandered, I felt a surge of panic as I remembered the crashing, stormy waves of the sea the night my life fell apart. I remembered running along the cliff top, trying to escape from the monsters that pursued me. Marcus had caught me as I collapsed in shock. He had taken me back to his house, cared for me, soothed me. I choked back tears that suddenly stung my eyes. This was stupid. It was time to move on, and this bath was supposed to be relaxing. Forcing all the bad and confusing memories from my head, I topped up the hot water and sank back into the bubbles, stretching out my limbs and sighing heavily, expelling all negative thoughts.

After a few minutes I shifted in the water, pulling myself more upright, and I opened my eyes to find the sponge. There was a man crouched beside the bath watching me with adoration in his bright blue eyes, and I screamed and jumped, crying out in shock and scrabbling for the bath handles.

"Jesus Christ, Jack you scared the life out of me!" I shouted, frantically finding a hold on the bath handles, coughing and spluttering as water splashed into my face and mouth.

Water slopped over the side of the tub, and Jack was on his feet bending over the bath to support me. I pushed his hands away and struggled to stand up, anger flooding through me.

"What the hell were you doing?" I shouted, shivering violently as my skin felt the cool air against wetness, "Why didn't you call to me?"

He lowered his eyes and ducked his head, stepping back and offering me a towel as I climbed out onto the bath mat.

"I am sorry, Jessica," he said, "I heard you in here, and you looked so peaceful I didn't want to disturb you." He looked down, and then back up, fixing me with his intense, hypnotic stare, "It will not happen again."

I was still bristling with shock but the anger was fading fast, and I spoke in a more gentle tone of voice.

"I'm glad you still find me attractive, but please warn me next time, Jack." I said reproachfully, "I nearly had a heart attack."

He stepped out of the bathroom while I dried my body, and when I walked into my bedroom a few minutes later he was sitting on the bed waiting. At first I didn't speak as I combed out my hair and applied moisturising lotion to my body. Jack simply sat still, watching. I turned my head a couple of times to check he was still there. This eerie stillness was very unnerving, but apparently it was a natural behaviour for vampires. I was trying to get used to it. Eventually I spoke.

"How was your day?" I asked.

"Uneventful," Jack replied, "I spent most of the day doing paperwork in the office."

"Oh," I said, "It must be strange to be quiet after everything that happened."

For the past four years Jack and Danny had been working undercover as gang members for werewolf mafia boss Seamus Tully in Scotland. They had finally closed down the operation when they killed the gang lord, and apparently all remaining members were now either under arrest or on the run. Jack and Danny didn't seem concerned about the ones that had escaped the law. They were confident that they would capture these criminals in time. I was still nervous, worrying that they might find us and take revenge on the death of their master. All I could do for now was trust that the Mason brothers were handling the situation.

"It is rather strange, yes," Jack agreed, still sitting like a statue.

I pulled on a pale pink vest and matching shorts, along with a soft blue cable knit cardigan, and motioned toward the door.

"Shall we go watch TV in the living room?" I asked.

He nodded, slid to the floor in a smooth, unnatural motion, and followed me from the room. I collected a drink and some snacks from the kitchen while Jack waited in the living room. We sat snuggled on the sofa as I had envisioned, and eventually retired to bed after a very quiet and boring evening.

4

I was lying on Redcliffe beach, listening to the gentle rolling of the waves. It was early evening, I could tell by the slight wind and the cooler temperature. The sun was low in the sky, and I felt the warmth of the sand beneath my body. A man was lying beside me, and I welcomed his embrace as he leaned over to kiss me. The kiss felt strange, different, and I realised with a shock that it was Danny. I sat bolt upright, pushing him away, and opened my eyes.

The bedroom was in darkness, and I panicked as I looked at the man sleeping next to me. It was Jack. Of course it was Jack, this was my bedroom at home, Danny had never been here. I closed my eyes and breathed in and out slowly and deeply. This was really starting to annoy me now. How could I stop these crazy dreams? They were so vivid, that was the worst part. It was like an altered state of reality, and I was angry with myself for fantasizing about my boyfriend's brother. Jack stirred and sat up beside me.

"Jessica, are you well?" he asked.

"I'm fine," I replied, still breathing deeply, "Sorry, Jack, I just had a weird dream."

"You are burning up," he said with concern, touching my forehead, "Are you sure it is not your wounds?"

I looked down at my bare stomach, glimpsing the angry red scars of Seamus Tully's claw marks where my vest had ridden up, and then I put a hand to the thick scar tissue on my neck. Nope, it was definitely not the wounds. They had healed remarkably well in a short time with a little help from some vampire blood. When I was on the brink of death right after Seamus attacked me, Jack had given me his blood to try and save me. It worked, but now I was worried that I wasn't completely human myself, even though Jack assured me it would have left my system by now.

"My wounds are fine, Jack," I said, "You know that."

He was silent for a moment and I knew he was thinking of a

response. I lay back down in bed. Jack lay beside me, pulling the duvet up over my body and gently stroking my cheek with his fingertips. I sighed and closed my eyes, enjoying his caress.

"There is something troubling you, Jessica," he whispered, "Please allow me to help you."

I felt a lump in my throat and tears sprang to my eyes. No, I would not be weak again. This was ridiculous. I fought to hide my emotion but it was too late. Jack slowly leaned forward and kissed my face.

"You are not weak to feel emotion, Jessica," he murmured, "It is a part of being human. Please allow me to help you."

The tears poured down my cheeks now, and I cried out in anguish and frustration. I jumped out of bed, throwing the duvet off, and I charged out of the bedroom, downstairs into the kitchen. The air felt cool against my skin and I welcomed it. It woke me up, helped me to chase away the tears and this stupid helpless need for support.

I switched the kitchen light on, grabbed a glass from the drainer, and turned the cold-water tap on forcefully, jumping back as water splashed up onto my bare skin. The tile floor was cold beneath my feet, and at first I focused on the sensation, until the cold seeped into my bones. I saw a pair of flip flops near the back door, and put them on, then picked up my hooded sweater from the back of a kitchen chair, and slipped it on over my shivering body. That was better.

"Jessica, please, I want to help you," Jack said from the stairwell where he stood in shadow, "You are not weak. Please talk to me."

Carrying my glass over to the table, I gulped the cold water and put my glass down, then turned to him. He was naked, and his body seemed to glow in the darkness, tormenting and tempting me at the same time. This was not a man. This was a vampire. I am in love with a vampire. Because of him I was almost killed, and now I am scarred for life, both physically and mentally. Because of him my life will never be the same again, and yet still I can't leave him. And now, to top it off, I am having erotic dreams about his identical twin brother, a man who has made it clear he wants to sleep with me. What kind of a soap opera is my life right now?

I sat down abruptly, dropping my head into my hands,

Love Kills

resisting the urge to lay my head on the table. Rubbing my eyes, I turned my head to look at Jack.

"Jack, it's late, or early, whatever, and I need to sleep," I said moodily, "And I can't sleep, because I keep having these stupid, ridiculous dreams."

"What dreams?" Jack asked gently.

I swallowed, thinking about my words. I felt anger now, and frustration, but at least the tears were gone. I took a deep breath. If I didn't tell him he wouldn't leave me alone.

"I keep dreaming about Danny," I said, heart pounding.

To say it out loud was embarrassing, as though I were a teenager confessing to my father. And that thought alone was enough to send a jolt of fear through me. This man who I was in love with, he was over a hundred years old. My thoughts were a tangle of confusion, anger, and sheer helpless love for the vampire. I watched Jack's face for a reaction, but he concealed himself well and I could only glimpse patches of white skin in the shadows, and the glow of silvery-blue from his eyes.

"It does not surprise me," Jack said quietly.

"Did you know?" I asked.

"No, but I had my suspicions." he replied.

"So what do you think of it?" I asked. I didn't even know what to say. I drank some more water.

"I think that you are struggling with your own feelings." Jack said, "You are in love with me, yet you lust after my brother, and this confuses you."

I nodded, amazed at how calm he was. Did this bother him at all?

"You don't seem bothered, Jack," I said, "Why?"

He shrugged, still standing on the bottom stair, reluctant to walk into the bright electric light of the kitchen.

"It is not for me to feel anything." he said, "Danny has told you how he feels. Now it is your decision whether you change your relationship with him."

My heart lurched. I stared curiously at Jack, but his expression gave nothing away. It didn't matter to him if I had sex with his brother. But it mattered to me that I was even considering it, even if it was in my dreams.

"And that's it." I said, "You just leave me to it?"

He nodded but didn't speak.

"I could sleep with Danny, with your brother, and you wouldn't be angry?" I asked.

"I would not be angry with you." Jack replied.

"And you and I would still be together?" I asked again.

"Yes." he replied.

I shook my head, ruffling a hand through my hair, catching my fingers in knots. The sharp pains of protest were actually a comfort. My head hurt. I really needed to sleep. I stood up and walked towards the stairs, past Jack, and back up to my bedroom.

"I can't handle this," I said, "I need to sleep."

I threw the sweater on the floor, kicked off my flip-flops and climbed back into bed, lying on my side as Jack slowly slid into bed behind me. He didn't try to cuddle me, and he didn't speak. I had left the kitchen light switched on but I didn't have the energy to walk all the way back downstairs. I closed my eyes, let out a deep sigh, and tried to sleep again.

5

The next morning Liz found me sat at my kitchen table with a strong cup of coffee, and heavy eyes. She opened the back door and walked in, dropping her handbag onto a chair.

"Morning, Jess," she said, "Are you alright?"

I looked up and smiled.

"Morning," I replied, "Yes I'm fine thanks. I just had a weird dream and didn't sleep very well."

Liz sat down and picked up the mug of decaffeinated coffee that I had made for her. She reached for a piece of toast from the rack in the middle of the table, and smothered it with butter and jam.

"Jess, don't you think a bit of counselling would do you some good?" she asked tentatively, "I mean, you went through such trauma, and nothing like this has ever happened to you before."

I nodded and picked up another piece of toast for myself.

"I'm fine, Liz, honestly," I said warmly, "Don't worry about me. It was just a silly dream, it didn't mean anything."

"What was the dream about?" she asked.

What could I say? Liz would be horrified if I dared confess that I had feelings for Danny. As it was, if she ever found out I had slept with Marcus, she would be so angry and disappointed. She had very strong morals.

"Oh it was just about what happened," I said lightly, "I suppose I was reliving the events. But don't worry." I added hastily as I saw her expression.

Liz left it, knowing that I wasn't willing to share. She did admit that she felt a little strange today, and then I started worrying about her. She sat behind the counter for most of the morning, and gradually she admitted that she was having some strange pains in her stomach. Her due date was two weeks away. I knew that the baby was imminent. Finally Liz phoned her midwife, who suggested she visit the labour ward at the hospital for a check up. Liz phoned Robert, who came and collected her, and they left with promises to phone me as soon as there was any news.

I tried to busy myself in the shop, sorting out the stock, tidying shelves, parcelling books for despatch to customers. What was happening to Liz? My phone was silent, the shop was empty, and there was a strange lull in the atmosphere today. Even the street outside seemed empty, although that could be explained by the grey, wet weather. The summer was drawing to an end, and so was the tourist season. Redcliffe would quieten down now as people returned to their homes and regular lives. Lunchtime came and went, and I ate a solitary sandwich and drank yet another mug of coffee. I was restless, yet I couldn't do anything. I had promised to run the shop while Liz was away, and that is what I would do. My fingers itched to phone the hospital but I knew they couldn't tell me anything. It was a waiting game.

By mid afternoon I was feeling increasingly anxious. I had sent a text message to Robert, hoping he would respond soon, but there was nothing. I raised my head from looking at the computer, and stretched my body. My neck felt taught around the scar tissue. I had only recently dared to start stretching my neck again, and it felt good as I tipped my head from side to side, massaging the raised skin with my fingers. The bell above the shop door jangled, and I straightened and turned my head, a professional smile automatically in place. Danny Mason walked into the shop, smiling, and my heart lurched. This was wrong.

"Hello, Jessica, how are you?" he asked, approaching the counter.

I smiled and tried to calm my shaking body. I could not let him see me like this.

"Hi, Danny, I'm fine thanks," I replied, "What are you doing here?"

His smile faltered, and his expression grew serious as he approached me. I kept the counter between us.

"Jessica, you seem anxious," Danny said, "Are you sure all is well?"

I realized he was scenting the air, and my body jolted in shock. I fought to regain control. I did not want Danny to think I was scared of him, or that I couldn't handle his being a

Love Kills

werewolf. I breathed a sigh of relief as I realised I had the perfect cover for my behaviour.

"Liz has gone to the hospital," I said, "Rob fetched her earlier. I think she might be in labour."

Danny stepped back and nodded.

"Ah yes, of course," he said, "Naturally you are concerned for your friend. She will be fine, you know that."

I nodded.

"I know that Danny, but I still worry." I said, "So why are you here?"

He laughed now.

"So many questions!" he exclaimed, "Am I not allowed to drop by and see a friend when I finish work early?"

I was embarrassed now, and I ducked my head and smiled. Of course he was just checking up on me. He was my friend after all. Ignoring the strange, hollow feeling that had begun in my stomach, I answered.

"Sorry," I said, "Ok, nice to see you. I am fine as you can see. How come you finished work early?"

Danny fixed his intense blue stare on me, and I shivered. Did he know about my dream? Had Jack told him?

"I have some pack business to attend to," he said casually, "So I thought I would come and see you first."

The doorbell jangled again as a group of customers wandered in. Danny stood to one side, pretending to browse the shelves. I greeted the customers, helped one with an enquiry, and served them as they bought some books after ten minutes or so. Danny waited the whole time. I couldn't help but feel nervous.

When the shop was empty I walked over to where he stood in the corner. I tidied some books on the shelf beside him, and picked up one that was in the wrong place. I could smell Danny's aftershave. It was a musky scent; different to the one Jack wore. Danny's somehow made me think of woodland and the outdoors. Jack's reminded me of a cosy fire on a dark night. The men were so alike and yet so different.

"I really would like you to visit the Ship again, Jessica," Danny said as he stood in front of me.

I looked up into his eyes. His face was serious, his expression gentle. My heart was pounding as I remembered that fateful night. I saw the wolves fighting, their voices barking and howling as I lay dying on the cold stone floor, with blood pouring from my neck and stomach. Closing my eyes, I fought back the horrible memories and forced myself to remain calm. My hand was touching my neck in an unconscious gesture of remembrance. I slowly lowered my arm and tried to hold Danny's gaze.

"I don't know, Danny," I said, clenching my fists, fighting to keep my voice from quivering, "I want to go back. I just, I keep remembering what happened…" my voice trailed off.

Danny put his hands on my shoulders, and then impulsively drew me against him in a warm hug. His body was so firm, so welcoming. Something seemed to relax inside me, a feeling of comfort and familiarity. I felt a strange flipping sensation, and a voice seemed to sigh through my head, whispering, "*Yes, this is our home. This is the life-force we desire.*" A pang of fear shot through my body, and I fought to suppress it. Danny seemed not to notice, and I kept my head on his shoulder as I hurriedly tried to regain control of my thoughts and myself. Finally I stepped back and looked into his eyes once again.

"Ok," I said, with a deep breath, "How about tonight? If Liz doesn't have the baby, and I don't have to visit the hospital, I will go to the pub tonight."

Danny smiled.

"Deal," he said, "And I will be there with you."

"Will Simon be there?" I asked.

"Yes," Danny replied, "Simon will be there. Now if you will excuse me, I must be going."

He hesitated by the door, and then turned back to me.

"I really do appreciate what you do for us, Jessica," he said, and then he left.

I was standing in the middle of the shop with a stray book in my hand, and Danny's scent lingering in the room. The ringing of the shop phone caught my attention, rousing me from my reverie. Liz! I scrambled to answer it, almost tripping over a table leg in my haste.

Robert explained that Liz was staying in the hospital. She was in the early stages of labour but the doctors wanted to monitor her and the baby after her recent experience. Liz didn't want me to visit; she told Rob it wasn't necessary. I protested, but he insisted that Liz was fine and I needn't worry. She knew I didn't like hospitals. I felt so mean, and yet relieved that I didn't have to hurry back to that place. I sent my love with Rob, and instructed him to phone me as soon as anything else happened. I would keep my phone beside me all night. Rob promised, and returned to his wife.

6

I had a promise to keep. I sent Danny a text message and gave him a time to meet at the pub. There was no use in procrastinating any longer. The pub was my local after all, and I had to return. The danger was gone. The wolves were my friends. I phoned Jack, and he explained that he had been called to a vampire meeting later that day. He couldn't accompany me to the Ship, partly for this reason, and partly because he wasn't welcome in the lair. Apparently he visited the place only rarely, out of respect for Danny's wolves. They tolerated him because of his brother, but they didn't necessarily like him, and many of the wolves openly hated vampires simply because they were ancient rivals. I assured Jack not to worry, that I would be fine with Danny and Simon. He promised to join me in the pub when he finished work.

When I closed the shop, I walked through our small storeroom, locking both internal doors before exiting into my kitchen. I barely noticed the microwave meal I prepared; it was simply food to fill the emptiness in my stomach. My mind was preoccupied with what I would see when I revisited the wolves' lair. I felt a dull sort of nausea, and the scar on my neck was throbbing as though my body was reliving the experience of having my throat torn. I forced the thoughts away, and banished the harsh sound of Seamus Tully's laughter. He was dead. Danny killed him. He could hurt me no longer. I was safe. I repeated these words in my head as I walked upstairs and changed into jeans and a t-shirt, brushed my hair, retouched my make-up.

I was still a little stiff in my movements but the short walk was good for me and I was greeted in the bar by a couple of people who knew me as a local. Sally Frost was standing at the bar and I went over to her. She is a nurse at the local hospital, we have been friends for a couple of years after meeting through Simon, and oh yes, she is Danny's third in command of the Redcliffe werewolf pack. She greeted me warmly with a smile and a hug.

Love Kills

"Jessica, how are you?" she asked, "Good to see you here again."

"Hi, Sally," I replied, "I'm ok I think. How are you?" I asked.

She nodded and I saw her nurse persona quickly scanning my movement and the scar showing above the neck of my t-shirt. I hadn't seen Sally since I left hospital. She had treated me on the ward when I was in intensive care, but she had given me some space to adjust to my new relationships. I like Sally for her empathy and her sensitivity to people's feelings.

"I am good thanks Jess," she replied. She hesitated. "Um, Simon's downstairs, did you want to see him?"

My heart lurched. Simon was in the wolves' lair in the basement of the pub. Well actually it was cut into the cliff face that the pub backed onto. And that was where I had almost died. Sally's expression was serious.

"I know it must be difficult, Jessica," she said quietly, "But perhaps you should come downstairs with me. This is a safe place and we want you to know that. You are part of our family now."

My heart was pounding and I struggled to stop myself trembling. Her beautiful blue eyes were large and appealing as she watched my reaction. I took a deep breath and nodded slowly.

"Go on then," I said, "You are right, I have to get used to this."

Sally walked beside me and then led the way down the cellar stairs and to the heavy wooden door set in the shadowy part of the room. I fought the fear that rose in my chest and concentrated on breathing slowly and steadily. Sally gently patted my arm.

"It's alright Jessica," she said, "Let me show you the Redcliffe lair as it should be. This is a place where you are safe and among friends."

Her language was so formal, not like Sally at all. This must be Sally the Wolf. I remembered how different she had been the day after Danny almost died because of Seamus. She had bristled with energy and power, her demeanour had been serious and frightening, and she had fought hard to defend her pack and her Master. Despite her petite frame, long blonde hair, and innocent face, Sally was a tough warrior, and I would not like to be on her bad side.

We walked down the passageway and into the first main room cut into the rock. It had rough stone walls and a flagged floor, and this was the room where Seamus had tried to kill me. I looked around now and shivered as I remembered. He had dragged me into the middle of the room to where Danny, Simon and Sally stood with his mate LuAnn who was their hostage. It should have been a straight swap, me for her, but Seamus changed his mind and attacked me instead. I hadn't seen Jack but I had known he was there. He had joined the fight and helped his brother to slay the enemy. Swallowing round the lump in my throat, I fixed my eyes firmly on Sally as she walked slightly ahead of me. I suppressed the echoes in my mind, ignoring the wolf howls and squelching sounds of blood splattering against the walls. The room smelt musty, which only increased my anxiety.

"Come this way, Jessica," Sally said, "I'll show you the rest of our lair."

Wondering how many lives had been lost in that cold, musty cave, I followed Sally through a door at the far end of the room, which led into another passageway. She pointed out rooms that were used as a kitchen, offices, living rooms, a games room. The wolves could use this as a home-from-home if they were struggling amongst human society. It was also used as a hostel for new wolves looking to join the pack, or newly turned wolves struggling to control their abilities. Sally opened a door further along the corridor.

"This is Danny's-" she said, and then stopped abruptly.

I looked into the room to see Danny and Simon sharing a passionate kiss in front of a desk. They both jumped apart and then smiled sheepishly at us and I gasped in surprise.

Sally finished, "-office. Sorry, boys I didn't know we were interrupting!" she said with a smile and a wink.

I stood awkwardly in the doorway, and Simon stepped away from the desk rubbing his mouth with the back of his hand. Danny ruffled a hand through his hair in a gesture identical to his brother, and then he stepped forward, smiling.

"Jessica," he said warmly, "it's good to see you here. I was going to meet you upstairs but I got waylaid." He looked meaningfully at Simon, who blushed and ducked his head.

I glanced at Sally who just smiled, walked into the room, and sat on the sofa adjacent to the desk, where Simon was now sitting. I was confused. She didn't seem at all bothered by their behaviour even though I knew she was in love with Danny. This must be a wolf thing. I cleared my throat and looked at Danny.

"Yeah, I bumped into Sally upstairs and she brought me down," I said, "Should I leave?"

Danny shook his head and moved towards me.

"No of course not," he said, "Simon and me were just discussing some pack business. Actually, Simon could you tell Sally please? I will give Jessica a tour." Simon nodded and turned his attention to Sally, and I followed Danny out into the corridor.

"Are you and Simon a couple now?" I asked, "Because he didn't seem to think so while you were away."

Danny smiled and showed me his irresistible, mischievous face.

"I told you, Jessica," he said, "I have no fixed romantic relationships. That is not my style. Simon and me are old friends who happen to share similar tastes, that is all."

We were in another large room now. This one was squarer, again with bare stone walls and a flagged floor. But in here there were chairs arranged in rows sort of like a meeting room. Against the far wall was a raised platform that reminded me of a stage in a school hall. There were three steps on one side, and what looked like two thrones on the platform. It looked very formal and quite old fashioned. As I peered at them, I could see ornate patterns carved into the wood of the thrones. They looked old, and very well worn. Danny followed my gaze.

"This is the throne room," he said, "There is my seat, and one for my mate, should I choose to have one. Either side of those are seats for my pack superiors, in my case Simon and Sally."

He turned round suddenly and I was aware of someone behind me. I turned and was faced with a woman who I vaguely recognised as a regular in the pub. She was tall with black hair and dark eyes, and her expression was angry. She was very intimidating and I had backed up against the wall before I realised. That made me angry but I knew she was physically stronger. She looked at me but spoke to Danny. "Why is the human in here?" she asked in a menacing voice, "This is not her place."

I felt what I could only describe as sheer power flow out from Danny. He hadn't changed but suddenly he seemed taller, bigger, and scarier as he spoke in a clipped, curt tone.

"You forget your place, Kimberley," he said, "Do not address your Master in such a way, unless you wish to challenge me. Do you?" His voice was rising dangerously and I shivered.

She hesitated and then turned her body towards Danny, softening slightly. Her voice was silky and seductive.

"No, Master," she said softly, "Forgive me." She ducked her head subserviently and then continued, "I am simply concerned for your welfare. The human poses a threat to our family and I wish to protect us, and you."

Danny smiled but it wasn't pleasant. In fact it frightened me.

"Jessica does not pose a threat to anybody," he said firmly, "least of all me. Step away from her, Kimberley, and leave us."

Kimberley started to move and then suddenly her hand was at my throat. She pushed me hard against the wall and I panicked, struggling to breathe. Before she could speak Danny grabbed her, yanked her back, and threw her across the room so that she skidded and crashed into the wooden chairs. I sank to the floor, hands to my throat, catching my breath, coughing and spluttering violently as my body reacted in fear. Danny was crouched above Kimberley, growling and snarling but still in human form. He punched her and the sound echoed through the room. She cried out and I heard her whimper and beg him for forgiveness. His voice was clear and terrifying.

"You ask my forgiveness?" he roared, slapping her face, "You should ask for Jessica's! She is my friend, and I welcome her here into our lair with a promise of protection. You will protect her as our own, Kimberley, or you will be cast out. What do you choose?"

Kimberley coughed and struggled to her hands and knees. I sat slumped on the floor, still trying to calm my breathing as I watched the drama. Danny was towering over her. She raised a tear-stained face to him and I saw blood glistening on her cheek.

"Master I meant no disrespect," she cried, "I am sorry. I accept the human if you insist."

She scrambled to her feet and approached me, offering her hand.

"Jessica I apologize for my behaviour," she said sullenly, "I cannot call you my friend but as long as Danny is our master then you are welcome here."

She hauled me to my feet and then walked quickly out of the room and up the corridor, her hair swishing from side to side. I heard her sobs as she retreated. My legs were shaking, and I leaned against the rough stone wall for support as I watched her leave.

"Jessica I am sorry about that."

I jumped to find Danny right behind me, his face full of concern.

"Are you hurt?" he asked.

I shook my head and then coughed again as my throat constricted. My previous wolf-inflicted wound was sore from the aggravation and I felt slightly nauseous. Danny saw me struggling.

"Here, come and sit down," he said, "I'll get you some water."

But as I tried to approach a chair the room faded around me. I vaguely heard Danny calling my name; my body went limp and all I wanted was to lie down. Then everything went black.

I woke lying on a bed in a strange room. I jumped to sit up and Danny was there with his arms around me.

"Jessica it's me, it's Danny," he said urgently, "You are safe, in one of our bedrooms. Please try to calm down."

I relaxed into his arms, feeling his warmth and strength around me. We were on a double bed in another room with rough stone walls. The walls were draped with hangings to try and conceal the stone, and the linen was a vibrant blue colour. There was a lamp switched on at the bedside table, offering the only light in the room, so it was subdued and slightly eerie. The musty smell was not so strong in here, and I detected a faint floral scent, perhaps an air freshener or candle.

Danny held a glass of water to my lips and I tried to hold it but found I was shaking violently. I let him gently tip the glass so I could sip from it, and the cold water was so refreshing it felt wonderful. He put the glass down and gently stroked my hair, cradling me in his arms.

"I am so sorry about this, Jessica," he said, "Kimberley is very territorial and seems to think I might choose her as a mate.

She saw you as a threat, believing that I wanted to bring you over into our pack."

I sat upright and turned to face him, ignoring the dizziness and the pains shooting through my neck.

"She sees me as a threat?" I said loudly, "Doesn't she know about Jack?" Danny nodded.

"Yes of course," he replied, "But Jack doesn't come down here very often and my wolves tend to disregard him as much as possible. Vampires are not welcome with wolves. They cause too many problems when it comes to power and control. Jack is tolerated because he is my brother, that is all."

I blinked and tried to focus my thoughts. My voice was croaky and I coughed again. Danny helped me sip some more water, moving forward to support me. Again something flipped in my stomach, and that mysterious voice drifted through my head, whispering, *"Accept the wolf. He is closer to your kind. Embrace his warmth and vitality."* I stiffened, staring at Danny warily, trying to process what was happening inside me. I knew it was power, energy, magic, something that I couldn't explain. All I knew was that Danny's closeness was suddenly very disturbing.

"But why would they think...I mean, have you said something?" I stammered, "What makes them see me as a threat?"

Danny was looking straight at me with his familiar deep blue, hypnotic eyes. It was as though I was staring at Jack and I struggled to collect myself. His voice was soft, gentle, and even sensual. I was very aware of his hands on my shoulders, the strength in his body.

"They know I am fond of you, Jessica," he said quietly, "I cannot deny that. And I have never invited humans into our lair before. My wolves are mistrustful because the females want to offer themselves as my mate. The position would elevate their individual power and control, and for them it is a desirable role."

I slowly took in what he was saying.

"They think that I want to be your mate?" I asked slowly.

Danny nodded.

"But that's crazy," I exclaimed, "I don't want to be a werewolf! I mean..."

I faltered, embarrassed and Danny smiled.

"It is fine, Jessica, do not worry," he said, "Of course you don't want to be a wolf; you are in love with Jack. I have no desire to change you in that way."

He stopped and swallowed slowly, then fixed that intense gaze on me again. "But I do have strong sexual feelings for you Jessica," he continued, "I cannot deny that. And the wolves know it. They are jealous because I do not show the same attraction to them."

The room spun around me. He was so direct. And I was taken by surprise. Danny had said words to a similar effect only recently, after I had discovered the brothers' big secret, but I had tried to forget about it. He was naturally very flirty and playful, always finding ways to touch and torment me. But I tried to treat him like a brother so he wouldn't get the wrong idea. He saw my face and moved back, his expression gentle.

"I am sorry Jessica," he said gently, "I shouldn't have said anything. Please let us forget it. How are you feeling now?"

I blinked and put a hand to my head. The dizziness was fading.

"Yeah I'm fine thanks," I said, "Maybe I should go home. Or see if Jack has finished his meeting."

I struggled to climb off the bed and Danny followed, keeping a careful distance but close enough to catch me if I fainted again. My legs were still shaking, but I gritted my teeth and ordered my body to obey. I was determined to move independently, and I did not want to faint again. I could not be so continually helpless. It was embarrassing.

Once in the corridor I hesitated, disoriented and not sure which direction to take. It was a maze down here, and I could see how safe and secure it must be against intruders. Danny gestured to my left.

"This is the way out, Jessica." He said gently.

We walked slowly along the corridor in silence. I glanced curiously into the open doorways that we passed. There was a TV on in one room and I saw two people lying on a sofa in front of it. I smelled food cooking in the kitchen as we passed, but it just made me feel nauseas after my recent shock. I used to be so strong, always in control. Yet since I met Jack and Danny all I seem to do is cry at the drop of a hat, and faint every time something upsets me. I felt ridiculous, and also very confused.

We were back in the entrance hallway, the one where I had almost died. I stopped in the middle of the room, staring down at a dark stain on the flags. This was my blood. I had lain here, bleeding from the neck and stomach, when Danny had fought Seamus Tully to the death. Closing my eyes I could hear the dim sounds of snarls and growls, turning to howls as wolves were slain. Simon and Sally had been injured but they healed quickly, so when they visited me in hospital it seemed like I was the only one to suffer. I took a few deep breaths, and when I opened my eyes Danny was standing silently beside me. I hadn't even felt his presence.

"The floor has been cleaned several times." Danny said, looking down at the stain.

"A permanent reminder I suppose." I said lightly, though my voice quivered.

"Come, Jessica, let us return to the pub." Danny said, taking my hand and gently leading me towards the door across the room.

I nodded.

"Yes," I said, "I need a drink."

7

As we walked back up the cellar stairs, my mobile beeped, alerting me to an answer phone message.

"Liz!" I exclaimed, "She might have had the baby. I'll catch up with you in the bar." I said to Danny. He nodded, and I hurried along the passageway and out onto the decked smoking area, pressing buttons on my phone to play the message.

I walked down the steps and into the car park, taking shelter by the pub wall. There was a brisk sea wind whipping up, and while it was still fairly warm, the salt stung my face and blew my hair all over the place. The familiar scents and sounds were soothing after the oppression of the wolves' lair, but as I lifted the phone to my ear, I noticed that my hands were still shaking. My stomach still felt strange, but the mysterious voice was quiet.

The message was from Robert. With a pounding heart I listened, thinking I could get Danny to drive me to hospital if need be, to save me running home for my car. But the quiet, controlled voice on my phone simply said that Liz was still in labour, it was progressing slowly, and I didn't need to visit her just yet. Robert was always so calm. I guessed he was really quite frightened about the birth of his first child, but he would never show his feelings to anyone. I returned his call, only to reach his answer phone this time, so I left my message.

I simply said I hoped Liz was all right, and he should phone again if they needed me at any time. I also said sorry I missed Robert's call, but that I had been downstairs in the pub, and mustn't have had a signal. Robert would know what I meant. Although he had never visited the wolves' lair, he knew where it was, and he knew about Simon and Danny. I didn't want to burden Robert with my drama, but I also knew that he was a friend and he would like to be aware of what was happening. I trusted him. He was a good man.

Ending the call, I locked my phone's keypad and slipped the gadget into the back pocket of my jeans. I raised my head and turned my face up to the sky, where the sun was setting in a spectacular burst of colour and warmth. I could feel the remains of the summer heat somewhere behind the sea wind. I shivered and rubbed my arms, wishing I had brought a cardigan. My body ached after the recent trauma, and I didn't know what to feel. I just wanted the whole sorry situation to be gone. I wanted my old life back, where everything was normal and boring and safe. Closing my eyes, I blinked back the tears that sprang up again.

"Jessica," a voice said, and my heart fluttered as I tried to decide whether it was Danny or Jack.

Opening my eyes I relaxed and smiled when I saw my lover standing before me. Dressed in his favourite black jeans and blazer, with a dark grey t-shirt underneath, I knew who this was. Danny's style of dress tended more towards surfer trends. He favoured baggy shorts and brightly coloured t-shirts where Jack preferred black jeans and dark coloured shirts. Jack's blue eyes were serious as he stared at me.

"What has happened?" Jack asked.

I shook my head, trying to speak. A lump had suddenly sprung up in my throat, and hot tears brimmed up again, despite my best attempts at self-control. Jack didn't speak. He simply stepped forward and wrapped his arms around me. I hiccupped, buried my face in his chest, and let the tears fall. I would not sob as my body wanted, but I allowed the tears their escape. Jack felt warm and safe and secure, and I pressed myself as close to him as I could. He rested his chin on my head and held me, not speaking until I was ready.

After a few minutes I slowly lifted my head and stepped back so I could look at him. I shivered again as the wind whipped around my bare arms, and Jack shrugged off his blazer and carefully draped it around my shoulders. It felt heavy on one side, and I realised with a jolt of panic that he was carrying a gun.

"Thanks," I said, drawing the jacket close and slipping my arms inside the sleeves, "I forgot my cardigan."

Unconsciously I was nervously touching the pocket that held Jack's weapon. He stepped close to me and slowly withdrew the gun, quickly tucking it into the waistband of his jeans and covering it with his t-shirt. I watched his actions but didn't question him. My mind was a whirl of confusion, and the mysterious voice was haunting me.

"What happened in there?" Jack asked again.

I took a deep breath, my shoulders shuddering with the force of it.

"Sally took me into the lair," I said, "We saw Danny and Simon. Then one of the women attacked me, because apparently she thinks I want to be Danny's mate."

Jack's expression turned from serious to angry, and I could actually feel a force of energy emanating from him. It made me shiver, and my skin crawled as though I had pins and needles. Something stirred deep down in my stomach, but I dismissed it as another nervous reaction.

"Did she hurt you?" he asked, stepping forward and reaching out to examine my neck.

I tipped my head to one side so he could see the scar tissue, and he muttered something incomprehensible.

"You have a bruise," he said, "I trust Danny is punishing her?"

"Well, he threw her across the room and punched her hard if that's what you mean." I replied.

"What else happened?" Jack asked, staring at me again.

He held my gaze so I could not look away.

"I fainted from the shock," I replied, looking down, "And I woke up in one of their beds, with Danny beside me."

Jack went very still, and I felt a cold, swirling mass of energy flowing around him. My skin prickled with a sensation like pins and needles, and I shivered. Jack fought to control his expression, but I saw the flash of anger across his face when he spoke.

"He said something that made you uncomfortable." Jack said.

"How do you know?" I asked, looking up at him, "Have you spoken to him?"

"No," Jack said, "But I know my brother, and I know he always takes his chances when he can."

His expression was grim now, and I distinctly felt the anger and jealousy that radiated from him. I shook my head, flicking my hair back over my shoulders. I was restless, I needed something but I didn't know what. The thought of going back into the pub had lost its appeal, but I also did not want to return home.

"Where do you want to go?" Jack asked, making me jump. Had he read my mind?

"I need to go for a walk, up on the cliffs," I said, "I need to stretch my legs."

Jack nodded, and turned to walk away.

"I had better tell Danny," I said, "I told him I was only coming outside to return a phone call."

"Shall I speak to him?" Jack asked.

I nodded.

"Yes please," I replied, "I'll wait out here. Tell him I need to clear my head."

I watched Jack walk around the building to the front door, and then I turned and wandered across the car park. Darkness was falling, and I walked over to the sea wall and stood there for a minute, staring out at the waves. Despite the wind, the sea was fairly calm this evening, and I lifted my chin and took several deep breaths, inhaling the salty air.

Turning my head, I looked across at the wide sweep of Redcliffe Bay. Orange light from the streetlamps reflected off the sea. I saw the bright lights of my favourite amusement arcade further along the promenade on the pier, and I could hear the loud noises of the slot machines and children's rides. Near the harbour, the fairground was still open, and I saw the carousel, the big wheel, and the waltzers in the distance. All of the familiar sounds of tourists drifted along to my ears, and I smelt hotdogs, candyfloss, and fresh cooked food from the restaurants. But I wasn't hungry.

Closing my eyes, I breathed in the sharp sea air, tasting salt on my tongue. It made me thirsty. My hair whipped across my face but I didn't move it. I felt a calm sensation sweep over me, and the atmosphere seemed to quiet down, dulling all the noises of human habitation. A voice drifted through my mind, gentle and warm and familiar.

"Hello, Jessica," said my mother.

"Lillian," I whispered.

My mother had spoken to me in my dreams over recent months, but since the incident she had not visited. I had missed her. Both my parents died in a car accident when I was six. It was part of the reason I didn't like hospitals, because one of my earliest memories was of being rushed into Casualty on a stretcher, having been a passenger in that same car. My heart leaped now as my mother's voice calmed me.

Love Kills

"I am here, child," she said, "It is time you trusted Jack. Please ask him to introduce you to the witch who may mentor you."

"But I'm not a witch," I insisted, "I'm just an ordinary human."

"You are not," she replied, "The reason you came here was to meet the Mason brothers. Unfortunately I did not foresee the incident with the wolf pack. That was an unexpected development."

I nodded, and opened my eyes. Lillian was still in my head. I could feel her like a shadow in my skull, an extra weight that I couldn't describe. It was almost like when your ears pop when you are in an aeroplane, or when you have a cold and your sinuses are blocked. She was different to how things normally felt for me.

"So you're saying that I was drawn here by some sort of fate?" I asked.

"Yes," she said, "Why did you choose Redcliffe above all the other towns in this country?"

"Because I liked it," I replied stubbornly, "Because it is a beautiful town, and I like the seaside."

"Yes," she said again, "You like the seaside because you have an affinity with the ocean. There are many revelations to come as you develop your abilities. Please, ask Jack to introduce you to Crystal."

"Crystal," I said cynically, "That's an original name for a witch."

"Do not disrespect us, Jessica," my mother retorted sharply, and I actually flinched at her tone, "I am still your elder, and Crystal is your superior. She will tutor you, but only if you are willing to learn."

I was still determined not to accept her words. And now my temper was raised by her admonition of my behaviour.

"You can't just appear in my life and start telling me what to do," I said, "I am a fully grown woman with my own mind. And besides, why would I need to develop my powers or abilities, or whatever you call it?"

She was quiet for a few moments, and I began to panic. I still wanted to speak to her.

"Lillian," I said tentatively, "Mum?" It felt strange to call her that, but it was true and I couldn't deny it just because she was dead and speaking from beyond the grave.

After a tense moment, her voice came again in my head, and I relaxed slightly.

"I am here," she said quietly, "But I grow weak. The decision is yours as you say. There is trouble coming, and it concerns Jack and his maker. You are the only one who can protect him, but you need to have control of yourself in order to do so."

I laughed.

"Me protect Jack?" I said, "You must be joking!"

"I am not joking," she replied seriously, "He is powerless against his maker. She is older and stronger, but she underestimates you. Take advantage of that, and you will defeat her and strengthen your relationship."

The wind suddenly buffeted me from the front, and I staggered back in surprise.

"Whoa!" I exclaimed, grabbing the grey stone wall for support, "Mum?" I said in a low voice, "Are you still here?" But she was gone. The strange sensation in my head had gone, and I was alone once more.

I slowly turned round to face the pub, wondering where Jack was. I had no idea how much time had passed, but it must have been a good 15 minutes or so. Sure enough, I saw him standing in the shadows, watching me. When I smiled he stepped forward, and I met him in the middle of the car park.

"Are you alright?" he asked, putting a hand on either side of my face, "Who were you talking to?"

I felt a familiar pang of emotion deep within my gut. It was not something I had ever experienced before meeting Jack, but now I knew that this was a symptom of being in love. The thought made me smile wryly to myself. A symptom sounded about right. Being in love was like being struck with a chronic illness. You could never get rid of it, but you might be able to manage it. There was just no medication that could dull the effects of this emotional roller coaster. Oh I was in a sorry state tonight!

"It was my mother," I said, "She finally spoke to me again."

He nodded, still staring into my eyes, assessing my mood. Apparently most vampires could not simply read minds using telepathy, but they could get a feel for what a person was thinking. They knew if someone was lying, or guilty, or feeling a certain emotion towards another, and they had enhanced abilities of perception when it came to judging people's thoughts.

"What did she say?" he asked.

I sighed, stepped back and looked around me.

"Let's go for a walk," I said, "I'll tell you about it later."

8

We walked out of the car park, along the pavement and past the pub. I walked with my arms wrapped tightly across my chest, hugging myself. It was my instinctual protective nature, to close in on myself rather than look elsewhere for support. Jack walked beside me, not speaking, but I saw his alert expression sweeping the area for trouble. Normally I would have commented but tonight I had no energy left to even care. There was so much to learn about the world I thought I knew. My head hurt with the weight of fear, unease, and just a little excitement at the new adventures that lay ahead.

I led us about five hundred yards from the Ship, to a grassy area that sloped down to the beach. Here there were a couple of picnic benches, a token litterbin, and a pathway that followed the line of the cliff, climbing a steep incline to the summit. I often walked up here when I had a headache, or wanted to be alone, or when I had things on my mind. Now it was a mixture of all those reasons that led me across the picnic area. I hadn't planned on having anybody with me, but it had now gone dark, and I was still reeling from my latest werewolf attack. I suppose the vampire bodyguard was kind of necessary under the circumstances.

As we climbed the hill I didn't even look around like I would usually. Content that Jack was being lookout enough for us both, and that I knew every inch of this particular place, I could focus on my own thoughts and feelings. I was aware that we walked up the gently winding gravel pathway. It was close to the cliff edge without being dangerous to tourists, and if you followed the path for its whole distance you would walk the ten miles into a neighbouring fishing village, although to reach it you had to walk through the dense forest that reached right to the cliff edge in places. This was a popular spot for hikers, birdwatchers, and even people that liked to spot ships out at sea. We often saw cruise liners, freightliners, and fishing boats at varying distances from shore, along with pleasure boats during tourist season.

To our left was a thicket of closely-knit trees and wildlife. The large expanse of greenery formed Redcliffe forest, and there were several nature trails marked out through the copse. Occasionally I had ventured amongst the ancient oaks, birch, willow and ash trees, but only on bright sunny days, and only when I had a companion. For some reason I always felt uncomfortable, even a little uneasy, about that place. I had never understood why. Tonight the trees towered ominously at our sides, black under the moonlit sky. Or maybe that was just my mood.

Reaching the top of the path, I slowed to a stop, panting with exertion after the climb. While I gasped and wheezed to catch my breath, Jack simply stood beside me, silent and unmoving. I glanced at him while I was bent over, and was struck again by his inhuman appearance. His skin seemed to glow in the moonlight, and I could see his eyes blazing. Yet I also knew that he only looked inhuman because now I was aware of his true identity. Gradually, my breathing slowed back to normal, and I straightened up, glad that Jack hadn't tried to intervene. I felt like a clumsy, stupid human, and I hated my weakness.

Hugging Jack's blazer around me for warmth, I walked off the path onto the grassy embankment, and I gazed out over the ocean. Under the moonlight the sea glistened with shades of silver, white and black. The waves crashed against the cliff beneath me, but I knew that this was a quiet night. There had been times in the past when the waves had almost rolled straight over this very path. I remembered once when we had such a vicious storm that the car park of the Ship was flooded, and even the smokers couldn't use their decked balcony because it was unsafe. I closed my eyes, and listened to the rolling waves, and the relaxing sound they made lapping against the rocks. It soothed me, and calmed my raging mind.

I jumped as Jack's arms slid tentatively around my waist. I hadn't heard or felt his presence behind me. But I didn't push him away. I relaxed just slightly, and tipped my head back to lean on his chest. He stood firm and silent, kissing me once on the top of my head. I stroked his arms, and shivered as I touched ice-cold skin. It was as though I was trying to warm him, although I knew that would never be possible. Opening my eyes, I stared out at the ocean, and saw the large, dark shape of a freightliner on the horizon. I was aware of the promenade streetlights reflecting off the waves to my right down below, and the blackness of the sheltered coves to my left.

Eventually, feeling more relaxed after hearing my favourite sounds of tranquillity and nature, I moved. I stepped away from Jack, and back over the path towards the tightly packed trees behind us. I stopped when I reached a clearing that was sheltered from the harsh wind, but I wasn't completely amongst the trees yet. I was close enough to the pathway to make a run for it if needed. It frightened me that I had to have an escape plan when I was talking to the man I loved. Finally I raised my chin and stared at Jack. He was standing across the pathway, still on the cliff top embankment.

"Do you want your jacket back?" I asked him, "Your arms are freezing."

"No," he replied, "I do not feel the cold. My skin is naturally cool to the touch."

"Ok," I nodded, hugging my arms around myself again, "So, do you want to hear what happened tonight?"

"Yes," he said, "If you are ready to talk."

My arms were actually starting to hurt from being hunched around me. I dropped them, and stretched out, swinging them around my body as I talked, flexing my fingers. They tingled with a sensation similar to pins and needles, but I ignored it. I told Jack about meeting Sally in the pub, about catching Danny and Simon in a passionate kiss, and then about how the werewolf Kimberley had attacked me. Jack stood still and silent throughout, never interrupting my words. He seemed to take in everything I said, and his expression was serious and thoughtful.

"So, that was my second visit to the wolves' lair," I finished, taking a deep breath, "I think I'll stay away from that place for a while."

"Do you mean the pub," Jack asked, "or just the lair?"

I tilted my head to one side, and sighed heavily as I considered Jack's question.

"The lair, I suppose," I said, "I don't really want to avoid the whole pub."

He nodded.

"And what about you mother?" He asked.

Here I was reluctant to speak. It was one thing to accept the reality of werewolves and vampires when they were physically attacking me. But to accept that the spirit of my dead mother, who just happened to be a witch, was actually holding conversations in my mind was something I struggled with. Jack saw the confusion in my expression, and suddenly he was there in front of me. I hadn't seen him move, and my heart lurched into my throat. He very gently put his arms around me, and gathered me against his body in a tight hug.

"She is real, Jessica," he said quietly, "I feel her energy around you. She has spoken in my dreams also, to warn me about protecting you."

I drew away from him in surprise, and looked up into his face.

"You have spoken to her?" I asked incredulously, "When?"

Jack stared at me with those brilliant blue eyes, and I almost lost myself in the depths of blue flame. I struggled with the urge to throw myself into his arms again. My lips twitched with the need to kiss him, and the force of my love was terrifying. I stood straight and stiff, willing myself to be strong. Jack spoke quietly, holding my gaze.

"Shortly after you told me she had visited you," he said, "She came to me and warned me that you were in danger. I knew that of course, but I was selfish. I allowed our relationship to deepen, and then you captivated Danny, and then we brought you into our turmoil," he hesitated, and I thought I saw moisture glistening in his eyes. He blinked, lowering his gaze, "I should have listened to her from the start," he said, "But then, I could not give you up so easily."

"Yeah," I said, laughing bitterly, "We were too wrapped up in each other. No one could have warned us about that."

I took a deep breath and shook my hair back.

"Anyway," I said brightly, "There's no point moaning about the past. It happened, we are still here, we should move on."

I wished I could feel as confident as I sounded. There was a storm raging inside me, and I didn't know whether it was my heart or my head, or both, causing me to feel so confused, angry and tormented. After a brief silence between us, I finally told Jack about my mother's conversation.

"And she told me I should meet your friend Crystal," I finished, "She said Crystal could be my mentor if I chose. Who is she?"

Jack had listened intently, and now he seemed to rouse from his unmoving state. He ruffled a hand through his hair, and my heart leaped again. That simple gesture was enough to make me melt. I was weak when it came to him. He made me think of rough, hard, sex, and doing things that normal people couldn't even comprehend. I suppressed those feelings and thoughts. Now was not the time.

"Crystal is my friend," Jack said, "She is a very powerful witch descended of an ancient lineage. Your mother is right. If anyone can help you unlock your powers, Crystal is that person."

I nodded.

"Fair enough," I said, "So do you have a phone number for her?"

"I do," Jack replied, "But I will ask her to visit you in the shop if you like."

"I suppose you could." I said reluctantly.

Suddenly I was afraid to meet this woman. I didn't know what to expect. She could be a full-on Goth, or even just an average looking person I could have passed in the street any day. But apparently she was the key to me developing my witch abilities, and I wasn't sure if I was ready.

"Jack," I said, "Could you teach me to fight?"

"You mean self defence?" he asked.

I nodded.

"Yes," I said, "I need to be able to protect myself from all these supernatural people."

"Good idea," he said, "I will teach you some techniques."

"And will you teach me about guns like you said?" I asked.

Shortly after I discovered the truth about Jack being a licensed gun carrier for the police, and about him being a vampire, he had briefly said he could teach me to use them. He could take me to the police headquarters where they had a shooting range. At least then I could be armed in an emergency. And I would know what to do with all the weapons hidden at the Masons' house.

Jack suddenly stiffened, and I heard a hiss escaping from his mouth. He looked all around him, his head moving in short, sharp bursts, totally inhuman. My heart lurched into my throat once again, this time in fear. I felt Jack's muscles tense as he held me protectively, and I was glad of his inhuman strength. Trying to follow his gaze, I heard a movement in the trees behind us, and my body was taut, trying to decide whether to flee or not. Looking at Jack's face, I saw his eyes glowing silver and the tips of his fangs protruding between his parted lips. I began to tremble, and ferociously willed my body to be still and strong.

My eyes focused on what looked like a large dog walking out of the trees towards us. Then I realised it wasn't a dog. It was a black wolf with silver highlights in its fur. And it was heading straight for us. It walked slowly, carefully, with grace and poise. Clearly it wasn't planning an attack just yet. Jack stepped forward, protecting my body. He spoke through clenched teeth, and I knew for certain that his fangs were extended because his voice sounded different, more menacing and slightly distorted.

"Do not even consider attacking her," he said, "You do not want to anger your master any more than necessary."

The wolf slowed, and tipped its head to one side, listening to Jack. He obviously knew that it was a Redcliffe wolf. Was it a man or a woman? I couldn't tell. My guess was woman, since apparently they were all upset with me over this whole mating thing. It was probably Kimberley, come to have another go. I didn't think she would be stupid enough after what Danny had done to her, but then I couldn't be sure.

Without warning the wolf suddenly launched itself at me. But Jack was much faster. He threw himself on the animal, throwing it to the floor and landing on top of it. I cried out in alarm, and just about stifled a scream. Although we were almost guaranteed to be alone up here, I did not want to alert any unsuspecting humans that might be out for an evening stroll. Jack was hissing and clawing at the animal, and it yelped and howled, as they rolled on the floor in a fight. I stood on the edge of the scuffle, helpless and clueless. What could I do? The answer was nothing. I just had to stay away from them. The wolf was still trying to attack me, but Jack wouldn't let it.

After what seemed like an eternity, but was actually only a few minutes, Jack gained an advantage and struck, tearing at the animal's throat. I jumped and gasped, terrified at the sight of my boyfriend feeding on a wolf. He was snarling and hissing, pinning the wolf to the floor, and I heard horrible wet, squelching sounds as he tore its flesh. I watched in horror as the animal's form began to shrink, and slowly shifted into a naked, bloodied, crying woman. It was Kimberley.

"Get off me!" she cried, shoving and punching at Jack.

He held firm, raising his head enough to glare at her. I saw blood around his mouth, and I fought the nausea that rose in my throat. I had to remember that he was doing this to protect me. She deserved it.

"I warned you," he hissed. "And you wouldn't listen."

"I do not take orders from a vampire!" she shouted. "She deserved a lesson."

I flinched at the venom in her voice. This woman really had a vendetta against me. I hadn't even spoken to her before tonight, at least not that I remembered.

"You will be dealt with by your pack leader," Jack said through clenched teeth.

He moved back slightly, as though he was going to lift her off the floor. She wouldn't give up the fight, however. Drawing her legs back in a lightening-fast manoeuvre, she kicked Jack hard in the stomach, sending him flying backwards.

"Jack!" I cried, running over to him.

Jack was on his feet in an instant, and across the clearing before I could blink. But Kimberley had fled. I just saw a naked woman running into the trees, followed by a hazy glow and then the swish of a wolf's tail as it retreated into the undergrowth. Jack gripped my arms, turning me to look at him.

"Are you alright?" he asked.

I nodded, and my gaze slowly moved up from his chest to his face. His t-shirt was soaked in her blood. It made a sort of abstract pattern from the neckline and ran in trickles into the fabric. My gaze settled on his face. His eyes were glowing blue flames, burning with passion in his white face. His mouth and chin were smeared with wolf blood, and his fangs glistened in the moonlight. I was terrified. I backed away slowly without realising, and then I saw Jack's stricken expression. I forced myself to stop, standing awkwardly in front of him.

"You, you have blood on your face," I stuttered, swallowing nervously, "And on your shirt."

Jack stepped back slightly so that he melted into the shadows. I was aware of him licking his lips, and then he raised an arm to wipe the blood away, lifting his t-shirt to mop it up with the ruined cloth.

"Jack," I said, "There's no point hiding in the dark. I need to see the real you. I have to get used to it."

He hesitantly stepped back out into the moonlight, and I forced myself to look at his face. I had to understand this vampire personality. This was Jack after all. And I still loved him despite everything. Jack pulled a mobile phone from his pocket, and I waited while he dialled a number.

"Danny," he said, "We just got attacked by one of your wolves."

He listened for a minute before replying.

"Yes," he said, "It was her. She was going for Jessica, but I intervened. Jessica is unharmed. Kimberley has taken refuge in the woods above the lair. You might want to intercept her before she disappears."

Jack put the phone back in his pocket, still staring at me. I took a deep breath and spoke in a voice that was only slightly shaky. It was an improvement.

"What do we do now?" I asked.

"Shall we go home?" Jack replied.

I nodded.

"Can we stay at your house?" I asked, "I need a change of scenery."

"Of course," he said with a smile. His fangs had retracted, and his face seemed less pale. He now looked human again, apart from the t-shirt.

"Jack," I said, "Your t-shirt. It's covered in blood. People will be suspicious."

He looked down.

"Oh yes," he said.

"Do you want your jacket back?" I asked.

"No." he replied.

In one smooth, agile movement, he whipped the t-shirt off and balled it up in his hand. I laughed, and felt my body tighten at the sight of his muscular figure. Those wicked thoughts jumped back into my mind.

"Jack!" I exclaimed, "Now people will wonder where your clothes are!"

He shrugged and grinned mischievously.

"Well," he said, "They will simply think I'm a sexy, half-naked, drunken tourist."

"Now you sound like Danny," I said wryly. But I didn't argue. If Jack was happy to walk around shirtless, I was happy to watch. There was just one more problem.

"What about your gun?" I asked.

Jack looked down as if he had forgotten it.

"Ah, yes." He said.

He removed the gun from his waistband and wrapped it up in the t-shirt, carrying both easily in one hand.

"Are we walking back, by the way?" I asked.

"No," he said, "My car is parked at the pub. I'll drive us home."

I was actually glad about that. My legs were starting to ache after the excitement of this evening. Right now I just wanted to soak in a bubble bath, and then tumble into bed. Fortunately we made it safely back to the car, and I sank into the passenger seat, closing my eyes as Jack drove us home.

9

When we turned into the driveway of the beautiful old cottage that was home to the Mason brothers, I opened my eyes. I always loved that first sight of this old grey stone building. The house had four spacious bedrooms, and Jack and Danny had owned it for more than ten years now. While they spent four years in Scotland working undercover, they employed a caretaker. She was a middle-aged mother of four, who now took on the role of cleaner once a week. In all honesty, Jack and Danny were out so often that there wasn't much cleaning to actually do, and what little there was I sort of picked up as I went along. I vaguely recognized Sarah, and on the odd occasions that I was home when she came, we would often have a cup of tea and a chat together. She was a lovely, comfortable sort of woman, and the kind who is totally at ease with her own life, and doesn't judge others.

Jack beat me to the front door and I followed him inside. He went straight down the hall into the kitchen, and then disappeared into their small utility room on the left. Kicking off my shoes just inside the door, I closed it and followed Jack. He had shoved his bloodied t-shirt into the washing machine, and was setting the wash cycle and pouring soap powder into the little drawer at the top of the machine. The only anomaly in this domestic scene was the small handgun sat on the counter top. I leaned in the doorway, arms crossed, watching him.

"It seems a waste to just wash your t-shirt, Jack," I commented.

He turned to stare at me.

"I suppose so," he replied.

He whipped off his belt, kicked off his boots, and pulled off his battered and dusty jeans, throwing them into the washing machine. Then he held out his hand.

"Jacket please," he said, "It needs a wash anyway."

Laughing, I wriggled out of his jacket and handed it to him. He looked quite comical standing on the tile floor wearing just his boxer shorts and a pair of white socks. But at the same time, he somehow looked incredibly sexy, and my body reacted even as exhaustion hit. Sighing, I straightened up.

"I'm going to have a bath and go to bed," I said, "I'm exhausted after today."

Jack nodded, rapidly emptying the pockets of his jacket, depositing keys, wallet and mobile phone on the counter next to his gun. He turned to put the jacket into the washing machine, speaking while he worked.

"That's a good idea," he said, "I will retire to bed also. I'll see you in the bedroom."

I turned and walked slowly through the kitchen, back down the hallway, and up the stairs. My feet dragged and my head was starting to hurt. My tense muscles were twitching and aching now, and the scar on my neck felt like a collar, thick and restricting. I could also feel a new bruise throbbing where Kimberley had tried to strangle me. My stomach was stinging in four sharp lines where the claw marks scarred my skin. I knew it was largely psychological, and I felt a surge of anger at the whole sorry situation. Why did I end up the victim? If I was a witch, how come I didn't discover my powers in time to save myself? Sighing again, I shook my head and smiled wryly. I almost spoke out loud to myself, but then remembered Jack would hear me. He wouldn't judge, but I wanted some proper alone time. I had to stop feeling so hard done by. This was a new adventure, a new phase in my life. I should embrace it, and make the most of my situation.

As I turned on the taps and put the plug in the bath, I remembered about Liz. My phone had been silent all the way home, and I suppose it had only been a couple of hours since I spoke to Rob. But a lot could have happened in that time. Worrying that my signal might have cut out, or my phone might have inexplicably turned itself off or drained the battery, I fumbled in my pocket. I cursed as I almost dropped it into the bathwater, and then stepped back near the sink. There were no messages and no missed phone calls. She was still in labour.

I put the phone on the edge of the white porcelain sink, where I could reach it from the bath if necessary. I didn't usually bring the phone into the bathroom, it wasn't my style, but tonight was an exception. My friend could give birth any minute, and I wanted to be there as soon as possible. Besides, once the excited grandparents descended on Redcliffe, I wouldn't get a look in. And there was Rob's sister, a mother of three who was very excited that her older brother had finally settled down. She had been sending over parcels of baby clothes and accessories for the last two months. Liz had a younger brother, who was not exactly a paternal type, but I was sure he would still be excited about the birth of his first niece or nephew. The families were very close, and I thought that was lovely.

I picked up a bottle of my favourite lavender scented bubble bath, and squirted a generous amount under the running taps. The bathroom was beginning to steam up nicely now, and I swirled the water around with my fingertips, to mix in the hot and cold. I always made the temperature just slightly too warm, so that I could acclimatize to it. If it was cold I got goose bumps and couldn't enjoy my bath. Satisfied that it was filling up nicely, I shut the door properly, and locked it. Normally I wouldn't bother, but I didn't want Jack walking in on me again like he did the other night. I had had enough shocks, and now I just needed a break. I stripped off my clothes. My t-shirt was quite dusty actually, and needed a wash, but it could wait. It wasn't surprising really, considering I had been threatened by a werewolf in a cavernous lair earlier this evening. My jeans actually seemed ok, so I folded them up and left them on top of the towel hamper that stood in one corner. I shoved my t-shirt and underwear into the dirty laundry basket. Jack and Danny kept telling me to treat this place like home, so I did.

I checked my phone once more, but it was silent. I didn't even have a text message from Simon, which was a surprise. Then again, maybe he was busy doling out punishment to their renegade werewolf. I shivered and dismissed that train of thought. It was not my problem, and certainly none of my business. The bath water was steaming hot, and the bubbles smelled lovely and inviting. I turned off the taps, checked the temperature with my hand, and then carefully stepped in. After pausing for a moment and allowing the water to envelope my ankles, I slowly lowered my body into the hot water. It was just slightly too hot, and I drew in my breath. Maybe I needed a bit more cold water. I made the adjustment, and finally sank gratefully into the silky, lavender scented bubbles.

Sinking down, I dunked my head under the water, and slid back up, rubbing the water from my face and slicking my wet hair back. Then I sank down again so the water lapped around my chin, and I let out a huge breath, letting my shoulders rise and fall. Maybe now I could finally relax. The room was quiet and empty, and indeed the house itself was silent. I couldn't hear any movement from Jack but I wasn't surprised. I didn't expect Danny to be home for a long time, if at all. Sometimes he slept over at the lair, or he stayed with Simon in his apartments above the pub. I turned my head to one side and stared at my mobile phone, sat inches away on the edge of the sink. It too, was silent. I was actually grateful. I didn't want my best friend to be in excruciating pain for hours on end, but I also knew that labour was a necessary part of having a baby, and that Liz could handle it. She was strong and practical, and she never let things get on top of her. Besides, Rob was a sensible, supportive guy. He would be the perfect husband and give her all the support she needed.

Closing my eyes, I took a few deep breaths, willing my body to relax. But it wouldn't happen. The room was still quiet, apart from the gentle popping sound of bubbles and the water lapping around my body. I was warm, and safe, and I could finally release the strain of that evening. But it wasn't so easy. I was tense all over. My muscles ached, and my head was spinning. I was certain that I would open my eyes and find Jack crouched by the bath again, staring at me. My skin prickled with anticipation and I slowly opened my eyes. The room was empty. The door was still shut and locked as I had left it. I sat up, cursing silently to myself. I dunked a sponge into the bath water, and squeezed it above my head, enjoying the heat and sensation of the water running down my face. I slid down and leaned back again, wetting my hair. I took several deep breaths, and tried again to relax.

It wouldn't happen. This time when I closed my eyes, I kept expecting to hear my mother's voice in my head again. She didn't speak to me. I knew that she had said what she needed tonight, and that she had exhausted her energy reserves in doing so. My instincts told me that until I developed my abilities, and unlocked the hidden powers I possessed, my mother could not fully communicate because she needed my help to do so.

Love Kills

Besides, she knew I needed rest, and now I was supposed to be getting that. It was partly why I had agreed to stay with Jack and Danny. I was a little nervous in case any more Redcliffe wolves took a dislike to me. There was nothing stopping them hunting me down at home if they wanted. At least here I had the full protection of their pack master, and of course my vampire boyfriend.

Eventually I gave up on my bath. I could not relax. I couldn't force myself to relax, and it would not come naturally. I splashed about angrily in the water, huffing and puffing as I rubbed shampoo into my wet hair. Then I let out some of the bath water, and reached for the showerhead that was attached to the bath taps. Using fresh hot water, I rinsed out my hair and applied conditioner, raking my fingers roughly through the tangles. I was in a foul mood all of a sudden. I was angry at my helpless situation, at my feeble useless body, and once again I was angry with Jack and Danny for putting me here. If they had left me alone, I could still be living a normal, quiet, human life.

I pulled the plug and climbed carefully out of the bath. It would not help matters if I slipped and fell now simply because I was in a bad mood. In fact, that would be ridiculous. Reining in my emotions a little, I calmed down as I wrapped a towel around me. I reached for my phone to check it again, and my heart leaped as I saw a little message symbol on the screen. I hadn't heard it beep, but then I could have been splashing in the bath at the time. I quickly accessed the text message. It was from Rob. He said, 'Liz still in labour, all good, phone you when baby is out.' I smiled as I typed a quick reply, 'Good, can't wait to meet baby Gormond, call me ASAP, take care.'

I cheered up a little as I dried myself. This baby would be a welcome distraction from all the drama around lately. I was determined to help Liz as much as possible, and I refused to let my supernatural friends interfere with that. Of course, my first priority was running the shop. Both Liz and me agreed on that point. While she was on maternity leave I was in charge. She would visit when she could, but I didn't want her taking on the stress of management when she didn't need to. I could handle it.

Feeling a little happier but not at all relaxed, I wrapped the towel around my dry body, tucking it into place. I rinsed out the bath to dissolve some remaining bubbles, and opened the window to let out the steam. Picking up my phone, I unlocked the door and stepped onto the landing. And I almost ran straight into Danny. He had just reached the top of the stairs, but he was moving faster than a normal human would. I didn't see him until I came up against a solid, hard mass, and felt his arms grab mine to steady me.

"Whoa," he said, "Sorry, Jess. I forgot myself."

Heart pounding, I stepped back and looked at him. I felt very self-conscious to be standing here wrapped in a towel. He couldn't see anything, but the heat in his eyes told me what he was thinking as he stared at me. He didn't blink, and it was unnerving. I swallowed nervously.

"Danny," I said, "Have you just got home?"

"Yes," he replied, "I'm going to bed."

"Alone?" I asked, and then mentally kicked myself, "I mean, sorry, none of my business."

I hurried past him, but stopped at Jack's bedroom door as Danny spoke.

"Yes," he said, "I am alone tonight."

I turned slowly to stare at him again. He sounded tired, and he hadn't even bothered to make any rude jokes or even to offer me his bed.

"Are you alright?" I asked, concerned.

He rubbed his eyes and ruffled his hair.

"I am fine," he said with a sigh, "I found the wolf, Kimberley. She has been detained at the lair and will receive due punishment."

I nodded.

"Ok," I replied, "Well, I should get to bed. I'm exhausted, and you look tired."

He stared at me for a moment longer, then nodded without speaking. I turned and walked into Jack's bedroom, feeling strangely lost. I had a strong urge to run over to Danny and fling my arms around him, to offer him comfort and support. But I couldn't do that. It was too intimate. I should only behave like that with my boyfriend. The lines could become blurred so easily and it scared me. I smiled weakly when I saw Jack lying in bed. He was watching TV, and had the remote in his hand. I guessed he was naked because his chest was bare, but I also knew he wouldn't expect anything from me tonight. I took my time applying moisturiser to my skin, carefully combed out my long, naturally straight hair, and then I slid naked into bed beside him, snuggling against his strong, warm body. I fell asleep almost immediately, with the sounds of canned laughter from a television comedy show echoing in my ears.

10

I ran through the forest, pushing myself harder and faster, dodging through the trees, and jumping nimbly over fallen branches and protruding roots. My body was lithe and supple, muscles moving like a well-oiled machine. The sun shone high above, but after it filtered through the branches the air felt cooler and fresh. Scenting the air, my lips curled in a snarl that resembled a smile. This was not my true forest. Mine was frozen, in both time and space. My own realm was flanked with huge snow-covered mountains, and the trees were pine, not oak or ash or hazel.

This world intrigued me. It was vibrant and alive, full of beasts. I was the only predator in my realm, and it was beginning to feel very lonely. Pausing momentarily, I glanced sharply around, taking in my surroundings. I was aware of smaller animals disappearing into burrows and nests, desperate to avoid capture and certain death. They were of no consequence to me at this time. I needed something bigger, something strong and worthy of my time and energy. Staring ahead, I saw the swish of a wolf's tail as it disappeared into the undergrowth. Throwing back my head and roaring with excitement, I shot after it, my tail straight out behind me, my head held high. The wolf was mine. He would surrender to my will.

I woke slowly, rolling over in bed, hearing a shrill ringing sound to my right. Jack was sitting upright beside me, and I was aware of him leaning over to pick something up from the bedside cabinet on my side of the bed.

"Jessica," he said quietly, "It is your mobile. It is Robert phoning."

I sat bolt upright, wide-awake suddenly, my dream forgotten.

"Rob!" I gasped, "Liz!"

I grabbed the phone from Jack and answered the call. Rob was speaking to me in a voice that was shaking with unshed tears, and so full of happiness that my heart lurched.

"Jessica," he said, "Sorry to wake you so early."

Love Kills

I glanced at the bedside clock. It was 03:10am. The bedroom was in darkness, and the only faint illumination came from the moonlight that crept around the edge of the dark grey curtains. Jack sat still and silent beside me, listening.

"How is she?" I demanded, "How are you?"

Robert laughed, and I heard a sob in his voice.

"I am brilliant!" he said, "It's a girl, Jess. We have a beautiful baby girl!"

Tears sprang to my eyes and ran down my cheeks. I had never experienced the birth of a baby before, and I certainly hadn't expected to feel such emotion. I choked back my own tears, and took a deep breath to steady my voice.

"That's fantastic!" I cried, "Well done! So tell me the details."

Rob laughed and cleared his throat. I could imagine him standing somewhere just outside the hospital, breathing in the fresh sea air that still drifted inland near the city. He was exhausted; I knew that much, and I guessed that he looked tired but ecstatic, probably standing outside wearing just his jeans and a t-shirt, no jacket. He was also probably starving, but at least now he could leave Liz and the baby for a few hours, and sort himself out.

"Her name is Amy Elizabeth Gormond," Rob said, "And she came out weighing 7lb 4oz. It was a natural delivery. Liz was amazing. She needed an epidural in the end because the contractions were so strong, but everything ran smoothly. The labour lasted for about 16 hours, but we can't be sure when she actually started. Phew!" he finished, "I am exhausted!"

I laughed.

"Ah, Rob," I said, "That is so amazing, I can't wait to meet her. And now you can go and sleep. How is Liz?"

"She is absolutely knackered, but so happy," Rob said, "You should have seen her crying, Jess. I have never seen her so emotional."

I smiled and felt warmth in my heart. I knew that my best friend was a strong and independent woman, but I also knew that she was born to be a mother. This was basically her vocation, and now it was a reality.

"Is she resting now?" I asked, "When can I come visit?"

Rob laughed, and I heard the quiver in his voice again.

"She was awake when I came outside," he said, "Amy went straight to the breast and I left them to sort out her first feed. Hopefully Liz can sleep after that, although she is determined to have a shower first."

Still smiling, I laughed at Rob's comment, and felt so much love for my best friend and her new baby. I couldn't wait to see them. But I would have to. Both Rob and me knew that if I dared leave the shop closed even for half a day, I would never hear the end of it from Liz. So I agreed to wait for the day, and I would go straight from work to the hospital. Rob ended the call, saying he had to phone all of their family members. I sat for a moment, staring at the phone in my hand.

"I suppose you heard the conversation?" I asked Jack, turning my head to look at him.

He was sitting so still beside me, and I couldn't hear him breathing, that at first it surprised me when he spoke. It was as though he melted into the shadows of the darkened room. The fact that he could conceal his presence even when sat next to me in bed was quite frightening, but I ignored that train of thought. Right now I was excited about my friend's new baby.

"Yes," he said quietly, "I heard Robert. That is fantastic news."

"I need to phone Simon," I said, dialling his number and putting the phone to my ear.

Simon was also keen to hear about the birth. He and Liz weren't as close, but they were still good friends, and Simon had a strange soft spot for children. Well, I suppose it wasn't really strange, more a natural yearning, but it was something I had never experienced. Whenever young families came into the pub, Simon would usually join in the games of chase with the children, or he would bring out some battered toys for them to play with. The parents loved him, and the pub had developed part of its tourist reputation because of its friendly and playful staff.

"Hello?" he answered almost immediately, his voice alert at once, "Jess, are you ok?"

I laughed. He automatically assumed the worst after our recent adventures. It was a very sad thought.

"I'm fine, Simon," I said, "Liz had the baby. They have a little girl, and she is called Amy."

Love Kills

I heard movement as he shifted in his bed. The sheets rustled, and he must have moved the phone closer to his ear, because it went muffled and then his voice came across louder.

"That's brilliant!" he said, "Are they well? Did it all go smoothly?"

"Yes," I replied, "She had a natural birth, Amy weighs 7lb 4oz, and Rob is really happy but exhausted. I'm going to visit them straight after work."

"Oh that's great," Simon said, "I won't visit at the hospital. I should imagine she'll be home fairly soon. I'll visit once they are more settled and the family have subsided."

Ending the call, I reached over and put my phone back on the bedside cabinet. My heart was racing. I was so happy, and I could not wait to hold the new little baby in my arms. I had never considered myself the maternal type, but since Liz became pregnant, something had been stirring within me. I realised that I did want a baby. But I didn't know what that meant for Jack and me. I hadn't dared broach the subject yet, but I guessed that he wasn't able to father a child, since he was technically an animated corpse. That thought sent shivers all through my body, and I shook myself.

"You want a baby," Jack said quietly.

I jumped, surprised at his clear voice in the darkness. I turned my head to look at him. He sat silhouetted in the moonlight.

"Yes," I said, "But now isn't the time to start that discussion."

"Very well," he replied, "May I accompany you to the hospital?"

"Yes," I said in surprise, "That would be lovely."

It shouldn't be unusual for my boyfriend to want to accompany me on such a visit. Yet I was surprised. Somehow I could not see Jack as a 'family' man. Even before I knew he was a vampire, he never seemed to show any interest in children. I choked back my uncertainty, and determined to enjoy these new experiences. We all had a lot to learn, and I should accept what was coming, and embrace it.

My mind wandered back to the dream. I had been chasing a wolf in the forest. I was not human; that much was clear. Shivering, I could even feel the sinewy muscles in my shoulders, muscles that humans simply didn't possess. It was more of a memory than a dream, and it unsettled me. Shaking my head, I forced it into the recesses of my mind. Baby Amy was my priority now, and I couldn't wait to meet her.

I yawned loudly, remembering that it was still the middle of the night, or early hours of the morning, and we still had work the next day. I lay back down in bed, cuddling in close to Jack as he lay down beside me and reached out his arm. Pulling the duvet up to my chin, which covered most of Jack's chest, I fell back to sleep. I slept soundly right until my alarm went off at 07:00am.

11

Waking slowly to the sound of my alarm, I reached over and batted my hand over the clock radio until I found the snooze button. Drifting off to sleep again, I was awoken what seemed like a minute later by the shrill sound of a pop song on the radio. Ten minutes had passed. It was time to get up. I had to factor in a walk to the shop this morning. Sometimes I would let Jack or Danny drop me off on their way to work, but today I needed some alone time. Dragging myself out of bed, I limped across the room, grabbing my robe from the hook on the back of the door, and fastening it round me before I could bump into Danny again. I heard the sound of water running in Jack's en suite, which told me he was in the shower. I would use the shared bathroom.

Twenty minutes later I joined the brothers in the kitchen for breakfast. Danny was sitting at the table munching his way through a massive bowl of cereal. I think it was bran flakes, or some sort of fibre based food. Jack sat opposite him, reading a newspaper. They had the radio switched on to a local breakfast show, and I listened to some commercial breaks as I looked in the cupboard for my breakfast cereal. Thanks to Danny and his enormous appetite, there was always plenty of snack food in the house. He especially liked cereal I had discovered, so I had several to choose from.

"Good morning, Jessica," Danny said, "There's tea in the pot if you want some."

"Morning, Danny," I replied, "Thanks."

I looked at Jack.

"Did you tell him about Liz?" I asked.

"Yes." Jack replied.

"It's fantastic news, Jessica," Danny said, "I will pay them a visit when they are ready."

I took a mug from the cupboard above the kettle, and poured tea from the black and white spotted pot that sat on the worktop. I found it incredibly quaint that Jack and Danny should brew tea in a pot. I forget how old they are. They did tell me that it was still a wonderful invention to have an electric kettle and teabags. These everyday necessities were things I had always taken for granted.

As I sat at the table between Jack and Danny, I noticed that Jack was drinking something from a glass tumbler. The liquid was dark red and seemed quite thick. My stomach lurched, and Jack saw my expression. He fixed his intense blue gaze on me.

"The effects of Kimberley's blood were short lived," he explained, "And rather than leave you alone again while I seek a donor, I am using my back-up supply of blood."

I nodded, trying to calm my body that was suddenly pulsing with adrenaline.

"You couldn't feed from me?" I asked, swallowing nervously.

"I do not think you would enjoy it at this time," Jack said quietly.

"No," I replied, "No, I wouldn't. This is really weird," I shook my head and smiled weakly, "Sorry, Jack. I know that you need it, and that it's normal for you. Ignore me."

He took another sip of the blood, and I wondered where it had come from. As if reading my mind, Jack answered.

"Sally introduced me to the people at the blood donor bank," he said, "We have an arrangement whereby I purchase supplies from them on a regular basis."

"Oh," I said, then ducked my head and set about eating my cereal. I tried to ignore Jack with his glass of blood, and ate determinedly, even though I felt slightly nauseas. It would pass once I was over the initial shock.

"Where do you store it, Jack?" I asked curiously, after a few minutes.

"I have a chest freezer in the garage," he replied, "I keep it locked."

After a swift breakfast, I set about collecting my belongings for work. I threw some items into my handbag, including a book I was halfway through reading, my hairbrush, lip balm and keys. I left a bag of clothes near the front door, and asked Jack to drop them off after work. They were for washing, and this was something I still did at home. There were some things that seemed a bit too familiar to be doing at my boyfriend's house

Love Kills

just yet. I had already fished out the clothes I dumped in the bathroom last night and added them to my bag.

Jack tried to give me a lift, but I insisted on walking. This was partly because I needed the exercise, and partly so I could think about everything on the way. Jack and Danny's house was situated on the coastal road, right on the outskirts of Redcliffe, on the main route to Plymouth. It would take me about half an hour to walk to work. The morning was beautiful and sunny, and quite fresh after the cool temperature and clear skies of last night. I was wearing a knee length red pleated skirt, with a cream blouse and thin red knitted cardigan. My shoes were black patent, with a low heel so I could walk comfortably. I felt quite chic and sexy in this outfit. It was a new one that I had bought on a recent shopping trip, a present to myself after the trauma I had been through. Jack loved it on me, and judging by his expression, I guessed Danny did too.

As I walked along the road, I lifted my face up to the sun and breathed in and out deeply, savouring the salty taste on my tongue. There was a slight breeze blowing, and it felt nice and refreshing. My heels clicked sharply on the smooth tarmac, and I enjoyed the silky feel of my skirt swishing around my bare legs. I nodded and smiled at the local postman as he walked past, and then I waved to a woman walking her dog across the road. She recognized me from the shop, and waved back, smiling broadly. I decided not to break Liz's news to anyone today. I couldn't wait to tell the women at the hair salon next door, and at the café two doors along where we bought our lunchtime sandwiches. But I wouldn't do it until Liz gave me permission.

Turning into the high street, I walked up the road and past our shop windows, turning my head automatically to check the place. Everything was in order, but I made a mental note to update the window display on one side. It had been there for over a week now, and was due for a change. Also I noticed some bare shelf space that needed filling. It would all keep me busy on a long day when I was desperate to visit my best friend and her new baby. This was for Liz as much as for me, I had to remember that.

Walking round the side of the terraced shops, I came to my garden gate at the back of the building. Letting myself into the kitchen, I locked the door behind me, and walked through the central storeroom, and into the main room of our bookshop, collecting the till drawer containing petty cash on my way through. It was time to start work.

12

I was on tenterhooks all day, waiting until I could close up and get to the hospital. I spent the morning tidying the window displays and restocking shelves, doing all sorts of little repetitive jobs to keep me busy. There weren't many customers today but I wasn't worried. We had a healthy turnover, which was more than enough to keep us operating smoothly. It was difficult for me not to tell my regular customers about Liz, but I wanted her permission first. When I closed the shop for half an hour and went to the café for my sandwich at lunchtime, I evaded the questions from our friends. They knew Liz had gone to the hospital, and I simply said I was visiting her that evening.

My lunch was a lonely one, and for once I was quite sad not to receive any visitors during the day. Simon often dropped by on his days off, but today he was busy with the werewolves. Apparently Danny had decided it was time to bring over some new recruits, which involved approaching selected humans. The process was delicate and I hadn't asked too many questions, because I felt it was none of my business, and I had enough to worry about. All I knew was that to turn a human, they were bitten by a wolf and had to wait until the next full moon to see if their body could handle the transformation. Sometimes it worked, and sometimes the human would develop complications if their body rejected it. In this instance they would end up in hospital quite seriously ill, and some would even die from their injuries. I did not want to think about my best friend potentially killing people, so I ignored it.

After lunch I half expected Marcus to visit me again. He was an interesting character. I had met him a few months after Jack. Marcus was a telecommunications business owner and a multi-millionaire. He lived in a huge mansion house in the countryside just outside of Redcliffe. I had mixed feelings about Marcus. I knew that he was attracted to me, hence our one night stand. I was incredibly attracted to him, and that bothered me. Surely, I should only find Jack attractive because I was in love with him. I was definitely not in love with Marcus, but I was fond of him. When he spoke to me, it was as though I was the only person in his world. He made me feel very special, and not in a silly or arrogant way. It would have actually been nice to see Marcus today, but he didn't come. He was probably busy with meetings in the city, or planning his next company take-over. He was a ferocious businessman, according to Jack and Danny.

The shop was empty. I had eaten my lunch, and those little jobs were starting to annoy me now. Standing up, I stretched my body, arching my back and stretching my arms above my head. After the incident with Kimberley last night, I was still feeling a little sore. It was nothing serious, just a bit of muscle strain, but it was irritating. Tilting my head from side to side, I fingered the thick scar tissue on my neck. With the sensation came a now familiar sinking feeling in my stomach, and then I felt a mixture of anger and sadness. My body would never be the same again. I would never be the same again.

Sighing heavily, I walked around the desk and wandered around the small shop, picking up a few stray books and putting them in the correct places. The atmosphere in here felt strangely flat and dead after the excitement of recent months. At the same time, I had the distinct feeling that this was the calm before another storm. It was a day just like this when two werewolves had visited Liz and me. They had left a terrifying message for Danny, which triggered the chain of events leading to my revelations and subsequent werewolf attack. At the time we only saw two scary looking women, but now I was far more knowledgeable. And poor Liz was none the wiser. I so badly wanted to tell her the truth, but where could I even begin? Especially now, when she had just become a mother. She had enough stress in her life, and she did not need me offloading information that she would struggle to accept.

I stopped and stared out of the door. The cobbled street outside was eerily quiet for this time on a Tuesday afternoon. I could hear the sound of people chattering and laughing, but they weren't shopping. They were all congregating on the promenade and the beach, enjoying the late summer sun. I felt nervous, and realized that I kept expecting someone to burst through the door. I didn't even know who I was expecting. Maybe it would be another renegade werewolf out to get me. I wouldn't stand a chance now, all alone in my shop. Or maybe there were other scary vampires, or strange witches I had yet to meet. I had to laugh at my own idiocy. Of course there were other non-humans for me to meet. But today, right now, I instinctively knew that I was safe, and that I should forget about my own trauma.

I cheered up as some tourists approached the shop, and fortunately the next few hours slipped by quite peacefully. Business picked up, I made some decent sales, and no one threatened or attacked me. Yet I couldn't help but wonder how many of my customers were actually human. A few of them looked at me suspiciously as I served them. They probably felt my eyes boring into them, or maybe they sensed my unease. A few times I had to shake myself and remember to be polite and professional. Besides, Jack and Danny had assured me that any vampires or werewolves wishing to visit Redcliffe had to clear it with them first. It was some sort of protocol. The Mason brothers, along with Marcus Scott, acted as sheriffs of the South West of England. They pulled rank because they were the oldest and most powerful of their kind in this area, and the local supernatural residents knew better than to argue. Which meant I was safe. Nothing was going to happen between now and my visit to the hospital to see my best friend and her new baby.

13

As I went through the daily routine of closing the shop, I kept glancing out of the window looking for Jack. He had promised to come straight from work and visit Liz, Amy and Rob with me. I was still a little anxious about taking my vampire boyfriend into a maternity ward, even though I knew it was ridiculous. He wasn't about to start attacking babies because they were so young and feeble. In fact, Jack told me that vampires needed adult blood to thrive, because it was stronger. I had to ignore the old Hollywood horror images that kept creeping into my mind. I locked the front door and turned the sign to say 'closed.' Then I took out the till drawer and began cashing up, and switched off my computer. I carried the till through to its small safe in the storeroom, locking the connecting doors behind me.

Finally I walked through to my kitchen, and pulled my mobile phone from my pocket. There was a text message from Jack. It read, 'Sorry, caught in a meeting. Be there soon. Love You.' I smiled and sighed heavily.

"You had better be here soon, Jack Mason." I muttered to the empty room.

I made a cup of tea, grabbed the biscuit tin, and headed upstairs to my living room. There was no need to change my clothes, as I felt perfectly comfortable. I did go to the bathroom and freshen up, splashing cold water on my face and fixing my make-up. Then I sprayed some perfume around me, and brushed out my long hair, enjoying the weight of it down my back.

My heart sank as I caught sight of the thick, red scar on my neck. I had forgotten about it for most of the day, but suddenly I was right back in that dark cave, having my throat torn out. I gasped, closing my eyes, trying to force the memory from my head but it pervaded. My heart was pounding, my body sweating in fear. Clenching my fists, I stood firm and gritted my teeth.

"It is over, Jessica Stone," I said to myself, "Be strong. He is dead. He won't hurt you any more. You will heal."

Blinking back tears, determined not to break down again, I turned my back on the mirror and drew my cardigan closer around me, buttoning it up. The material was thin, but it still felt very comforting. I fought the urge to wrap a scarf around my neck. For one thing, the weather was too warm for that, even if I chose a lightweight chiffon scarf. And for another, I refused to let fear rule my life. I had to accept these scars, and move on. I walked back into my living room, sat down heavily on the sofa, and picked up my mug of tea, reaching into the biscuit tin for a chocolate digestive. After munching half a dozen biscuits and gulping down my brew, I felt much better.

My mood dipped again when there was still no sign of Jack. Muttering to myself, I picked up my mobile phone and checked again for messages. There were none. Gulping down the last bit of tea from my mug, I dialled Jack's number. It rang out and eventually the answer phone kicked in.

"Jack, you had better be on your way," I said firmly, "I give you ten minutes, and then I'm going without you."

Ending the call abruptly, I took a deep breath, and dialled Danny's mobile number. He answered almost straight away.

"Hi, Jessica," he said cheerfully.

"Danny," I said, "Are you with Jack?"

"No," he replied, "I thought he was on his way to the hospital with you?"

I swallowed the lump in my throat. My emotions were taut, and I was not about to lose control again.

"No," I said, "He text me an hour ago to say he was in a meeting. Now he isn't answering his phone."

"Oh," Danny said quietly, "I know that his vampire partner wanted to discuss something with him. Maybe she kept him a little longer than expected."

Vampire partner? My heart thudded hard in my chest. What the hell was a vampire partner?

"What are you talking about Danny?" I asked.

He was silent for a few seconds, and I thought the phone signal had cut out. Then he answered.

"Jack works with another vampire on police cases," he said, "Her name is Angela Gold and she has been on the task force now for about three months. I thought he told you about her."

"No, he didn't," I said tightly, "Look, it doesn't matter," I continued, glancing at my watch, "I've got to go to the hospital, otherwise I'll miss the visiting time. Jack can explain himself later."

"Do you want me to accompany you?" Danny asked.

My body jumped as adrenaline surged through me.

"Um, no," I said in surprise, "Thanks, but I don't need a chaperone. I just wanted Jack to show some support as my boyfriend. Never mind."

I ended the call, with Danny promising to chase Jack and find out what was keeping him. My head was whirling with this new information. I knew it was nothing unusual for Jack to have work colleagues that were female. And I suppose, given the circumstances, he would obviously work with other vampires. After all, he had told me he wasn't the only one in the profession. I supposed Danny also worked with other werewolves, but that was a question I would save for later. What really bothered me was the secrecy, and the fact that Jack could let me down on something like this. It may not seem important to him but it was to me. I needed him to show solidarity, to be there as my partner while we welcomed the new baby into our lives. Perhaps he just didn't understand the human world anymore. Or he was using it as a convenient excuse. I was determined not to let him off so easily.

I picked up the yellow 'new baby' gift bag that had been hidden behind my sofa for the past few weeks. Inside there was a pretty yellow knitted cot blanket, a brown teddy bear with a white comforter attached, and a greetings card for the new baby girl. I had bought the presents a month ago, but the card I had bought on my lunch break once I received Rob's news. I decided to stop at the hospital shop en route and pick up a helium balloon as well. Liz would laugh, but I knew she would enjoy it. Checking my reflection one last time in the hall mirror, I walked downstairs, slipping on my shoes that I had kicked off in the kitchen. Grabbing my handbag, I locked the back door and walked down my path, and out into the road behind our building. My small, red Ford Fiesta was parked right outside my gate.

Once I was out of Redcliffe and driving along the coast road to the hospital, I sighed heavily. Jack Mason was in big trouble. He probably didn't even realise it. I was seething with anger, but it was mostly directed at myself. Only six months ago, I had been a confident, independent, happily single woman. Now I was crazily in love with a vampire, and I was upset that he wouldn't accompany me to the hospital to visit my friend's baby. It was absurd, and I felt stupid. And that made me even angrier. Tears sprang to my eyes suddenly, and I slammed my hand against the steering wheel, crying out in anguish.

"What the hell is wrong with me?" I said out loud, "How is he doing this to me?"

I jumped when my mother's voice drifted into my head.

"You are in love with a vampire, Jessica," she said gently, "Your emotions will never be calm again. I am sorry, but that is what he means to you."

"Mum?" I asked. I glanced at the passenger seat, half expecting to see her there. She wasn't, but I distinctly felt her energy in the car, and it calmed me a little.

"You mean this is how it will be from now on?" I asked, "I hate it!"

"No, Jessica," she said, "Once you meet with Crystal, and learn to erect a psychic defence barrier, you can control your emotions better. But you will never be rid of the Mason brothers. You can run, but you will always return. That is what they have done to you."

She sounded sad, and again those easy tears sprang to my eyes. I blinked furiously, glancing around at the vehicles on the dual carriageway. I must focus on the road. It would be stupid of me to cause an accident now. Taking several deep breaths, I felt myself calming down a little. My skin was tingling, and I felt a cool breeze in the car.

"Is that you, Mum?" I asked.

"Yes," she replied, "Forget your troubles for a while. Enjoy the new baby."

And she was gone, just like that. I almost missed the turn off for the hospital. Cursing under my breath, I managed to exit the A-road without causing a pile up. I heard a car horn beeping furiously behind me, but irate drivers were the last of my problems. I ignored them.

I drove into the car park, and followed the signs until I was closer to the maternity unit. I felt the usual anxiety as I neared this clinical building. My scar was throbbing, and even the faint scar on my stomach seemed to sting a little. It was just my imagination, or repressed memories or something. I fought the urge to touch my healed wounds. What remained was purely emotional, and mental. It would take longer to deal with those. The hospital was nothing to be afraid of. Breathing deeply to calm my body, I drove through a barrier, stopping to collect a parking ticket on my way. I parked close to the building, under a streetlight. The sun was still shining, but it was sinking in preparation for dusk. I was always careful never to be too vulnerable late in the day. I realised now that I had more to fear than rapists and murderers. Again I suppressed those thoughts. I should be happy. I would be happy.

Walking into the building, carrying my brightly coloured gift bag, I smiled at a couple as they went past. The man was holding an infant carrier containing his newborn baby, and he had a large overnight bag slung over his shoulder. He was smiling, but he looked exhausted. His partner was close behind, shuffling uncomfortably towards the exit, but she smiled radiantly at her new baby. I smiled warmly at them both, and my heart lifted. I found the signs directing me to maternity, and then remembered I wanted a balloon. Luckily the shop was situated close by, and was still open. I purchased a large, bright pink balloon with the words 'baby girl' emblazoned across it, and then continued on my mission.

Climbing two flights of stairs, I found the ward where Liz was staying. I remembered to silence my phone before I went in. I was not in the mood for Jack to be phoning me now, which I was sure he would. There was a new text message, but I ignored it. I would read it after my visit. I stopped outside the secure door, and pressed the buzzer.

"Hello?" a pleasant female voice answered.

"Hello," I replied, "Um, I'm here to see Elizabeth Gormond. My name is Jessica Stone."

There was a pause.

"Ah yes," the woman replied, "Come on through."

I heard the mechanical buzzer, and pushed open the door.

Rob had text me the ward number and room in which to find Liz. The helpful nurse at the desk in the corridor pointed me in the right direction. I walked around a corner, entered a small room containing about eight beds, and I saw Rob sitting on a chair at the far corner by the window. I smiled warmly and hurried over.

"Hello!" I said loudly, "Where is she?"

Liz was sitting in bed, wearing her favourite 'Cookie Monster' pyjamas. Her short black hair was groomed as always, but I saw the telltale signs of childbirth in the way it stuck out in odd places. Normally, Liz made sure it was neat and tidy, and always under control. Her face was pale but she was smiling. In her arms lay the most beautiful baby girl I had ever seen. I am not joking. I had no experience of children, but my heart literally skipped a beat, and my maternal clock suddenly woke up. I had to hold this baby.

Rob turned round and stood up, smiling like the proverbial Cheshire cat. His eyes were bright beneath his black-framed glasses, and I saw dark shadows betraying his lack of sleep.

"Jessica, you made it," Liz said, "Here she is!"

She held out her precious bundle, and I hurriedly handed over my gift bag and balloon to Rob. He laughed at the helium monstrosity I presented him with, but I was too busy gazing at the baby.

Amy was swaddled in a pale pink blanket, and wearing a tiny white knitted hat. Her skin was blotchy, and her moon-shaped face was wrinkled in an odd way that was totally adorable. One tiny hand stuck out from the folds of blanket, and I gazed in awe as she clenched and unclenched her fingers, making tiny squeaking sounds as she was passed over to me.

"Oh, Liz," I whispered, "she is gorgeous," I turned my head, smiling broadly, "and, Rob, well done!"

And just like that, I was experiencing a whole new kind of love. This baby was not a blood relation. She was not my daughter. But I already loved her like my own, and I would do anything to protect and care for her as she grew up. Once again my emotions amazed me. And somewhere in the back of my mind I wondered, would it have been like this if I weren't with Jack, and if I hadn't experienced near death at the hands of supernatural creatures?

14

I spent an hour at the hospital talking to Liz and Rob. They told me all about the birth. It had been quite straightforward up until the end, when Amy became distressed. There had been talk of a possible caesarean but eventually Liz managed a natural birth, and she was happy about that.

"Ooh, Jess," she said, wriggling her body, "It doesn't half hurt!"

I laughed.

"Well you did just push a baby out of your body, Liz," I said, "What were you expecting?"

Liz grinned widely, and gazed at her daughter, still snuggled comfortably in my arms.

"I know," she said softly, "And I'd do it again. She is so perfect, I can't believe she's really ours."

I glanced at Rob, who was gazing at his daughter and wife with such naked adoration in his eyes that I felt a lump in my throat. Ducking my head, pretending to coo over the baby, I hastily blinked back the tears. I had never seen Rob as a romantic type before. He and Liz were always such a practical, no-nonsense couple. But I could see the pure love and devotion between them, and my heart swelled. I resolved to protect my best friend and her daughter from all of the horrible things I had discovered about the people we knew.

After about half an hour, baby Amy grew restless and started whimpering. I handed her back to her mother, and watched in awe as Liz deftly lifted her loose pyjama top, and put the baby to feed on her breast. She was so natural, and she kept up her conversation with Rob and me the whole time, apart from a little intake of breath when Amy first latched on. Finally it was time for me to leave. There was still half an hour left of visiting hours, but I wanted to leave the family to themselves.

"Shall I visit again tomorrow, Liz?" I asked, "Or will you be home?"

Liz glanced at Rob.

"I should be home tomorrow," she replied, "We are waiting for a doctor to check us over, and then we'll be away."

"Great," I said, "Well, send me a text message, or phone if you can, and I will visit wherever you are after work."

Liz and Rob nodded, and I stood up, leaning over to kiss Amy, who was now fast asleep in her mother's arms. I gave Liz an awkward hug, and kissed her cheek, mindful of her precious bundle. Then I turned to Rob who had stood up.

"I'll walk you out, Jess," he said.

We walked out of the ward and back to the door that led out into the stairwell. I turned to say goodbye to Rob, but he opened the door and walked out with me, down the stairs.

"How are you getting on with Jack?" he asked.

I looked at him sharply as we descended the staircase. There was nobody around, but I spoke quietly.

"We are fine," I said, "Why?"

Rob inclined his head.

"I know it must be difficult, learning to live with his…habits," he said, "And you have no one else to talk to about it. Just remember I am here."

I nodded, and stopped as we reached the main entrance.

"Thanks Rob," I said, "I appreciate it. I'm not about to add more stress for you now. You have more important things to worry about."

Rob nodded, and took his glasses off, cleaning them on his t-shirt.

"Just remember I am here," he said again as he breathed on the lenses and carefully wiped them, "I'll do what I can to help."

I blinked back those tears that threatened once again, and then impulsively threw my arms around him, hugging him tightly. He returned it, still holding his glasses in one hand. Rob felt strong, and warm, and was just so familiar that it was a relief to know I still had someone I could trust. He was going to be a brilliant dad.

"Go on," I said, standing back slowly, "Get back to your wife and daughter."

He smiled warmly.

"Yes," he said in wonder, "I'm a father. I still can't believe it."

I laughed at his expression, and lightly punched his arm.

"You'll be a fantastic dad," I said, "And Liz is a wonderful mother. Go and enjoy it."

He replaced his glasses, then leaned forward and kissed me on the cheek.

"See you tomorrow Jess," he said, then turned and walked back inside the hospital.

I stood for a few minutes, staring blankly at the doors. His life had just been turned upside down for completely different reasons to mine. His was a normal progression, the next step in his marriage, and a culmination of his little family. I wanted a baby. Suddenly I realised what people meant when they talked about the 'biological clock,' and what it really meant to be broody. I physically ached to have my own baby. And now I didn't even know if that would be possible, certainly while I was dating a vampire.

Shaking my head, I roused from my reverie and turned to walk to my car. The car park was still fairly busy, with couples exiting the hospital carrying their newborn babies, and visitors coming and going from various departments in the building. I felt perfectly safe out here, even though at this point I didn't know who was human and who was not. It didn't matter. Surely for now I didn't need to worry about another attack from a vampire or werewolf.

I remembered what had happened with the vampire that made Jack, when I was healing from my werewolf attack only weeks ago. Emily Rose was an old, French vampire, who had turned Jack after she fell in love with him. Although he escaped her, she had somehow made a psychic connection with me, and had tormented me on several occasions. This was a result of me carrying Jack's blood, which he had given me to prevent me from dying from my injuries, and partly because of my natural witch heritage. I knew nothing more about the technicalities, but I knew that she hadn't given up on us yet. Apparently she hated Danny because he kept Jack away from her, and now she hated me for the same reason. It was only a matter of time before she returned for another attack.

For now I was safe. Jack's blood had long since left my system, which meant Emily Rose lost her connection with me. I really needed to learn more about my abilities and myself. It was imperative, I knew, because otherwise I would be wide open for attack. The Mason brothers were dangerous people to have a relationship with. As I thought about this, I remembered that Jack had let me down. I had told Liz and Rob that he was stuck in a late meeting at work, but I was sure my anger had shown. That was why Rob had asked me about Jack.

I got into my car and pulled my mobile phone from my handbag. There were three text messages, a missed call from Jack, and an answer phone message. Grimacing, I locked myself into the car for security, and dialled the answer phone number.

"Jessica," Jack's voice said, "I have upset you. I will be at home when you are free to talk. Tell me if you wish to see me tonight."

I deleted the message, my heart racing. He hadn't apologised. There was no remorse in his tone. He probably only knew he was in trouble because Danny had told him. I was seething. Checking the text messages, I read one from Jack sent about ten minutes ago. It simply said he was waiting for my call. Another message was from Danny, telling me he had spoken to Jack. And the third message was from Simon, asking me to phone him after I had seen Liz. I smiled. He wanted all the gossip about the new baby. Maybe I would stop by the pub and see him.

I drove home in a daydream. Luckily the roads were quiet since rush hour had finished and most people were now back home from work, or out enjoying their holidays. It was dusk, and the streetlights were starting to switch on. I could feel a change in the air, as summer prepared to subside and make way for autumn. We were in September now, and I usually liked this time of year. It was a time when the tourists started to retreat, and Redcliffe became a quieter, more peaceful town in their absence. I enjoyed the tourism of course, that was one of the reasons Liz and me moved down here. It was essential to our trade. But it was nice to take a breather for a few months of the year, and take time off from work. Of course I had no time off for the next few months, at least not while Liz was with the baby. At the moment she was torn between staying off for a year, or returning after six months and putting Amy into a nursery. I thought we could manage to hire an assistant, but Liz was reluctant, ever careful where our shop was concerned.

Without even thinking about it, I had pulled into the car park of the Ship. It was fairly empty, which was a good sign. I would appreciate the pub being quieter tonight, so I could have Simon's full attention. Not bothering to return Jack's phone call, I checked my reflection in the rear-view mirror, then got out, straightened my clothes, and walked into the pub. I choked back the rising anxiety in my throat. I was safe. This was a safe place. Everything was fine. Walking into the main bar, I breathed a sigh of relief when I saw Simon. He saw me, smiled broadly, and indicated that my favourite table near the fireplace was free. I smiled and sat down, waiting as he fetched us some drinks, and came over.

15

Simon walked over to our table and placed a large glass of red wine in front of me. He sat down opposite and took a huge gulp of lager from his glass, making a satisfied 'ah' sound when he had swallowed. I laughed.

"You ready for that, Simon?" I asked sarcastically.

He nodded, and I lifted my glass in a salute and took a large sip for myself. The warm, rich taste soothed my raw nerves, and I took a deep breath, feeling the tension in my shoulders ease just slightly as the wine slid down into my stomach. I sipped again a couple of times before we spoke.

"Come on then," he said, "Where are the photos?"

"Oh yes, the new baby!" I said in mock surprise, and rummaged for my mobile.

I found the photos I had taken, and showed Simon, who cooed over them in such a comical way that I laughed. It felt good to be normal with him again after all that we had been through, and indeed, what we were still experiencing. He was still my best friend, and I still loved him. We talked about Liz, Rob and Amy for the next ten minutes, and I enjoyed my glass of Merlot. When we had finished our drinks, Simon half turned in his seat, catching the attention of one of the young barmaids. She caught his eye and jumped to attention, and I knew immediately that she was a werewolf. She nodded at Simon's gesture, and hurried to fetch us some more drinks.

"We get table service now?" I asked with a raised eyebrow.

Simon grinned.

"Well, now you know my secret, I may as well use it to our advantage." he said with satisfaction.

I watched as the girl set our drinks down on the table, ducking her head obediently to her master. Simon is Lieutenant to Danny, second in command to the Redcliffe werewolf pack. He was basically their leader while Danny was away for four years on an undercover police job in Scotland. Now the wolves were struggling to accept their true master, because Simon was the one that had been there for them. Apparently Danny was working hard to restore his power base, despite Simon's obvious dedication to his master.

Simon stared at me, his pale blue eyes showing intelligence beyond his twenty-six years. His soft blonde hair fell in natural waves, and I noticed it had grown longer over the summer. It looked a bit unkempt, and actually enhanced his appearance. Not that Simon needed any enhancement. He was the ultimate heartthrob surfer guy, and it was a damn shame he was gay. I knew that he was suspicious about my mood.

"What happened?" he asked, "I know it can't be about the wolves. They have been warned."

I shivered at his hard tone of voice. It was difficult to see Simon as a disciplinarian, but I had seen him as a wolf, and he was scary. He knew something was bothering me, and I couldn't hide it from him.

"Jack never showed up tonight," I sighed, "He said he would come to the hospital, and then he got stuck in a meeting."

"That's not all of it," Simon said.

"Apparently he has a vampire partner at work," I said, "And he never told me. Danny didn't think it was important," I took a deep breath, "But I don't like the sound of her, even though I know nothing about her. Does that sound crazy?"

"No," Simon said seriously, "You have a right to be suspicious. Have you spoken to Jack about her?"

I shook my head.

"Actually I was so busy being angry with him that I ignored my phone and came here," I admitted, "I suppose I should give him a chance to explain."

Simon inclined his head.

"Yes," he said, "You should. He has to work with other vampires, Jessica. And he works with shape shifters and witches. So does Danny."

I smiled sheepishly, and gulped my wine. It was already going to my head. I should walk home and leave my car at the pub. Finishing the drink, I stood up.

"You are right Simon," I announced, "I will go and speak to him, and I will stop being angry. I'm annoyed with myself now."

He laughed and stood up.

"Shall I walk you home?" he asked, "You look a little unsteady."

"No, no," I said, "I'll phone Jack and get him to meet me. I only have to walk round the corner. Besides, if anyone's going to attack me now I'm sure my 'witchiness' will kick in again, don't you think?"

Simon stared at me thoughtfully.

"I don't know Jess," he said, "You haven't exactly embraced your abilities yet. We don't know what you are capable of. Maybe I should walk with you, just in case."

I felt a rush of stubborn independence. I was sick of these men having to look after me all the time. What happened to the independent, self-reliant Jessica Stone of old? She had been replaced by this emotional wreck of a woman, who seemed to need men in her life just to function. I needed a break.

"Simon," I said firmly, turning to look at him squarely, "This is a nice town, with mainly nice people in it. For the sake of the very short distance to my house, along brightly lit, busy streets, I will take my chances. You don't need to baby-sit me."

He held his hands up and stepped back.

"Ok," he said, "Fine. You win. But promise me you will phone Jack first so he can at least meet you, and be there if there are any problems."

I nodded.

"Deal," I took my phone out, "I am dialling his number now. See you tomorrow Simon."

He watched me go, and I turned and walked out of the back door on to the smoking deck. Outside I breathed in and out deeply, tasting sea salt and actually enjoying the smell of cigarette smoke. It seemed to calm my nerves, and the warm fuzzy feeling from the wine subsided a little. I was glad. I did not need to be drunk for my conversation with Jack. And I shouldn't be drunk after only two glasses of wine, even if they were large ones. I looked longingly at my car, but I wouldn't take the risk. I would never forgive myself if I hurt somebody. It was fine on the car park and I could collect it after work tomorrow.

Jack answered just before the answer phone kicked in.

"Jessica," he said, "Where are you?"

"Hi, Jack," I replied, "I'm at the Ship, I came to see Simon. Will you meet me at home please?"

"Yes of course," he replied, "Are you well?"

"I'm fine," I said, "We need to talk. I'm leaving my car at the pub and will be home in about ten minutes." My stomach growled loudly, and remembering I was hungry, I added, "Make that twenty minutes. I need food."

He didn't argue or ask more questions. He simply accepted my words. This was good. I wasn't in the mood to argue. But we could at least talk like civilised adults. It felt good to let go of some anger, and I lifted my head, shook my hair back over my shoulders, and set off across the car park and onto the promenade. Crossing the road, I walked in the direction of the main shopping street, where I would walk round to the road at the back of our buildings. There was a fish and chip shop where I could get some food on my way.

I dodged a group of rowdy men, possibly a stag party judging by their raucous behaviour. They laughed and cajoled each other, and I knew they were looking at me in that predatory way that drunken men have. I ignored them and carried on, stepping into the warm, familiar takeaway establishment. This was my regular haunt, and the staff smiled warmly when I walked in.

"Hello, Jessica!" boomed the jovial voice of Bob, the owner, "What can I do for you tonight?"

Smiling, I made polite conversation and ordered a portion of chips with curry sauce on. My stomach was rumbling very loudly and I was ravenous suddenly. I felt a jolt of surprise when I found myself ordering a large sausage to accompany the food. Bob frowned and hesitated.

"Are you sure about that?" he asked curiously, "I thought you were vegetarian."

"I am vegetarian!" I said with a gasp, "I don't know why I just said that. Ignore me, Bob, it's been a long day."

He smiled and served up my chips and curry sauce, but he stared at me thoughtfully for a few minutes while he worked. Shaking my head, I turned to look out of the window, and saw the drunken group of men wandering around outside. I took my food gratefully, and started eating as I left the shop.

When I turned into the bottom of my road, I jumped as someone bumped into me, throwing his arm loosely around my shoulders. My first instinct was to steady my food, and then I glared at the man who was grinning down at me. My heart thudded hard in my chest but I didn't feel afraid. I was angry at the intrusion, and I just wanted him to leave me alone.

"Aw'right darling," slurred a cockney male accent, "Do you live round here?"

I clicked my tongue loudly in annoyance and shook my head. The man reeked of whiskey, and I guessed he was from the stag party. They had obviously been drinking for several hours by now, and he had decided to take his chances with me. Taking an exaggerated deep breath, I smiled politely, and slowly lifted his arm from my shoulder, dropping it by his side, careful not to drop my food. He staggered a little, still grinning suggestively.

"I am not interested," I said, "Thank you."

I started to walk away from him, but he stopped me.

"Come on love," he said, stepping a little too close for comfort, "How about a little hospitality?"

He leaned in close to my face, and I realised he had effectively pinned me against the rear wall of one of the terraced shops. I was holding one arm out to the side, balancing my tray of chips out of his reach. The building was in darkness because the apartment above was used for storage. I didn't need to scream, not yet. This guy was drunk, and I didn't think he could really be a threat. I was certain that he was actually human, and the fact that I had to acknowledge these thoughts was very amusing.

"I'm not in the mood," I said, smiling sweetly, "Now please leave me alone."

Staring at him, I willed him to step back. He stared at me, and some sort of comprehension crept across his face. I saw a movement in the shadows behind him, and I slowly shook my head. I did not need Jack interfering. He would only make the situation worse. The man seemed to realise I was serious, and he moved back from me. Without a word he turned and walked away, following the group of friends he had separated from. I watched him run across the road, and I heard their cheers and catcalls as he rejoined his group. I sighed with relief, and turned to face Jack.

16

He was in front of me in an instant, grabbing my face, staring into my eyes. I saw the blue fire burning in his, and his fangs gleamed in the streetlights. I smiled weakly, and my heart thudded painfully in my chest. I hadn't realised I was holding my breath before. I had gone into an automatic defence mode. And I had defended myself, without any need for protection. It felt good.

"Are you hurt?" Jack asked urgently, looking me up and down, touching my face with ice-cold fingers.

I shook my head.

"No," I replied, "He was just a drunk tourist. I deal with them every year."

Reluctantly, Jack stepped back, and I watched as his face returned to a human expression. It was unnerving, but I knew that it was normal for him, and I had to get used to it. This was the real Jack, and I needed to know him. I shook my head and walked briskly up the road, turning into my garden with relief. We didn't speak until we were standing in my kitchen and I had locked the door securely behind us. I automatically kicked my shoes off and left them in a pile near the door, dropping my handbag onto the bench that sat against the adjacent wall. Looking around my cheerful, slightly dated kitchen, I smiled. This was my home. It was safe, and warm, and familiar. I thought about baby Amy and my heart swelled.

Jack was standing near the stairs. He was so still that for a moment I forgot he was there, even though I had switched the light on and he had no shadows to hide in. He just had that unnatural quality, and he was watching me intently, waiting for me to break the silence. Looking down at the fast food tray I carried, I realised with surprise that I had eaten all my chips. I hadn't even tasted them, just wolfed them down. My body shivered violently and my stomach flipped. Forcing myself to remain calm, I walked over to the sink, discarding the empty container in the bin. I picked up a glass from the drainer, turned on the cold tap and filled the glass. Gulping down the fresh water, I put the glass down, wiped my mouth with the back of my hand, and walked past Jack and up the stairs. Although I couldn't hear him, I knew he followed me.

In the living room I walked straight over to my floor lamp and switched it on. Then I mechanically closed the curtains on the two windows, one which looked out onto the shopping street below, above the shop, and the other which looked out towards the sea at the end of the road, beyond the promenade. I turned round to find Jack standing right in front of me, staring. The heat was burning in his eyes again, and my body responded automatically. I wanted him. I needed him with a raw energy that seemed to unleash itself. Grabbing his head, I crushed my lips to his, feeling the sharpness of his fangs against my mouth. It only excited me more. In the back of my mind, something said this was wrong; I should stop. But instinct had taken over, and I wanted to be free. I was a caged beast, and he was my salvation.

Jack returned my frantic kisses. He was ravenous for me and I knew it. I had the power and love of this man in my hands, quite literally. This vampire would kill for me. I didn't know why. At this point I didn't want to question it. I just needed him. His jacket fell to the floor with a thud, and in some distant recess of my mind I realised he was carrying a gun. I should have been alarmed, but I wasn't. I shrugged off my cardigan and dropped it to the floor, desperate to be rid of the clothes that restrained me. Jack followed, ripping off his t-shirt and jeans, until we both fell naked onto the floor. I sat astride him, revelling in the feel of him against me. His hands touched my skin, caressing me, growing frantic as I moved faster on top of him, smiling as I saw him surrender completely to our lust. Finally we cried out together in ecstasy, clinging to each other, riding the waves of pleasure for as long as we could. I was in the clouds, flying through the air. I was all-powerful. He was mine. The climax passed and I collapsed on top of Jack, gasping for breath, laughing at the sheer intensity of our actions.

"That was..." I said breathlessly, rolling off him to lie on the carpet, "That was…amazing!"

Jack laughed and turned his head to look at me.

"You were like a crazed animal," he said, "What happened?"

"I don't know, but I liked it." I replied.

We lay side by side, and I listened as Jack's breathing slowed almost immediately. Still catching my breath, I shifted onto my side to look at him. His eyes were blazing with blue flame, and his skin was pale. He was beautiful, and I felt a lump in my throat. It was a mixture of happiness and grief. I was happy to be with a man I loved, and who loved me completely. I was certain of this. But I was sad because a human part of me had perished. I didn't know if it happened after my werewolf attack, or when I battled with Emily Rose, or even if it happened gradually once I accepted the truth about Jack being a vampire. It was time to move on. With the birth of a new baby, I had to become a new person. I had to accept my fate, embrace it, and learn what I needed to survive and thrive. Once again my stomach lurched, and I fought to suppress the panic and excitement that rolled inside me.

"You look so serious, Jessica," Jack said softly, reaching up to stroke my cheek, "What is wrong?"

I shook my head and blinked back tears.

"Nothing," I gasped, "I just realised that things have changed. I have changed. And I have a whole new way of life to experience. With you."

I leaned down and kissed him softly on the lips, then slowly struggled to my feet. I was not graceful. I got to my knees, used a nearby armchair for support, and finally managed to stand up, giggling at my clumsiness. Jack simply stood. One moment he was lying stretched out on the floor, and the next he was upright and standing beside me. It was so unfair. I shook my head at him, and walked off into the bedroom, grabbing my dressing gown from the hook on the back of the door. Returning to the living room, I sat down on the sofa and waited while Jack pulled on his jeans and sat on the adjacent armchair.

"What did you want to talk about, Jessica?" he asked.

I took a deep breath and lifted my face to look at him.

"Why didn't you tell me about your vampire partner?" I asked.

He shrugged.

"It wasn't important," he said, "She is simply a work colleague."

"OK," I said, "But surely you could have mentioned her."

"Why?" he asked, genuinely surprised, "She is of no importance to us."

"Well," I said, growing impatient, "She kept you away from me tonight when I needed your support. I wanted you to be a proper boyfriend and visit my friends and their baby at the hospital."

My anger was growing again, and I choked it back. I was determined to be an adult about this, and not to let it ruin our intense lovemaking session.

"I am sorry about that Jessica," Jack said quietly, "It was a professional matter that needed urgent attention. I cannot share details. It is classified."

I tipped back my head and closed my eyes, breathing deeply to calm myself. Something felt different. I could hear an echo in my head, and I thought it was my mother but I wasn't convinced. It was a warning sound. I needed to be suspicious. There was a new energy stirring deep within my body, and I didn't understand it. But somehow I knew that it was a sleeping part of me that had woken up. It was about to make its presence known.

Opening my eyes, I turned to look at Jack again. He actually jumped and stood up.

"Jessica," he said sharply, "What has happened to you?"

"Nothing," I said, "Why? Do I look different?"

Jack's fangs were suddenly extended, and he actually hissed in a defensive gesture. Instinctively I hissed back, and then jumped to my feet in surprise, both hands clasped to my mouth.

"What the hell was that?" I cried.

Jack was shaking his head, already standing across the room from me.

"I don't know," he said, and his Irish accent was growing thicker with his agitation, "You are different, Jessica. Something has changed."

I ran out to the hallway and looked in the mirror. My face was pale. My hair was shining, and my green eyes were bright and clear. In fact, I looked pretty amazing actually. I looked ethereal. I did not look human. There were no obvious changes. I hadn't sprouted a second head; I still resembled my human self. But there was something animal-like about me. And I could feel a pressure deep within my body. It was as though I was freezing cold and burning hot at the same time. I was trembling, and I lifted my hands, watching the tremors shuddering through my body. The building was stifling. I had to escape. I had to run.

Bursting into my bedroom, I grabbed a pair of jeans from the floor and pulled them on, not bothering with underwear. I pulled a clean t-shirt from the drawer and ran downstairs. My body was desperate to be outside. I had to obey my instincts. Jack followed me, grabbed my arm, but I shook him away and he didn't stop me. He simply followed. Grabbing my house keys, I shoved my feet into the nearest pair of shoes, and ran out of the house. Jack followed at my heels.

"Jessica," he said, trying to restrain me, "Jessica, what are you doing?"

"Let me go!" I shouted, pushing him away, "I need to run!"

Slamming the door, I turned and ran down the garden path, out into the street, and down the road towards the promenade. My feet slapped against the paving slabs, jarring my body because I wasn't wearing running shoes. It didn't matter. I instinctively turned towards the cliffs behind the Ship. I could run freely up there, and disappear into the woods. That was what I needed. Fresh air, earth and foliage. I didn't stop running until I reached the top of the cliff. It was almost the exact spot where Kimberley had attacked us only last night. That seemed like weeks ago. Time seemed irrelevant.

I bent over, gasping for air, trying desperately to catch my breath. Although I wasn't completely unfit, I wasn't really an athletic, or even a sporty kind of person. I was more likely to be found in a library than in a gym. But I had found a burst of energy, it had propelled me up the steep hillside, and now I was paying the price with my human body. I heard movement and glanced up, grabbing my wild hair and holding it back from my face. I wasn't afraid of attack. I knew that Jack had followed me. He approached me cautiously, slowly, not sure what to do.

"Jessica," he said hesitantly, "Is that you?"

I laughed. What a ridiculous question.

"Of course it is me," I said scornfully, "What were you expecting?"

He moved closer, watching me intently. There were no streetlights up here. There was a residual glow from the brightly lit town below us, and the bright moon above. I wondered if it was a full moon. I had no idea. The sea was rolling against the cliff side. It sounded quite peaceful tonight, calm and relaxed even. I was not calm and relaxed. The storm was raging within my body, and something had to give. I could feel a ball of pure energy growing inside me, and it was getting stronger and stronger as I focused on it. I knew that it was a part of my natural ability. It was my power. I just had to accept it. But I didn't know what it was.

Closing my eyes, I was transported far away from here. There was a forest, and I was running through it. I was free, and strong. I was a hunter. The trees were tall and majestic, rich, green pine trees. They grew thickly, close together, but I knew the path that wound through them. This freezing cold place, on the edge of the earth, was my home. There was a cave in the mountainside. It was the place in which I would sleep. It was a resting place, just another secret retreat on my journey.

"Jessica," I heard Jack's voice nearby, low and urgent, "Jessica, speak to me."

Opening my eyes, I was back on the cliff top in Redcliffe. I was kneeling on the grass, my knees cold as the wind whipped around me. But I didn't feel the cold. I opened my mouth to speak, and chills ran up and down my body.

"You cannot consume me, vampire," I said, "I will conquer you. And your wolf."

Jack reared back, defensive, hissing at me. He dared not attack until he knew what possessed me. He did not want to hurt the woman he loved. But I was far more than that weak, human woman. I had strength and power, and energy that had been released. It had been locked away inside me for all these years. And now, finally, the vampire and the werewolf had unlocked it.

"Where is Danny?" I asked, and my voice sounded strange, a lower pitch, an accent I didn't recognize.

"He is at home," Jack replied, "Why do you ask?"

"Call him here," I commanded, "He must know the truth."

"What truth?" Jack asked, "What are you?"

I threw back my head and laughed. My voice was rich and deep, and I loved the way it rumbled through my body. Rising slowly to my feet, I stretched my arms above my head, shaking my hair back, holding Jack's gaze. I saw the way his body instinctively reacted to the sight of mine, and how he was excited all over again. He had unlocked my true self. Now I could finally reveal it to him.

"Call him," I said again, "And I will tell you."

I turned and stalked towards the cliff edge, and stood watching the sea as I heard Jack take out his mobile phone.

"Danny," he said urgently, "Come to the cliff above your lair. Something has happened to Jessica. She seems... possessed," he listened for a moment and then I heard him say, "It is not my maker. This is something older, and it demands your presence."

I smiled and continued to stare out over the sea. Far off in the distance I saw a cruise ship, lit up on the horizon. I was breathing in and out deeply, and my body felt powerful and free. Stretching again, I felt the energy pulsing through me. I could almost feel white hot sparks shooting from my fingertips, though I did not know what to do with them. I too had secrets, and I had finally revealed them to myself. I wanted to show Jack and Danny. They should know that I was not merely a weak, powerless human. Oh no, I was far more than that. I had a strength that came from Source. It was part of the ultimate creation of life. I had finally discovered it.

Five minutes later I heard Danny approaching. I smelled his scent on the wind. His wolf was strong and musky, and my lips curled into a predatory smile. I wanted to play with the wolf. He would be a worthy toy. I knew that he had been in the lair below us. I felt his energy as I ran up the cliff side. In fact, I felt the energy of all his wolves, including Simon. If I made a connection through Danny, I could control the entire Redcliffe pack. They would be mine to command.

"Jessica," I heard Danny's voice, identical to his brother, "I am here as you requested."

Turning slowly, I surveyed the two brothers standing side by side on the gravel path. They kept a careful distance from me. They were unsure whether I had been possessed by a vengeful entity, or whether I was simply channelling a mischievous spirit. They certainly did not understand what they had done for me. I laughed again, savouring the sounds. It was good to experience this human body. I had taken it for granted all these years, and never really appreciated it. Lifting my head, I delicately scented the air. Levelling my gaze I saw Danny stiffen, and his beast rose instantly.

"What are you?" he growled, "You are not human."

I opened my mouth and growled a reply.

"No," I said, "It would appear I am not. You were right, both of you," I walked forward slowly, stepping over the rough ground delicately. Both men edged away from me warily, and my smile widened. I enjoyed their fear. It strengthened me.

"You told me I was a witch," I said to them, "You said I hold a great power within. Well, you have finally unlocked that power."

I drew myself up to my full height, standing straight and proud.

"I am a snow tiger," I declared, "And you, wolf, are my plaything."

17

The wind seemed to rise from nowhere, whipping across the cliff top and sending my hair flying around my head. Lifting my chin, I fixed my gaze on Danny, watching his expression change from mild unease to a more primal fear. He growled, low in his throat, and my tiger heard him and responded. Opening my mouth I howled a reply, and it was a blood curdling sound. Deep in the recesses of my mind, my human self was screaming "No! This is wrong! Stop it!" I wasn't going to stop it. The tiger was my creature, and she was beautiful. I could see her in my mind's eye, standing at the entrance to a dark cave of grey stone. Her coat was silver-white, streaked with darker shades of grey and black. She belonged in a time and place far removed from where we now stood. Swishing her tail, I saw her bright, dark eyes almost glowing in the icy surroundings that were her home. Then she sprang forward, and I knew that she was using my body as her portal into this scene.

"Jessica," Jack said cautiously, stepping closer to me, "Jessica, can you hear me?"

Turning my head slightly I curled my lips in a smile. I knew that my eyes were glowing; I could feel the heat. I felt a sheer strength running through my body, an energy and power that were mine to control. The tiger would give me all of this, in return for some fun with the wolf. I could accept that. I spoke to Jack.

"I am here, Jack," I said in a voice that did not sound like mine. It was deeper, husky, with a growl at the back of my throat, "The tiger is my animal. She is a part of me, and she has finally woken. Now she wants to play."

I fixed my gaze on Danny again, who was now standing defiantly before me, preparing for a fight. I felt his energy and power spilling out around me, and it was warm and exciting. It smelled like the forest, and the trees, and I wanted to chase him. My tiger wanted to chase him. My human conscience seemed to find a voice, and somewhere in my mind I reasoned with myself. What was I doing? I was not a shape shifter. I could not physically become the tiger. Yet I knew with certainty that she belonged to me, and I to her. She wanted to use my body now. My human self was defeated, as the tiger pushed her way forwards.

I stepped closer to Danny again, and my tiger advanced upon him. Although I couldn't physically see her, I felt that she was around me like a cloak. Her warm, exotic energy wrapped around my body and attached itself to me, so that to Danny and Jack, she was clear to see. Something instinctive told me that only the supernatural creatures would see my tiger. Humans were not evolved enough to trust in their senses. They would ignore the tingles down their spine, or that feeling of discomfort. They would dismiss it as a cold chill, or a draught. In truth it was energy, pure and brilliant. And this energy needed an outlet.

"Jessica," Danny said warily, "What are you going to do?"

I threw back my head and laughed. My power spiked around me, and when I looked at Danny again, I threw it at him in a great, hot ball of fire.

"We are going to play," I said, "That is what she wants."

I suddenly leaped at Danny, pushing him to the ground, straddling him as we fell. Jack shouted and jumped beside us, and Danny didn't know whether to push me away or not. I knew that had I been any other person, he would have hit out in defence. But this was me, a woman he cared for, and he was confused. It made him clumsy. The wind was howling across the cliff top now, and it was my energy that had invoked it. I could feel a pressure in my chest that burned and strained for freedom, and I had to release it.

Danny pushed me to one side, so I landed on the ground beside him. He scrambled back, jumping up and retreating towards the trees. I stood smoothly, with grace and agility that I did not possess as a human. My tiger glowed around my body, becoming brighter as I gave her more strength. She growled again, and the sound must have been terrifying coming from my very human seeming body. Jack grabbed my shoulders, putting himself in front of me.

"Jessica," he said urgently, staring into my eyes with his burning blue ones, "Jessica, please stop this. You cannot control it."

For a moment I felt a soothing sensation wash through me, a sense of cool and calm amidst the storm of my power. I almost relaxed in his arms, but my tiger knew what he was doing. She hissed angrily at him, and I pushed him away so hard that he staggered back with the force of it.

"Do not try to distract me, vampire," I said in that eerie voice, "It is not you that my tiger seeks. She needs something warm and alive to give her strength."

Looking past him, I fixed my gaze once more on Danny. This time he retreated fully into the trees, and I scented the air delicately. My tiger could smell where he was, and that he was still in human form. This would be fun. We would bring his beast out to play. I ran into the forest, aware of Danny running ahead of me. He was either trying to outrun me, or he was taking us deeper where we would not encounter any humans. I could run faster with the strength of my tiger. She was young and strong, and very agile. Behind us I was aware of Jack following, but he was of no concern to us. This game had no place for vampires.

I charged into a small clearing, where Danny was facing me, panting with his exertions. We had run quite a distance, and were now deep into the forest, in a part where the trees grew close, and humans dared not venture. We had lost Jack somewhere behind, and I knew instinctively that he was now searching for us, using all of his vampire senses and flying through the woods. He would not find us for a while. We had leaped over fallen trees and damaged trunks, skipped across a stream or two that ran down to the river, and skirted round the giant trunks of the ancient oaks, ash and sycamore trees that graced this land.

Danny took a fighting stance, preparing for battle. He had no idea what we wanted, but he was anxious, and determined to bring me back to my senses. He did not realise that I felt more alive than I had my entire life. I had power. I was strong. I was not human after all. Smiling, feeling the heat glowing in my eyes, and my tiger cloaking my body, we stepped forward stealthily. I threw out all of my power, and it felt like silver sparks of lightening shooting from me. Danny fell back as though he had been hit.

"Jessica, stop!" he cried out, "Please stop! I will lose control."

I laughed.

"That is what we want," I said, "Come out and play, my wolf friend. Show my tiger what you have to offer."

Danny raised his head, and I saw his wolf eyes glowing amber in his still-human face. He growled again and bared his teeth, and I felt a thrill of excitement pulse through me. It was working. We were pulling the wolf out of him, forcing him to transform. And he was fighting against it, determined to keep control of the situation, even though he had lost that a long time ago. I kept on throwing sparks of energy at him, watching his body convulse and jerk in response. He growled and shouted, trying to stand up and then falling back to the ground as he fought the change. I felt his power swirling around us, and then I felt it sweep wider. He was searching for his pack, to use their energy for support. He certainly was strong, and my tiger grew even more excited.

Suddenly we were attacked. Jack swooped in from somewhere higher up, and I heard his voice in my head.

"I am sorry, Jessica." he said, and then he bit my neck.

Screaming with pain, I immediately turned my attention to the vampire. The tiger screamed with me, swishing her tail, snapping at the vampire to try and send him away. But it was too late. Our bond was broken, and the tiger disappeared just as suddenly as she had arrived. The wind dropped, Jack stepped back, and I stared at him in shock. My head was pounding, I clasped a hand to my bleeding neck, and for a moment I didn't know where I was.

"Jack," I said weakly, "What happened? Where are we?"

And then my knees crumpled, my body gave up, and I fell to the ground, unconscious.

18

A shrill beeping sound woke me from sleep. Groaning and muttering, I rolled over in bed and batted ineffectually at my radio-alarm clock. After a few seconds I found the snooze button and pressed it, then flung my arm above my head. It was too late. I was awake. My head ached and I felt like I had been drinking. Turning my head slowly to the side I saw that the bed was empty. I sensed a presence in the room, and I turned back and opened my eyes. Jack was sitting in the wooden armchair beside my dressing table. He was staring at me with a terrifying expression on his face. My heart immediately jumped into my throat, and I sat up in bed. Jack's skin was white, his eyes were glowing silver, and he was doing nothing to disguise his inhuman heritage. He was angry with me.

"Jack," I said in a croaky voice, "What happened?"

I coughed to clear my throat, but Jack never moved. Only his mouth responded.

"You tell me, Jessica," he said in an icy tone that chilled my body.

I wrapped my arms across my chest, rubbing at the goose bumps that had suddenly risen in response to Jack's presence. Closing my eyes, I thought back to what had happened the previous night. I had returned from the hospital, been with Jack, and then something had changed. I remembered pulling on my clothes and running out of the house and up onto the cliff top. Jack had followed me, and then I demanded Danny's presence, but why? Slowly, the memories resurfaced, flashing through my mind in a crazy montage.

"Danny," I said, "The tiger. What did I do? Did I hurt him?"

"You did not hurt my brother," Jack said in that same icy tone, "How did you hide such a powerful creature from us Jessica?"

I shook my head, and then stopped as pain shot through it. I needed water, and food.

"I didn't hide it Jack," I replied, "I didn't know she was there."

Slipping out of bed, I walked through to the bathroom and mechanically switched on the shower. While the water warmed up I took care of business, deep in thought. I was a witch. There was no doubt about it. First I was having visions in my dreams, and then I was holding conversations with my dead mother. Now I had discovered that I had an animal familiar and she was a snow tiger of all things. I never even knew they existed. This was crazy. And I had to get ready for work. While the thoughts whirled around my head, I climbed into the shower, enjoying the hot water pounding on my body. It loosened some of the tension, and I took care to lather up my favourite citrus scented shower gel and use my body buffer.

This time I wasn't surprised to find Jack standing in the bathroom when I pulled back the shower curtain. He didn't hand me a towel, so I reached for it myself, carefully stepping onto the bath mat so I didn't slip on the tiled floor. Jack was standing near the window, staring at me across the small space. If he was trying to make me uncomfortable it was working, but I refused to back down. He had no right to be angry with me. It wasn't like I did any of that stuff on purpose. When I had dried my body, I wrapped the towel in a turban on my head, and walked back into the bedroom to apply moisturiser and get dressed. The only sign that Jack followed was a blur moving past me, and then he was seated once more in the chair, watching me as I went about my morning routine. He never even seemed distracted by my naked body, which actually upset me more than the vampire mood swing. Finally, I broke the silence.

"What do you expect me to say, Jack?" I asked, turning to face him from across the room.

I was laying out clothes on my bed as I spoke. A glance out of the window showed a day that was overcast and possibly cooler, so I picked out a knee length dark blue a-line skirt, a coordinating fitted top with long sleeves, and my black lace up boots which almost reached my knees. That way I could avoid wearing tights, but I should still be warm enough. I pulled out some underwear from my drawer, and spoke as I slipped on my French kickers and a matching black lace bra. I kept eye contact with Jack as I spoke, watching his face for any signs of reaction. I had chosen the underwear in part to see if I could get through his angry façade, but he was fighting the desire, though I saw the telltale signs of him weakening.

"I am not sorry for what happened," I said, "Because I didn't exactly plan to do it. Why are you angry?"

He stood slowly, in his characteristic smooth, fluid motion. He was still dressed in yesterday's clothes, and his hair was unkempt. I reckoned Jack could do with a shower before work as well, but his mind was on other things. He finally spoke.

"You kept that animal a secret from me," he said coldly, "From all of us. Why?"

Fastening my skirt, I looked up as I smoothed it out, straightening my top where I had tucked it into the waistband.

"I didn't know about her," I said, "Do you really think I could hide something like that from you?"

"Yes," he replied, "You tried to hurt my brother. I want to know why."

I took a deep breath, and glanced at the clock.

"I did not hide anything from either of you, Jack," I said again, "Apparently you were right. I am a witch, but I still don't know exactly what that means. All I do know is that something snapped last night, and all of a sudden I was taken over by this massive tiger."

I walked round the bed and picked up my mobile phone from the dressing table, glancing at it. There were a couple of text messages and half a dozen emails. I would check them later. I carefully ignored the angry vampire standing behind me, and I kept a distance as I walked back around the bottom of the bed and out of the bedroom door.

"I need breakfast," I said over my shoulder, "Are you coming downstairs, or are you going to stand there being angry all morning?"

As I walked slowly down the stairs, I felt his presence rush up behind me, and I huffed as he once again flew past me in a blur. I was starting to feel quite grumpy myself. My head was aching, my stomach was rumbling, and I felt detached from my body. It was sort of like a hangover, but I felt distant from my surroundings. I was later to learn that I needed grounding, because my earth energy was all over the place. My angry boyfriend, who was now seated at the kitchen table as I entered the room, helped none of this.

My first task was to fill a glass with cold tap water, and gulp it down. Feeling better already, I set about filling the kettle and switching it on, and then I poured cereal into a bowl and added milk. When the kettle boiled I made a cup of tea, and carried my breakfast over to the table, sitting opposite Jack.

"You accept that you are a witch," Jack said quietly.

I looked up, chewing a mouthful of cereal.

"Yes," I said after a pause, "I suppose I do."

"You knew nothing about the snow tiger before last night," he said in that same quiet, cool voice.

"No," I said, "It was a complete shock to me."

"You have no ulterior motive for my brother," Jack said, "Or for me?"

I put down my spoon and stared at him. The anger was building in my own chest now, born of frustration and confusion.

"What possible ulterior motive could I have, Jack?" I asked sharply.

He shook his head.

"I don't know," he said, "Perhaps you wish to control the wolf pack. Or maybe you want to destroy us for what we are. There are many reasons we attract enemies."

That was it. I had had enough. Standing abruptly, I grabbed my empty bowl and mug, carrying them over to the sink and throwing them roughly into the washing-up bowl. It was a wonder they didn't break.

"Why the hell would I want to destroy you both?" I asked angrily, "I didn't even know what you were until you dragged me into that fucking mess with Seamus Tully!"

Jack sat still, apparently unruffled at my outburst.

"You are telling the truth," he said thoughtfully.

He stood up and moved to the back door, reaching for the key to unlock it.

"Perhaps we should speak later," he said quietly, "We both have work to attend to. Goodbye, Jessica."

And he was gone, swiftly and abruptly. The door banged shut behind him, and when I looked out of the window I saw nothing. I didn't even see his car parked on the street outside, so I guessed he was walking home. Or maybe he flew. Sighing heavily, I rinsed the dishes clean, locked the back door, made another cup of tea, and carried it through to the shop. It was time to start work. My personal life could wait.

19

The day was dragging. My morning was spent feeling tired and lonely, drinking several strong mugs of tea and munching biscuits. I had a strange sort of tummy ache, as though something was churning inside me. My fingertips still throbbed with energy, although it wasn't as strong as it had been last night. I could feel the snow tiger confined to a place deep within. I couldn't explain it, but I could feel it. Instead of feeling nervous or agitated, I was actually excited. Here was my power. I had the strength of a true tiger, an ancient species no less, and she would be mine to control once I understood how to work with her. I was not sure what the implications would be with Jack and Danny, but at this point I didn't care. At least they could stop seeing me as a helpless human.

Liz phoned shortly before lunch, and informed me that she would soon be home, Rob would be cooking an evening meal for me, and that I should visit directly after work. I obeyed, my mood brightening at the prospect. Liz sounded amazing considering she had only given birth two days ago, but then she was a natural mother. She never let things bother her, and always had a positive response to a negative situation. I wondered what she would think about my current situation if she knew the truth. She would probably run away screaming from me. Actually no, Liz wasn't a coward. She would weigh up the situation, deal with the truth as she saw it, and then set about planning a solution. If only I could tell her.

I was surprised that Simon didn't come to visit me. He had been very protective of me for weeks now, and I knew that my outburst last night had upset more than just Danny. My tiger had wanted all the wolves; that was why she went for their leader. I wondered if Simon was angry with me too, and whether he had transformed into a wolf and gone hunting as a result of my actions. I still couldn't comprehend what I had actually done. Initial research on the Internet didn't yield anything promising. I kept being directed to obscure websites for role-playing games, or magical supply stores, or various social networks for witches and pagans. I tried searching through the books in our limited Mind, Body and Spirit section, but most of these were self-help manuals. I needed to speak to an actual witch, one who could give me some relevant information.

After a substantial lunch, I was once again surfing the web for anything of use, and my mood was darkening again. I still felt hungry. I had a strange craving to eat meat, and it was very unsettling. It had taken all my self-control not to order a chicken sandwich or a BLT in the café. Even the women had looked at me curiously, obviously noticing something was wrong. I managed to evade their questions and made a hasty retreat back to my shop.

It was as though the events of last night had drained me of all energy, and I needed food to replenish that. Returning from the kitchen munching on an apple, I looked up as the doorbell jangled and in walked a customer. I saw immediately that she was not here for retail purposes. She was a bit taller than me, perhaps about 5' 7" and her skin was very pale. The black pinstriped business suit she wore, along with her perfectly styled, sleek black hair accentuated it. I knew she wasn't human. It was an instinctive knowledge, and my heart beat a little faster. I didn't think she was a threat, but given recent events, I wasn't about to take a chance.

"Hello," I said warily, "Can I help you?"

I had walked back around my desk, putting the solid wood between us, but I remained standing. The woman was now standing in front of me, smiling warmly. Her eyes were an unusual shade of blue, almost purple, and they were captivating. Her hair was pulled back in a ponytail, and she had an air of confidence and control that I instantly envied.

"Hello, Jessica," she said, "It is a pleasure to finally meet you. I am Crystal Waters, and my friend Jack Mason thought we should talk."

She held out her hand, and I was totally thrown. This was the witch? She looked like a businesswoman. But then, her striking eyes and the power that flowed around her were easy to discern, at least for me. I smiled in response, and my defences lowered a little. I should be able to trust her, because Jack did. Then again,

Love Kills

did I really trust Jack at the moment? That was a question I didn't want to answer.

"Hi," I faltered, "Um, sorry, you surprised me."

Crystal laughed, and the sound was pretty and reassuring. I felt a moment of dizziness and then the room settled, and my heart rate slowed a little. There was definitely an energy here that I hadn't felt before. The atmosphere felt alive suddenly, almost crackling with static electricity. Flexing my fingers, having dropped the half-eaten apple onto my desk, I could feel the invisible sparks wanting to shoot out of my fingertips again, like they had last night. I gasped, not wanting a repeat performance.

"Don't worry," Crystal said, "Your tiger is quiet. She is content after last night's excitement."

"How do you know?" I asked.

"Jack phoned me this morning," she replied, "He was very agitated, and he told me what happened," she lowered her head and raised her eyebrows at me, "We had better start your training soon I think," she said, "It seems you have quite a power within you."

My eyes flickered to look at the door, where I could see a few people approaching. Crystal turned as well, and then spoke quietly to me as three customers walked in, chattering loudly.

"Now is not the time," she said, "I will return on Sunday, at around 11:00am, and we can talk then. Is that alright with you?"

I nodded, lost for words. She had taken control of the conversation, and somehow I was willing to let her. She looked to be in her late thirties, but I guessed there was far more wisdom than meets the eye. Whatever she was, I felt comforted, and I took the business card she handed to me.

"Phone me if you have any problems in the meantime," she said, "And don't worry. I will explain everything to you."

She turned and walked quickly out of the shop, her high heels clicking sharply on the wooden floor. I breathed out slowly, and looked at the business card. She was a lawyer. Her name was Christine Waters, and she had a string of letters after her name, none of which I understood. The customers soon distracted me, and fortunately business picked up in the afternoon. I finished the day feeling a lot happier, more refreshed surprisingly, and looking forward to my dinner with Liz, Rob and baby Amy.

20

Having closed up the shop, I walked through to the kitchen and straight upstairs. The weather was definitely cooler today, so I changed into a pair of dark blue jeans with a t-shirt and cardigan. My mobile phone was still silent. I had resisted the urge to send Jack a text message, and for some reason, I didn't actually dare to phone him. I couldn't deal with his black mood if it was anything like the morning. It would just wind me up in defence, and we would be worse off. I was embarrassed to contact Danny, but I desperately needed to speak to someone. Finally, I phoned Simon. His mobile rang out, so I tried his landline, which again yielded no answer. I tried the bar phone at the Ship, and a young woman answered.

"The Ship public house, Jen speaking," she said cheerfully.

I recognised her as one of the teenage bar staff. We had spoken a few times, but I didn't think she liked me.

"Jen," I said, "It's Jessica Stone. Is Simon there please?"

There was a pause, and then she replied in an icy tone.

"Simon is busy at the moment," she said, "Can I take a message?"

I breathed out slowly to calm myself. Something was definitely wrong.

"Jen," I said, "I'm sorry about whatever happened last night. I need to speak to him. Please, will you get him for me?"

"No, Jessica," she said more loudly, "He cannot speak to you. Our Master forbade him. I must go." And she hung up the phone.

I stood for a minute, stunned. Danny had forbidden Simon to speak to me? This was ridiculous. Simon was my friend, never mind being Danny's subordinate. I felt anger spread through me, followed by intense irritation at the stupidity of these men. No, they were not men, they were wolves, and I must remember that. Clearly I was witnessing the arrogance of pack animals, or rather the pack animal leaders. I was trying to decide whether to visit the pub, and defy Danny's stupid instruction, when my phone beeped indicating a text message. It was from Liz, telling me dinner was ready and I'd better hurry up or else. Smiling, I walked back downstairs, pulled on my trainers, grabbed my bag, and left. As I walked down the garden path I replied saying I was on my way.

Parking on the kerb at the bottom of Liz and Rob's driveway, I looked around me as I climbed out of the car. The streetlights were coming on early due to the dark and miserable day. I could feel moisture in the air, as though rain were threatening but not quite making it through. I shivered, and wrapped my cardigan around me, tying the belt round my middle. Soon I would have to dig out my jacket and coat ready for winter. It would certainly be a strange one this year. I saw people parking up on their own driveways up and down the street, as they returned from work and after-school clubs. Children and parents chattered loudly, shouting at each other about their day or to fetch the shopping out of the boot, or to hurry up and get that front door open, I need a drink after today! Smiling, I dropped my keys into my handbag and walked up the drive to my friends' house.

Rob met me at the door, followed by the smell of something delicious cooking in the kitchen. I caught a whiff of herbs, tomatoes and garlic, and my stomach rumbled loudly.

"Evening, Jessica," Rob said, laughing when he heard my stomach, "Hungry I take it?"

I laughed.

"Yes," I said, "Hi! Oh I'm starving. Hi, Liz!"

I walked through to their living room and found Liz sitting in an armchair, feeding Amy. The room was cosy and warm, full of greetings cards declaring congratulations for the new baby. The huge pink helium balloon floated in one corner of the room, the coffee table was strewn with muslin squares, baby wipes, a half-empty glass of orange juice, and envelopes containing opened mail that had been discarded for the moment. Liz looked up, smiling broadly. I reached down to stroke Timmy, the Gormond's tabby cat. He arched his back and rubbed his head against my legs, always happy for some attention.

"Hello," Liz said, "How are you?"

Pulling off my cardigan now I was in a warm room, I dropped it across the back of the sofa and sat down.

"I'm fine thanks," I replied, "How's my little girl?"

Liz looked down at her daughter and smiled indulgently.

"Hungry as always," she said, "All she does is eat and sleep."

"Sounds like a good life to me," I said, and laughed.

We chatted for a few minutes while Rob retreated into the kitchen to make drinks and check on the food. He didn't cook very often, but when he did it was always a proper hearty meal, and I was really looking forward to it. I asked Liz how she was doing, and she told me a little about her experiences of breastfeeding.

"Oh Jess," she said, "They don't tell you how much it hurts. My toes curl every time she latches on."

I frowned.

"Is that normal?" I asked, "I mean, have you spoken to your health visitor?"

"Oh yes," Liz replied, "And I've checked the forums online. Apparently it should ease after a few weeks, I've just got to get on with it until then."

"Can't you give her a bottle?" I asked, and Liz exclaimed loudly in reply.

"No!" she gasped, "Hey, this is the natural way to feed our children, and if we can survive labour then we can survive this. I'll deal with it." She finished firmly.

I nodded, not understanding at all, but pretending to for her benefit. This whole motherhood thing was a mystery to me, and I felt pretty helpless as a friend to Liz. It wasn't as if we could go through the experience together. But she was strong, and she had already joined a group of local new mothers to share with. I didn't have to worry about Liz. But I did feel a little left out. This was something I could not truly be a part of, at least not for a long time.

"I'll just go and give Rob a hand with the drinks," I said, standing up, "Do you need anything?"

Liz shook her head, shifting Amy in her arms. The baby drew back and squealed a little, then rooted for Liz's breast almost straight away. We both looked at each other and laughed. Amy was adorable. Shaking my head, I walked into the kitchen.

"Do you need a hand, Rob?" I asked, walking over to the kettle.

He had set out three mugs with teabags in, and I fetched the milk from the fridge after switching on the kettle again. It seemed he had boiled water but not poured it immediately, and that made for a bad brew.

"No, it's all under control Jess," he replied, stirring something in a pan and checking something else in the oven.

I stirred the tea aimlessly, and jolted when I heard Rob behind me.

"Jess," he said, then more loudly, "Jessica! What's wrong?"

Turning, I stared up into his kind, gentle face. His eyes looked tired, which was obvious with a new baby in the house. I didn't want to burden him with my problems. But I couldn't help it. The words tumbled out.

"There was an incident last night," I said quietly, almost whispering, "I sort of discovered I have an animal familiar. It's a snow tiger."

Rob stared, swallowed, and stepped back so he leaned against the kitchen cupboards. Taking off his glasses, he began mechanically to clean them on a corner of his t-shirt. I knew by now that this was a nervous gesture, a way for him to bide time while he processed some new and shocking information. After a few minutes he put them slowly back on, pushing them up close to his eyes.

"So you are a witch then," he said in the same half-whisper.

I nodded.

"Yes," I replied, "And I attacked Danny."

Rob's eyebrows shot up.

"You did?" he said incredulously, "What happened?"

We both jumped as Liz's voice called through from the other room.

"Oi, you two," she shouted, "Where's my brew, I'm parched!"

I glanced at Rob, and then hurriedly picked up two mugs of tea.

"I'll tell you more later," I said quickly, "Danny's fine but they are both angry with me."

Loudly I called out to Liz, "Sorry, I'm coming!"

Rob dished up our food shortly after that, Amy went to sleep tucked into her crib, and we all sat at the dining room table and enjoyed a delicious wholesome meal. Liz nodded approvingly when she saw my plate piled high. My appetite had been greatly reduced recently, and she had been worried that I wasn't getting any nourishment. She also ate heartily, and we joked about how she needed even more food for the baby now that she was breastfeeding. The evening finished very nicely, and I felt happier and warmer by the time we finished. I didn't stay too late because I could see they needed their own time, and Amy took a lot of attention. I promised to visit again the next evening, but I would wait until after dinner so Rob didn't have to cook again.

He followed me out to the car when I left, under pretence of saying goodbye. I had hugged and kissed Liz, and had cuddled baby Amy while she slept in my arms. I stepped out into the cool night air, wrapping my cardigan tightly around me again, and rummaged for my keys. Rob walked beside me down the drive, and spoke only after he had checked there was nobody within earshot.

"So," he said to me, "What happened with Danny, and this...tiger?"

Unlocking my car door, I opened it and turned to face him.

"She just sort of woke up," I said, "I don't know what triggered it. I suddenly got the urge to run, and I ran up onto the cliff top above the Ship."

Rob nodded, urging me to continue.

"I demanded Danny's presence," I said, "so Jack phoned him. And when he arrived, my tiger decided she wanted the wolf to play. I threw everything at him, metaphysically. I can't explain it. I had sparks shooting out of my body, and I aimed them all at him."

Rob put a hand on my shoulder, warm and comforting.

"How did you break the connection?" he asked gently.

"Jack bit me," I said, my voice breaking, "I had chased Danny into the woods. He was about to transform, and Jack stopped it. And now Danny has forbidden Simon to speak to me, because he thinks I did it on purpose and I caused chaos with the wolves."

"So, what now?" Rob asked.

I shrugged, and then shook my head, smiling weakly.

"Don't worry Rob," I said, "I'm sorry, I shouldn't have said anything. You get back inside and take care of your family. I'll sort this out."

He stared at me for a moment, and then slowly stepped back, nodding.

Love Kills

"Yes ok," he said, "But if you need help, and I can offer it, then call me."

Nodding again, I climbed into my car and watched Rob as he strode back up the drive and in through his front door. I waved when he reached the door, and waited until he had closed it. Then I pulled out my mobile phone. There were still no messages. I didn't want to just drive round to Jack's house. I was afraid of what might happen. And it looked like I couldn't visit the pub. I didn't want to make the situation worse. I could not simply go home and forget about it. Sighing, I sent Jack a text message, asking if I could visit. Then I started the car, and drove off out towards the coastal road that led away from Redcliffe. There was only one person who might listen to me without being judgemental. And he might actually offer some constructive help.

21

I had only visited Marcus Scott once, and that was the night he rescued me from Jack. It was the night when Jack had arrived on my doorstep, battered and beaten, had tried to attack me for blood, and Marcus had appeared in time to stop him. He had subsequently transported us back to his mansion in the countryside, where Danny lay dying in a guest bedroom. After some pretty horrific scenes that I would rather forget, Jack saved Danny's life through sharing blood, but both men remained unconscious all night. It was Marcus who then took me into another room, and explained the truth about their kind. Memories flooded my mind as I drove automatically. It wasn't hard to find Marcus' house again. I turned into the lane that led from the coastal road, and saw the house hidden amongst the treetops. It was a huge, modern structure, and it was well concealed from public view. I guessed this was to protect Marcus' regular non-human guests. Apparently he was fond of entertaining fellow vampires, and occasionally shape shifters if he felt the gesture served a purpose.

Pulling into the long, sweeping driveway, my courage failed as I drove closer to the front door. There was a new Jaguar parked in the drive; a sleek, dark grey machine. I wondered if Alice was home. She was Marcus' human assistant. They told me that she was mostly human, but she had partaken in blood sharing rituals with Marcus to preserve her youth, since they had met in the sixties and fallen in love. She didn't want to become a vampire, but she did care for Marcus, and she lived with him in a very strange but apparently very agreeable arrangement. She worked as a PA for his telecommunications business, and I knew that they were intimate, though not exclusive, partners.

I was about to drive right round the ornamental fountain that sat squarely in front of the entrance to the house, when the door opened and Marcus stood on the top step. Smiling, ducking my head briefly, I waved and carefully parked my car behind the Jaguar. As I climbed out of the car, trying desperately not to catch my foot in the seatbelt or some other clumsy disaster, my heart beat faster. Marcus made me feel like a giddy, awkward schoolgirl, and I hated it. He appeared to be younger than me, having been turned into a vampire at the age of twenty-three. He was older than Jack and Danny, and had grown up during the Victorian era. I didn't know Marcus' actual age, and I wasn't sure he remembered either.

"Hi, Marcus," I called as I approached the door, "Sorry, is this a bad time?"

He smiled and shook his head, but his body remained still. He never wasted energy on movement.

"Not at all, Jessica," he said in a smooth, rich voice, "Please come in."

I stepped past him and into the dimly lit hallway, catching my breath as I caught the scent of his expensive aftershave. It was musky, sultry, and with spicy undertones, and my body reacted before I had time to even register my desire for the vampire. Marcus closed the door quietly and turned to face me. I stood awkwardly, not sure what to say. He broke the silence.

"I had a visit from Jack today," Marcus said, "He told me about last night. Do you want a drink?"

I nodded, and when Marcus gestured towards his living room, I hurried across the square entrance hall with its white walls and black and white tiled floor. This place reminded me of that first night. I had entered the house in a daze, following Marcus, Jack and Alice. Then we had heard screams of pain from upstairs, and Jack had literally flown to assist his brother. I had run up these stairs to see what was happening, and that was when my life fell apart. Turning my head away from the stairs, I focused on entering Marcus' comfortable, modern living room.

"Please, sit down," he said, gesturing to the large, black leather sofas, "What drink would you like?"

"Um, could I have a coffee please?" I asked, sitting down tentatively.

Marcus' expression changed, and I blushed as I realised he had meant an alcoholic drink.

"Oh, sorry," I blustered, "I'm driving, I can't drink. How about water?"

He smiled, and his eyes sparkled mischievously. He saw my clumsiness, and he was enjoying it. I frowned.

"Do not worry Jessica," Marcus said, "I will fetch you some coffee. It is so rare that I entertain humans, I forget you are sensitive to the effects of alcohol."

He disappeared, and I looked around the room while I waited. The house was completely silent. I guessed we were the only ones home. Marcus' living room was a very contemporary design. Besides the two large black leather sofas, there was a very expensive ornamental fire on the wall, the kind that lit up electronically and you operated with a remote control. On one wall was a huge LCD flat screen TV, and surround sound speakers had been carefully arranged around the room, so discreetly that you barely noticed them. There were floor lamps to offer dim lighting, and the only other furniture was a coffee table set on a thick white rug in the centre of the room, and a couple of bookcases made of a dark-stained wood that looked black. The shelves contained vases and ornaments that had been chosen to blend in with the monochrome décor. Although it wouldn't be my personal choice, it felt quite comfortable. There was a large window at one end of the room, and French windows at the other, and both were shuttered with heavy white curtains.

Marcus returned, and the only evidence as he entered the room, was the smell of coffee from the mug he was carrying. I took the drink thankfully, and Marcus sat on the adjacent sofa, watching me as I sipped the fragrant brew. It was clearly an expensive brand, rich and strong, and I savoured the taste on my tongue.

"Is Jack still angry with me?" I asked after a minute.

"Yes," Marcus replied, "Though he is being an idiot."

I laughed and then checked myself. This was serious.

"You don't believe I was hiding my power then?" I asked.

"No," he said, "You were clearly unaware of your abilities. I have met witches like you in the past."

"What do you mean, witches like me?" I asked curiously.

"Those who are raised as human," Marcus said, "And only awaken their powers when they meet other nonhuman creatures."

"It is possible then?" I asked, "I thought these sort of powers would manifest at puberty or something. I mean that's what all the stories say."

Marcus smiled and laughed softly.

"The stories are told by humans," he said, "They write what they want to hear. It is all very romantic, until they meet the real supernatural beings."

My heart skipped a beat and thudded in my chest. I was not human. I was a witch. He told the truth, and I could no longer deny it after last night's incident.

"Can you tell me anything about this?" I asked, "I am totally lost, and I can't speak to Jack."

Marcus nodded. He stood, in one smooth fluid motion. He never disguised his vampire heritage. Among humans he was seen as an eccentric but very attractive businessman. His vast wealth and his intellect, and indeed his supernatural abilities, all helped him to disguise his true nature just enough so as not to raise suspicion.

"Come," he said, "Let me show you something which might help."

I put my mug on the coffee table, stood up more slowly, wincing as my knees cracked, and followed Marcus out into the hall, and across to another door. He opened it and ushered me into another room. It was his study. Walking in, I stopped and gasped as I gazed in awe at the floor to ceiling bookshelves that covered all available wall space. Books were tightly packed onto the shelves, and there were no spaces that I could see. The only gaps in the room were the French windows on the opposite wall, which were now covered with heavy brocade curtains in shades of gold and dark red. In one corner stood a huge antique wooden desk, on which sat a laptop computer, assorted files, a telephone and a few books. The modern technology looked quite out of place in this room that was decorated to resemble a Victorian library.

I saw Marcus watching me from the doorway, a pleased smile on his lips. This was clearly his favourite room, and he was glad that I appreciated it too. I saw a comfortable looking sofa sat in front of the bookcases adjacent to the desk. It was covered in the same brocade of the curtains, and the carpet was a deep pile in a rich oriental pattern. I guessed that this was also an antique, or at least an expensive import. The only thing missing from this room was an ornate fireplace. The modern house didn't have chimneys. But somehow, the room didn't miss it. The books were impressive enough, and I desperately wanted to run to the shelves, trail my fingers across the ancient spines, and immerse myself in the smells and sights of the written words before me.

Marcus cleared his throat and walked over to the shelves, pulling out a book almost straight away. He carried it over to the desk and placed it beside the laptop, opening it and leafing through the pages. He stopped, putting his finger on the page at the paragraph he wanted. Then he looked up and beckoned me over.

"Here," he said, "Come and read this. It might help."

I did as he instructed, walking as if in a dream. All my life I had longed for a room like this, and now I was standing in one and it wasn't even a museum. I was stunned. The book turned out to be an ancient volume about witchcraft. I read the paragraph Marcus pointed to, and it said that a witch's familiar need not be the traditional black cat. It said that if a human had suffered a shock or trauma, and they were truly a witch, then the event might trigger an awakening for their familiar. The animal could be anything, but it had already been chosen for the witch by powers of magick. I found that hard to comprehend, but how else did I explain last night.

"Who wrote this book?" I asked Marcus, straightening up and stretching my aching neck.

"Anonymous," he replied, "It was a witch I am sure, because everything written has been true in my experience. Humans simply see it as an occult book, with no true meaning."

I nodded.

"So, it's like some sort of delayed reaction to my attack from the wolves?" I asked.

Marcus nodded again.

"Yes and no," he said, "You are still suffering from their treatment. It may not show so much physically, but emotionally your wounds are raw."

He held up a hand as I opened my mouth to protest.

"Do no argue with me," he said, "I feel your pain, and your sadness. You grieve the loss of your human life, yet until last night, you struggled to accept that you truly are a witch."

I shook my head, unsure how to answer. Leaning forward again, I continued reading. I stumbled over some of the words, since it was written in an old form of English, and Marcus helped me on a few occasions. The passage told me that a human might experience vivid dreams, or visions, which was a sign of their powers awakening. I remembered what had happened before I met Jack. Clasping my head, I walked out into the middle of the room, crying out my frustration in an agonized wail.

"This all makes sense!" I cried, "But, hang on," I said, turning to look at Marcus, "I had dreams about Jack before I met him. I didn't even know it was him in the dream until after I heard the truth. What does that mean?"

Marcus spoke from his position behind the desk. Again he didn't move, except to speak, and his body was perfectly still. I was more aware of my own shuffling, nervous, twitching limbs.

"Perhaps you crossed paths with a vampire unwittingly," he said, "It is possible that you saw one in passing, and your power recognised it. You said that your dreams never showed a clear figure."

I nodded agreement.

"Yes," I said, "It wasn't clearly Jack until much later. In one of the dreams it was you, but now I know why."

As I stood there staring at Marcus, contemplating his inhuman appearance and processing the information I had just read, my body began to tingle. At first it felt like pins and needles that quickly spread up my legs, and into my arms. Then it felt like ice shooting through my veins, and then fire. I stood rigid, holding out my arms and stretching my fingers. Everything happened so quickly that I cried out in surprise, and in an instant Marcus stood before me.

"Jessica," he said urgently, "What is it?"

I bent over, crying out, as my body seemed to convulse with the strength of whatever was shooting through me.

"I don't know!" I cried, "It burns. It's freezing. My body is on fire!"

I was on my knees now, almost crying with shock at the sensations I was experiencing. For a terrifying moment I thought the tiger had woken again, but when I thought about her, she appeared to be lying beneath a huge tree, content, her tail swishing from side to side. She did not want to play tonight. There were no living things nearby to entice her.

"Jessica," Marcus' voice said firmly in front of me, "Open your eyes. Look at me."

Slowly, painfully, I did as he instructed. He was crouching in front of me, and I looked directly into his ice blue glowing eyes. They looked silver as his power flowed through him. He reached out a hand and tentatively touched my cheek. I jumped as a jolt of static electricity sparked at his touch. He reared back, and I fell backwards, and then scrambled to my feet, pressing my back to the door in an effort to find something solid to hold onto. Marcus rose slowly to his feet, his gaze never leaving my face.

"You need to disperse some energy," he said steadily, "Direct it at me if you must. It is burning because you are new to your powers, and cannot control them."

"I don't know what you mean," I whispered, tears springing to my eyes.

"Yes, you do," he replied, "Direct your power at me, Jessica."

My fingers were tingling, and I felt the sparks of power shooting out like I had last night. At that time it had been my tiger attacking the wolf, shoving the power into Danny and trying to force his transformation. Now there was no tiger, only me, and I was facing a vampire that didn't transform into anything. But I could move him. As soon as the thought struck, I knew what to do.

"I'm sorry Marcus," I said, raising my hands.

Sparks shot out of me, and straight into him. The force of my power shoved him so hard that he flew across the room, hitting the wall with a resounding thud, and when he fell to the floor, books tumbled down after him from the cracked shelves.

"Marcus," I said, hiccupping with emotion, "Marcus?"

He rose suddenly, and I jumped. He flew through the air and was on top of me before I realised. Instinctively I raised my hands, pressing my palms to his chest, and directed my power at him again. He was forced backwards, but the strength had faded. He stopped himself and stared at me with those glowing silver eyes. He smiled, and I saw his fangs glistening. His expression was pure predator.

"No, Marcus," I whispered, backing up to the door again, "Please don't."

But he did. He struck, grabbing my shoulders and plunging

his fangs into my neck, tearing open the wound that Jack had inflicted the previous night. I screamed, trying to push him away, but he was too strong. He fed, and I felt the most amazing, orgasmic sensation at his touch. My screams faded into a moan of pleasure, and after only a few minutes, he released me so that I fell back against the door, my legs weak. I stared at him, and saw droplets of my blood on the corners of his mouth. He smiled and slowly licked his lips, and I shivered convulsively. My power was gone. I felt human again, and my knees buckled.

"You took my power." I whispered, trying to raise my arms as I slumped on the floor.

Marcus crouched in front of me, his eyes still glowing.

"Yes," he replied, "It was all I could think of to help you."

"You enjoyed that," I said, regaining my voice, "Why did you turn all predatory on me?"

Marcus smiled and his expression sent shivers coursing through me.

"It was a natural instinct," he said, "It has been many years since I feasted on a witch. They usually thwart my attempts."

"I can see why," I said, pursing my lips.

I tried to stand up but I couldn't even use my arms to raise me from the floor. Marcus lifted me gently, carried me through to the living room and lay me on the sofa. I was too weak and battered to protest. He fetched me a glass of water, holding it to my parched lips. Then he fetched a first aid kit and cleaned my wounds, covering them with a small, square padded bandage.

"My apologies, Jessica," he said as he worked, "I was a little over-enthusiastic, and my bite was jagged."

"It's ok," I replied, "My neck is enough of a mess, I probably won't notice."

I was slowly regaining my senses. Strangely, I didn't feel frightened with Marcus. I knew that he wouldn't hurt me in any real sense. This was simply an outlet for our energy. His feeding had dissipated the electricity within me, and for now I was grateful. We had come a very long way from our first meeting all those months ago. Eventually I felt well enough to stand up, after drinking another cup of strong, hot coffee. We didn't speak about the witchcraft. I was exhausted, and I really needed to sleep. Checking my watch, I realised it was almost 11:00pm.

"I had better go," I said, "Thanks for your help Marcus."

He nodded.

"Anytime," he said, "You are welcome to use my library whenever you please. Just be warned that I often entertain guests that might alarm you."

His smile showed a hint of fang, and I smiled and laughed.

"Yeah, well, I could probably handle it now," I said, "I suppose I'll tackle Jack and Danny."

Marcus stood on the doorstep and watched as I climbed carefully into my car and started the engine. As I set off down the drive, I passed Alice, returning in her private plate red BMW. She smiled and waved, and I returned the gesture. Then I headed back towards Redcliffe, and steeled myself to face my angry vampire boyfriend.

22

Driving along the coast road, I fought the exhaustion that threatened to take my body. It was actually a better idea to stay at Jack's house since it was closer than mine, and I really shouldn't be driving in this state. Luckily the road was quiet, and ten minutes later I turned into the Masons' enclosed driveway. Both of their cars were there, parked side by side. I pulled up behind Jack's 4x4 so that at least one of the cars was free for a quick departure if the emergency arose. I was still unsure of their professional obligations, but I knew they had to be ready at short notice if a supernatural crime was committed in our part of the country.

I walked slowly along the drive and climbed wearily up the wide stone step that flanked the front door. Then I hesitated. Should I ring the bell or use my key? Shaking my head, I fumbled for the key in my handbag. Jack and Danny were expecting me, so I might as well just let myself in. The house was in darkness, but I could hear the TV in the living room. Switching on the hall light I closed the door behind me, and then turned right and entered the adjacent room. Danny was lying sprawled across the sofa, and Jack was reclining in the armchair on the far side of the room. They were watching an action movie, and both turned their heads towards me as I entered. In the darkness their faces looked inhuman. Jack's skin was pale, which meant he was either hungry or he wasn't bothering to use his magic. I was guessing the latter, since I doubted he would sit watching TV if he needed blood. A growl rumbled in Danny's throat, very quiet, but enough to make me jump. Ok, so he was still angry.

"Um, hi," I said uncertainly, determined not to show my fear, "How are you both?"

"Fine," Danny said abruptly, turning back to face the TV.

Jack stood up slowly, and I retreated into the hallway, not wanting to be close to Danny at this time. Although he had barely spoken, his growl had called to my tiger, and I felt her stir deep within me. Since I still didn't understand exactly where she was, or how this magic worked, I wanted to get away from Danny until I could learn to control it better. Plus I really needed to sleep. Turning towards the stairs, I turned my head to look at Jack as he walked out of the kitchen and approached me. He walked at a human pace, careful not to alarm me, but his skin was still white and it was impossible not to see him as a vampire.

"I am exhausted, Jack," I said, "I can't handle an argument now."

He shook his head once.

"I am not angry with you Jessica," he replied, "Perhaps we could talk properly tomorrow?"

I nodded, and started climbing the stairs slowly.

"That would be great." I said unenthusiastically.

Jack followed me upstairs, but as we reached his bedroom door he surprised me by suddenly shooting out a hand to touch my neck. I froze, catching my breath, and my power buzzed in my fingers. Jack's cold fingers pulled back the collar of my cardigan, revealing the white bandage on my neck.

"Who bit you?" he asked, and then he leaned closer, sniffing me.

I jumped and moved away, opening the bedroom door and walking in. Clenching my fists, aware of the magic flaring at my fingertips, I strode towards the bed. My heart was racing, and I struggled to remain calm. I did not want to excite him by acting like a victim, or a prey animal. I had learned that much already.

"It was Marcus," I said, staring at him steadily, "I went to see him."

"Why?" Jack asked, standing in the doorway.

I shrugged, dropping my handbag to the floor and retrieving my mobile phone to place on the bedside cabinet. The magic began to subside, and I relaxed very slightly, shrugging off my cardigan as a flush of heat swept over my body.

"He was the only person I could talk to," I said simply, "Since I can't tell Liz all of this. Oh, and apparently Simon is forbidden to speak to me." I added loudly, hoping Danny heard me. I was sure he did.

"I know about the wolves," Jack said calmly, "Danny is simply protecting them until we know more about your familiar."

Love Kills

He turned and closed the door quietly, and I shook my head and started stripping off my clothes, pulling on the shorts and camisole that I wore as pyjamas. Jack watched as I moved around the room, but he didn't speak. The atmosphere was strained, although it wasn't as negative as it had been that morning. Now it felt tired, which was probably because of me. I sensed that Jack didn't know what to say, but that he was trying desperately to regain control of the whole situation. Ignoring him, I walked into the en suite bathroom to remove my make-up, brush my teeth, and get ready for bed.

Jack was lying naked in bed, with the duvet pulled up to his waist when I re-entered the bedroom. I climbed in beside him and lay down; pulling the duvet up over my shoulders and tucking it round my chin. I felt so alone, and my eyes suddenly stung with unshed tears. After a moment the bed moved as Jack turned to face me, and I felt his arm slide across my waist, drawing me close to him. He nuzzled my neck softly, kissing my cheek.

"I love you, Jessica," he whispered, "I want to help you with this."

The tears spilled over, and my shoulders shook as sobs convulsed through my body. I couldn't speak, and I struggled to catch my breath and reply. Jack simply cuddled me closer as I turned over to face him. Burying my face in his chest, I cried out all of the frustration and fear that had been building during the last twenty-four hours. He kissed my head, wrapped his arms tightly around me, and waited for me to calm down. Eventually I fell asleep, unable to talk or even think any more about my current problems. I slept deeply, dreamlessly, and felt a whole lot better in the morning.

23

I saw Danny briefly the next morning. He handed me a mug of steaming, strong coffee when I entered the kitchen, and we shared a companionable breakfast. I didn't ask him about the wolves and his orders to Simon. It didn't seem right to start an argument at this time of the morning. All I wanted was a couple of quiet days at work, and some time with my best friend and her baby, before I met properly with Crystal and started my witch training. Everything was buzzing round my head, and I was so nervous about my tiger waking up when I saw Danny, that I couldn't help but jump and tense up when I was close to him. Sitting at the table as we both shovelled cereal into our mouths, Danny broke the silence.

"I know you didn't mean to hurt me the other night, Jessica," he said quietly, glancing up, "Your strength surprised me, and I reacted defensively."

Staring at him, I realised that this was an apology of sorts. Danny wasn't prepared to forgive me entirely, because he still felt I had purposely been hiding my abilities, but he was willing to call a truce. I nodded.

"Thanks," I said, sipping my hot drink, "I really don't want to do that again. I am meeting with Jack's friend Crystal on Sunday and she will teach me more about being a witch."

"Good," he replied, "She can show you how to channel your power and control your beast."

My heart thudded at his choice of words. I went hot and the room spun. Dropping my spoon, I focused on the smooth pine table, gripping the edges of it and breathing slowly and deeply while I calmed down. Danny watched me curiously.

"What did I say?" he asked, confused.

"You said it was my beast," I replied, "That makes it sound like I'm a were-animal."

He sat back, staring at me thoughtfully.

"You will struggle to accept that you are not human," he said, "You are definitely not a were-animal. But you are a shape-shifting witch. Now you must learn to control your animal. Crystal will explain."

Looking at him, I reached for my coffee with a shaking hand. The mug was empty and I cursed softly. Without a word Danny stood up, taking my mug. He walked over to the coffee machine with both our mugs, refilling them. He silently handed mine back to me, and I thanked him shakily and sipped the hot brew. I watched as Danny gulped his without even feeling the scalding heat. I could feel his power around him, and I could almost see it glowing. I think he was doing it for my benefit, or maybe for my tiger. He was reminding us that he was the stronger beast in this room, and that he would not beaten again. I almost smiled at his male pride, but stopped myself. I would do anything for the quiet life right now.

I looked up as Jack entered the kitchen from the utility room. He had been out to the detached garage, to collect some blood from his secure freezer. I watched as he opened the medical pack and sucked the liquid out smoothly, with no noise. There was no emotion in his face, no appreciation of the life force that he was drinking. It could have been a mug of coffee for all the attention he paid to it. I noticed that he carried a second blood bag in his other hand, and once he had drained the first one, he drank from that too. His skin seemed to transform as it darkened until he was tanned and glowing just like Danny. Both men stood side by side, staring at me with their glowing blue eyes, and I sat transfixed. Then I roused myself, glancing at the clock on the wall.

"I should get to work," I said uneasily, "Um, see you later?"

Danny nodded and watched me as I left the room. Jack followed me, picking up the overnight bag I left in the hallway. Picking up my handbag and slipping on a cardigan, I walked out to my car with Jack beside me. He slung the bag easily into my back seat, and then leaned down to give me a kiss as I sat behind the wheel and adjusted my seat.

"Shall I come to your house tonight?" Jack asked, "Or do you wish to stay here?"

I thought for a minute.

"Would you come and see baby Amy with me?" I asked, "Liz and Rob were asking after you."

He smiled and his face lit up. I caught my breath at his beauty. I wanted to see more of this Jack, happy and excited.

"I would love to meet the new baby," he said warmly, "I shall come to the shop before you close, and we can go from there."

Smiling, I accepted his kiss, and when his lips touched mine, it quickly escalated from a quick peck on the lips, to something deeper and more sensual. We broke away from each other with huge difficulty, both groaning with frustration.

"I must let you go to work," Jack gasped, his eyes burning with blue flame, "Tonight we will be together."

Nodding, I regained my composure, forcing my body to calm down.

"See you later, Jack," I said huskily, "Have a good day."

He watched me reverse down the drive, and waved as I turned onto the main road. I tasted his kiss on my lips all day. It was excruciating and exciting both at the same time.

24

Still trembling when I arrived at the shop, I made a cup of tea and busied myself with the morning duties. Thankfully I had a busy schedule, which involved packing up Internet orders, checking some paperwork, and ordering more stock, and I had several customers in quick succession that kept my mind off my personal life. Gradually I calmed down, though I could feel an undercurrent of pent up energy deep within my body. It felt a little like anxiety, and a little like excitement, as though I were eagerly awaiting a big event. I didn't know what that event might be, but instinct told me it was an unpleasant one. I sighed and turned my mind back to the daily normality of work.

At just after 1:00pm the doorbell jangled and I looked up to see Simon entering the shop, smiling in his usual mischievous way. My heart beat faster, and I smiled warily, not sure what to expect. I could feel an energy emanating from him, and it was wild and warm, full of heat and danger. But it was also friendly. How had I ever seen Simon as human before? It seemed so obvious now. The shop was suddenly filled with the warm, comforting smell of chips smothered in salt and vinegar, and I eyed the brown paper bag he was hugging as my mouth watered and my stomach rumbled loudly. In his other hand he was carrying a little cardboard tray with two cardboard cups of coffee, and it smelled like my favourite mocha.

"Hi, Simon," I said, "Mm, something smells delicious!"

"Hey, Jess," he replied, "Yep I brought lunch. I reckoned you would probably forget to eat."

I laughed. He knew me so well. Whenever something troubled me, and I was alone at work, I usually forgot all about lunch. It was only when I began to feel faint that I would remember about eating. This morning I had immersed myself in work and had forgotten about everything else in my life for a few precious hours. Fortunately the shop was quiet while we ate, and I fetched plates and cutlery from the kitchen. Simon was happy to eat straight from the paper bag, but I insisted on some form of etiquette in my workplace. It was bad enough to stink the place out with chips, but it couldn't be helped and he had made a good choice. We had bread and butter with it, and I soon filled up on the substantial meal.

"Sorry I couldn't speak yesterday," Simon said sheepishly, "Danny forbade all of us from speaking to you."

"It's ok," I replied, shovelling chips into my mouth, "I haven't really spoken to Danny, but I guess he changed his mind?"

Simon nodded, also munching on a hefty chip sandwich.

"Yes," he said, "He phoned me this morning. That's why I came round. What exactly did you do the other night?"

He stared at me with pale blue eyes, and once again I admired his longer, sun kissed wavy blond hair. It suited him, but I wondered if he would have his seasonal haircut soon. Then I shook myself. There were more important things to worry about than Simon's hair.

"Apparently I woke my animal familiar," I said, "Did you feel it?"

Simon shivered.

"Yes I felt it," he said, "We all did. It was chaos. I almost had young wolves transforming in the pub, and one or two in the streets. We only just got to the lair in time."

I felt faint and the room spun.

"You mean that I made them transform?" I asked weakly, "I am so sorry Simon."

"Yes," he said, and his expression hardened, "It was a tiger, I felt that much. When you threw your power at Danny he called on me and the other wolves for support. Sally and I did our best to keep everyone human, but the weaker ones succumbed. It was a nightmare."

"How did he call on you?" I asked, intrigued.

"We have a psychic link," Simon explained, "Between Danny, and me, and Sally. We can communicate basic instructions, and if one of us is threatened, we call on the others for support. Our power connects us."

I nodded. It made sense, but I knew it would take months for me to truly understand the process between my supernatural friends. I may never learn or comprehend the truth about what they were.

"Well," I said with a sigh, "I have to accept what I am now."

"A witch." Simon said it with no emphasis. He was simply stating a fact.

"Yes," I said, "And I have met Jack's friend Crystal. She will teach me what I need to know so I can stop that happening again."

"Good." Simon said, and returned to his food.

We finished our lunch and chatted about normal things for a while. Simon told me some gossip about a few people we knew, I talked about Liz and Amy, and eventually Simon left. He said he would see me later, but I didn't know exactly when. I would avoid the Ship for a while, at least until my powers were more under control. There were too many wolves working there, and I would only cause more trouble. Besides, I wasn't sure I could face them all yet. I wondered what Sally would have to say when I saw her. I hoped she wouldn't be angry. Sally was a small woman, but she was strong and powerful. Even in human form she could be terrifying, which seemed at odds with her vocational career as a nurse. She was a formidable commander for the Redcliffe pack, and she, along with Simon, was madly in love with Danny. The Mason brothers were just adored from all angles it seemed.

Thankfully my afternoon was steadily busy, and I didn't have to think about everything while I served customers and dealt with enquiries. A few people who came in asked about Liz, and I happily passed on her good news and received their best wishes. By the time I closed the shop I was looking forward to visiting my human friends that evening. I was a little nervous about Jack meeting the baby, though I knew that was silly. I just didn't see him as the paternal type.

As it turned out he surprised me. He appeared in the shop at 5:10pm, and waited while I closed up at half past. He helped me to move some tables around and reorganize a few shelves, and then we went through to my apartment. I quickly changed clothes, wanting to wear my comfortable jeans and t-shirt again, and Jack sat with me while I ate a quick meal. It was nothing special, just baked beans on toast, but I wasn't much of a cook and I was eager to go visiting.

When we arrived at Liz and Rob's house, I felt a little nervous again, but I quashed it. Jack was the perfect visitor. He actually took a real interest in the baby, cuddling her and cooing over her. I relaxed a little, and enjoyed watching him with Amy. He was like a different person, so soft and gentle. Even Liz seemed surprised, and she nudged Rob and made jokes about what great parents Jack and me could be. I smiled and laughed along with them, but I saw Jack's curious look. There was another awkward conversation to save for later.

We stayed for a few hours, chatting about various topics of interest. Rob told us some things about his new projects at the university. He was technically on paternity leave for a few weeks, and although the academic term didn't start until later in the month, he was already preparing his schedule and lessons. Alongside teaching students he was embarking on a new research project in partnership with a professor at a neighbouring university. It was some sort of study about graduates and the economic climate, and was to be used by the government in their plans for future developments. Liz was clearly very proud of her husband, and I smiled to see her glowing features as she gazed upon her little family. She had everything she ever wanted, and I felt such warmth for my best friend that for a moment I felt tears stinging my eyes.

"Are you alright, Jess?" Liz asked, staring at me curiously.

"Yes," I said, blinking furiously, "Just a bit of dust or something in my eye."

I regained my composure, but I saw Jack and Rob watching me. They knew the truth about my feelings, and it was disconcerting to know that these men knew so much about me. I had never been one for sharing emotions before, and now I couldn't seem to stop.

When we returned home Jack didn't try and discuss anything with me. There wasn't much to say. We had both experienced a lot of energy in a short space of time, but we couldn't really talk until I had met with Crystal. I changed into my pyjamas and joined Jack on the sofa, watching a comedy panel show as we stretched out together. I relished the opportunity to do something normal and boring, and I did not want to ruin it with serious talk about our metaphysical problems. Everything else could wait a little longer.

Eventually, Jack grew restless. He began stroking my bare arms, and I shivered as goose flesh rose in response to his caress. When he kissed me softly on the top of my head, I roused myself, my body already responding. I met his lips hungrily, and we soon lost our clothes, and forgot all about the TV, as we enjoyed each other in the most intimate and perfect way that we could. I was anxious that another orgasm might trigger the tiger like it did the previous night, but once we started I couldn't stop.

"I can tame your beast," Jack whispered, nibbling at my ear, "Just say yes."

I shivered and moaned at his touch, and felt the sharpness of his fangs on my skin. He would bite me, take my blood, and that would dissipate the rising heat of energy I could feel building inside me. Marcus' wounds had already almost healed, so there was room on my damaged neck.

"Yes," I sighed, reaching up for more kisses, "Do what you must. Feed from me."

As I rode him, eyes closed, liberating my body with abandon, he grabbed my head and drew me close. I glimpsed his fangs just before he struck, but his bite was full of passion and excitement. My tiger reared up at first, wanting to beat him down. He held firmly to my body, and I moved faster on top of him, focusing only on the sensations of pure pleasure. I forced my tiger to calm down, and she retreated with a snarl as I cried out and gasped with ecstasy. The energy flowed all around us, and the air crackled with electricity. It was intense, and amazing, and finally I collapsed on top of Jack on the sofa, happy and satisfied.

25

I was standing on Redcliffe beach, staring out to sea. Immediately I looked to my left and saw my mother standing beside me. Yes, it was a dream. They had finally returned. This time I smiled, happy to see her, sure that for now at least, I needn't worry about attack from vengeful werewolves and vampires. I was wrong of course. When would I learn that life with the Mason brothers was never quiet? They were incapable of living peacefully, simply because of their species. Even their own kind sought to destroy them because of the threat they posed as vampire and werewolf side by side. The typically proud and quarrelsome vampires clashed often with the strong and territorial werewolves, and I was to learn more about their immense tempers and huge egos over the coming years of my relationships with such creatures. For the time being, I was blissfully clueless and happily in love.

"Hi, Mum." I said, feeling the warmth of the sun on my skin.

Lillian's eyes were sad, and her pale face held an anxious expression as she stared at me. My happiness quickly turned sour as I awaited her words of warning.

"My child," she said, "There is more trouble to come. It is not yet over."

Sighing, I watched the gently rolling waves, glittering silver in the sunlight atop the green-blue water. I tasted salt on my tongue, and it was sharp and refreshing.

"What is to come?" I said wearily, "Haven't I been through enough already?"

She clasped her hands, imploring me with her large green eyes. Her features were an older version of my own, right down to the scattering of freckles across my nose which seemed to join during the summer months, and caused much consternation to my fifteen year-old self when I wanted to impress the boys and pretend to be eighteen.

"She has not finished with you Jessica," Lillian said, "She will attack, and soon."

Love Kills

I frowned, trying hard to think about who she meant. Danny had Celine Toulouse imprisoned still in the Redcliffe lair, until he decided what to do with her. He had killed her alpha male Seamus Tully, and his mate LuAnn Moor. Celine was weak and powerless, and I doubted that she even cared about me now that her lovers were dead. She was now trying to seduce Danny so that he would free her and take her into his pack. Who else might want to do me harm?

"It is the vampire," my mother said quietly, "She seeks her child."

Slowly it dawned on me, and my heart sank.

"Emily Rose," I said, "She is after me now?"

Lillian nodded.

"She never really left before," she said, "She lost her psychic connection with you, but she knows where you are. She is planning her attack, and you must be prepared."

I stood straighter, rolled my shoulders, and took up a defensive, proud stance.

"Well then I am ready for her," I said, "She cannot take Jack away. He doesn't want her anymore."

"It is not so simple, my child," Lillian said sadly, "She made Jack. He is her vampire to control. He cannot disobey her command."

Now I was confused.

"What," I said, "You mean, if she calls, he must follow?"

"Yes," she replied, "You must stand firm, and do what is necessary. Be prepared. Be alert. And do what you must."

She was gone, just like that. I was alone on the beach, and a storm was brewing. Sighing, I stared out to sea as the dream faded into blackness.

Next morning I woke promptly when my alarm sounded. Jack was lying in bed beside me, lightly stroking my arm. I smiled and wriggled, murmuring nonsense as I roused myself. The dream was echoing in my head, or rather the conversation with my mother. She always seemed to speak in vague terms, almost like riddles. Was there something about being a ghost that meant you couldn't simply say what needed to be said? Or was it that we humans (or witches) needed to exercise our brains and our intelligence, rather than expect to be spoon-fed the information we needed? Whatever, I felt slightly irritated and very anxious about her warning.

"How are you, Jessica?" Jack asked in his gentle voice.

I shivered when I heard his faint Dublin accent, and my body instantly reacted to his touch and his tone. Smiling, I rolled over to face him. We were both naked in bed, and I felt a lot better than I had recently. It actually felt like some of my wounds had healed more just overnight. It must be the vampire's touch.

Jack frowned as he focused on my neck, then his gaze travelled lower. I dropped my head to see what he was staring at. I was sporting new bruises, and a few neat red bite marks.

"Oh," I said softly, "Did we get a bit carried away last night?"

Looking up at Jack, I saw his stricken expression.

"Jessica," he said, "I am so sorry. I forgot myself. Please tell me the truth. How badly are you hurt?"

"I don't know." I whispered.

Moving very slowly and carefully, I levered myself into a sitting position, and swung my legs out of bed. The cool morning air hit my skin, and I drew in my breath sharply. Jack was beside me in instant, crouching on the floor beside my legs.

"What is it?" he asked, "What did I do?"

I smiled, and laughed gently, touching his head and enjoying the silky feel of his short hair.

"You did nothing," I said, "It was the cold air hitting my skin. It surprised me, that's all."

Standing up, I discovered that my body felt great. I didn't feel the bruises or the bite marks. They were simply there, marks upon my skin, memories of our night of passion and pleasure. Inspecting myself in the full-length mirror, I peered curiously at the neat puncture wounds scattered over my body. I could almost be a dot-to-dot drawing, albeit an abstract one. Jack had not only bitten my neck, but my arms, legs, chest, stomach, thighs. In fact he had bitten me almost everywhere there was a vein within easy grasp. And all of those places were now marked with the results of his desire. I wasn't angry, or scared, or confused. It just felt right, and even natural, to be this way.

"I'm fine, Jack," I reassured him, "It doesn't hurt. In fact I feel great!"

Eventually he allowed me to shower and dress, and I sent him off to work, promising him that I was healthy and happy. I was. Well, apart from my mother's warning. But for now that would be my secret. I didn't want to worry Jack until I knew more about what I was dealing with. Besides, once my witch training started properly, I could handle it. Whatever was necessary to remove Emily Rose from our lives for good, I would do. I was strong. I would not back down for the man I loved.

26

Over the next few days I focused on the business, and set up a proper plan for how I would manage the shop in Liz's absence. I was glad of the distraction from my personal life, and by the end of the week I was actually starting to feel almost human again. I spoke to Liz on the phone during the day, and visited her in the evenings, and we discussed the situation. I was prepared to work six days a week until Liz could return part time once Amy was older. But it would be difficult, not least because I knew instinctively that something big was about to happen, and that would inevitably impact on my availability to work. For now I kept quiet, trying to establish just how Emily Rose might attack, and when it could be.

I spent two nights at Jack and Danny's house, and gradually Danny seemed to relax around me. He was still alert and tense, especially if I made any sudden movements. I could feel his energy rolling around the room whenever we were close, as if he were erecting psychic barriers against my tiger. When I asked him, he said that was exactly what he was doing.

"I know that you did not intend to attack me the other night, Jessica," he said, "I am simply taking steps to protect myself and my pack."

At least he wasn't angry with me, and he and Jack seemed to accept that I hadn't hidden anything from them. Simon also seemed a little distant, but he assured me it was nothing to do with our friendship. I knew that things would settle down eventually, but still I didn't tell them about my mother's warning. They would only try and protect me, and might risk Liz finding out about us. I was not ready to put my best friend in danger, and certainly not her newborn daughter.

I was sitting at my kitchen table, reading the newspaper and sipping coffee, when Crystal arrived promptly at 11:00am on Sunday morning as she had promised. She appeared at my back door, knocking quietly but firmly. Today she was wearing a long blue velvet patchwork skirt and a cream coloured blouse which seemed loose and shapeless, but which somehow accentuated her female form into something sexy and desirable. Even a firmly heterosexual person like myself couldn't help but notice. Draped around her neck was an assortment of pendants that I recognized as crystals. One was purple and looked like amethyst, another was clear, and a third was a strange dark green colour. They all seemed to shimmer and pulse with their own energy, and my fingers tingled as I resisted the urge to reach out and touch the necklaces. Crystal was also wearing a silver pentagram pendant, several sparkling bracelets, and a large pair of earrings set with amethyst and marcasite stones, finished with feathers that were a glossy black colour. The whole effect was striking, even breath-taking.

Crystal looked the epitome of the modern witch, and that was actually more reassuring that her pinstripe business suit. Smiling politely, I let her in and offered her a drink, gesturing for her to sit at the table. She accepted a cup of coffee, and when I had made two fresh mugs and placed them on the table, I sat opposite and waited for Crystal to speak. Once again my eyes were drawn to the pendants, especially the clear one, which hung on a long length of black cord and rested between her breasts.

"Tell me exactly what you felt the other night, Jessica," Crystal said gently, staring at me with her strange violet eyes, "I have heard a version of the story from Jack, but I need to hear about your experience before we begin."

I jumped, almost knocking my mug over. Frowning, I flushed red with embarrassment and Crystal smiled.

"You are drawn to my clear Quartz," she said, touching the crystal, "You feel its power."

Nodding, I swallowed, unsure what she was talking about. I felt dizzy and my fingers were tingling. My whole body seemed to tremble with excitement.

"What exactly are we beginning?" I asked, fighting to remain calm, "I mean, I only know you because of Jack. How did you come to be a witch?"

She smiled, and it was peaceful, warm and comforting. I immediately felt tension ease from my shoulders, and a cool breeze seemed to waft through the room, bringing the scent of lavender and fresh air. I stared at Crystal in confusion, knowing that she was responsible for this. She simply sat in her chair, holding the mug of coffee in her hands, returning my gaze.

"I was always a witch, Jessica," she replied, "Fortunately for me, my mother practised her arts and she raised me to embrace my heritage. I have been a witch all my life."

I nodded.

"Ok," I said, "Now this might sound stupid, but I have to check. How old are you, exactly?"

Her gaze was steady as she spoke. There was no scorn in her voice. She accepted my questions, no matter how insignificant I felt they sounded.

"I am thirty-six years old," she said, "Witches are not immortal in the human sense. We inhabit mortal bodies, and we are prone to human afflictions, as you have discovered."

I leaned back and drew my cardigan close around me, realising that she was looking directly at the fresh bite marks on my neck. My skin was healing faster than normal, but Jack's impressions were stubborn to leave me. I took a deep breath. There were so many questions and I didn't know where to start.

"Ok," I said again, "I kind of understand that. You mean that witches still exist even after death?"

"Yes," she replied, "Like your mother, we can communicate through the use of magic and our natural abilities."

My heart thudded at her reference. Clearly Jack had told her about my visions.

"What exactly did Jack tell you?" I asked.

"It was not only Jack that told me about you," Crystal said, "I spoke to your mother recently."

The room spun. My heart jumped into my throat, and I sat up straight.

"When?" I whispered, "What did she say?"

Crystal's expression softened again, and she reached across the table and gently took my hand in hers, prising my fingers from their grip on the edge of the wood. Her hand was warm and comforting, and I felt her power flow into me like honey. Again I smelled lavender, and I began to calm down.

"What are you doing?" I asked, "What is that I can feel?"

"It is magick," Crystal replied, "I am using natural Earth magick to calm your nerves as you process this information."

As she stroked the back of my hand, I felt Crystal's soothing energy. It washed over me and through me, and all of my wounds ached and stung momentarily, as though my nerves were reacting to her touch. Squirming in my seat, I jumped up and backed away, stopping when I hit the kitchen units. I stared at Crystal, who returned my gaze, not speaking until I calmed down.

Gradually she explained her part in my recent experiences. Apparently my mother had approached Crystal from the Other Side, a mysterious spirit realm where people went to after death. Witches were able to communicate with others of their kind, and occasionally with humans and even some supernatural creatures. Crystal explained that it took a lot of magick and power to keep a connection, which was why my mother's conversations were brief and confusing. People in the spirit world did not speak in human language, so they had to translate when they spoke to living relatives. This explained a lot to me about what I had heard of fortune tellers and mediums in popular culture.

Crystal began my training by introducing me to the practice of meditation. I wanted to jump straight in and perform spells, but she stopped me with her gentle smile and calm words.

"You must learn to harness your own abilities," Crystal said, "before you turn them on others again."

Crystal took me through a guided meditation where I sat in a chair with my feet flat on the floor, breathed deeply in and out to slow my body, and I could reach a vibrational frequency on which to speak to the spirits and energies around me. I would have found all of this very hard to accept, if it weren't for my experience with the tiger earlier that week. After that, and my attacks from werewolves and vampires, I was finding it much easier to believe what Crystal told me.

At first I struggled to relinquish control of my human experience. I couldn't simply relax and meditate for a while, but eventually I found a sense of peace and a strange freedom. I went into a trance of sorts, and while I was still aware of the room around me, and of Crystal's gentle voice at my side, I was away in a strange, foreign land. I was walking in a forest of tall, green pine trees. The air was cold and crisp, and I knew that humans did not frequent this part of the world. The climate was too extreme for all but the most hardened explorers. Looking down, I saw that I was wearing only a white dress that flowed around me and reached down to my ankles. I was barefoot, and my arms were bare, but I felt no pain and no extreme temperatures.

I looked up, admiring the beauty of the trees, so graceful and magnificent. The sky was a clear, deep blue, and the sun shone brightly above everything. The ground at my feet was frozen solid, but nature still functioned. Beneath the packed dirt and mud, I could feel roots from the trees, and water from an underground stream, and the atmosphere felt alive with beings that I couldn't see, but I could feel. It was like sparks of electricity shooting all around me, but they weren't mine. They signified all of the little creatures that humans have banished into folklore and fairytale. But I knew they were there, and they knew about me. Some were playful, others mischievous, and some were simply curious or indifferent to my presence in their land. I knew that this was a place still on Earth, but it was separated by magick, protected from intrusion.

Coming out into a clearing, I looked up and surveyed a tall, craggy mountain of blue-grey rock. It towered high above me, almost blocking out the sun, and I saw snow on the higher slopes and ledges. About twenty feet above my head, I saw the entrance to a cave, and my heart lurched as I recognised the lair of my tiger, my familiar. Sure enough, as if in answer to my call, she walked slowly out of the darkness, and stood staring down at me, her tail swishing lazily. She was magnificent. A tall, graceful beast, her white fur seemed silver in the bright light, and she had darker stripes across her back and neck. These alternated from grey, to silver, to black. Her large eyes glittered with intelligence, and she licked her lips, showing me a large pink tongue, and massive sharp teeth. There was no menace in her stance. She was my friend, my familiar. She knew me, and had known me all my life.

We spoke in a language without words. Humans always felt the need to be noisy, to make their presence known. Spirits and other beings knew better than to waste their energy. They simply thought their words to each other, and understood the language by instinct. My tiger was called Suri. She lived in this frozen country, patrolling the forest and keeping it safe from intruders. She hunted, and played, explored and slept all within this vicinity. But she had seen Redcliffe through my eyes, and she was curious about the wolves. She had met true wolves in the past; those that did not take human form. Now she wanted to play with the werewolves, using me as a vessel.

"You cannot just play with them," I said, feeling no fear, "They are my friends."

Suri stared at me with her huge head on one side. She blinked her yellow eyes, and then very slowly and deliberately started climbing down the mountainside until she stood before me.

"They are not our kind," she said simply, "What use do they have?"

"They don't need a use," I said, "I like them. We share common interests. I spend time with them, because that is what friends do."

"You mean, like a pack?" she asked curiously.

I frowned.

"Not like a pack, exactly," I said, "We are sort of like a family, but not related."

She still didn't understand. Suri lived a solitary life up here, but she was happy with that. If a mate came along she might be interested in producing a family with him, but it wasn't necessary. She did not understand the concept of friends. I eventually asked her to trust me, and not to frighten the wolves again unless I asked. Somehow I wanted to keep her on my side, and I wasn't above considering a possible future attack if I felt threatened. She agreed, and I could almost see her smiling, showing her huge white teeth.

"Very well," she agreed, "I will remain quiet unless you call me. I am your beast, your animal. When you are in trouble, I will help."

And with that she walked past me, and disappeared into the forest. I watched her slow, deliberate walk, and then she hesitated, and turned her head to look at me. Just before she vanished into the trees, she threw back her head and let out a blood-curdling howl, and all the forest knew that Suri the snow tiger was on the prowl. She commanded their respect, and their fear. This was her land, her kingdom, and she was my protector.

I came out of my trance slowly, gradually seeing the kitchen, my table, and Crystal sitting before me, staring intently at my face. Her large violet eyes were anxious, and she smiled when I opened my eyes and blinked, shaking my head as I woke.

"Whoa," I said, "That was bizarre."
She laughed.
"You met your familiar?" she asked.
I nodded.
"Yes," I replied, "It was crazy. I spoke to her, and I know that she is real. How can she be real? How can any of this be real?"
Crystal tipped her head to one side.
"Jessica," she said sternly, "After everything that has happened to you recently, do I really have to explain the metaphysical world?"
I laughed, and stood up, shaking out my limbs and loosening my body.
"I suppose not," I said, "I can't really ignore the truth anymore."
"No," she agreed, "You cannot. Now, let us continue."
And with that, she began explaining about the local witch coven, the various forms of witchcraft that were practised, and how it all fit into human society. Crystal told me the truth behind many of the old fairy tales and folklore. She told me about the witch calendar, a cycle of festivals that ran at various times of the year, which celebrated changes in season and the power of nature. The more she spoke, the more comfortable and familiar I felt in her presence. It was as if I had been away on a long journey, and I was finally home. Now, I could truly be myself once again.

I asked again about working spells, and what tools I would need. Crystal regarded me with the indulgent smile of a teacher surveying her favourite pupil.

"You do not need tools in order to weave magick," Crystal said, "The ability lies within you, Jessica."

"I know, you said that," I replied impatiently, "But what about potions and amulets, and all that stuff?"

Crystal shifted in her seat, shaking her hair back and settling her hands on the table.

"I will show you all of that in good time," she said, "Your true magick is the power you feel. It is the energy that unsettles your supernatural friends. It is the power of your animal familiar. This is strong magick, and you have it literally at your fingertips."

My heart beat faster at her words. I really was a powerful being. I knew it. Memories flashed through my mind. I remembered a boyfriend from when I was a teenager. He had told people he was a witch, but no one believed him. He told me that I was also a witch, and that I was hiding great powers deep within. Now his words came back to me in a rush, along with a dozen other previously dismissed occurrences and conversations. Crystal advised me to meditate at least twice a day to strengthen my control, and I promised to obey. We agreed to meet again the following week, when she would take me to a meeting of her local coven.

"You can make some new friends," Crystal said, "And be among your own kind."

"Sounds great." I replied with a smile.

As she opened the door to leave, Crystal hesitated. Then she removed the quartz pendant from her neck and handed it to me.

"Here," she said, "Take this. You will learn more about crystals as you develop. They contain great power and magic of their own, since they contain the wisdom of ages. This is one of the most powerful kind, and you were clearly drawn to it when I arrived."

"Thank you," I said with a smile.

Accepting her gift, my fingers closed around the large chunk of crystal. It was about two inches long and an inch wide at the top, tapering into a graceful point where it had been shaped by a machine. I could feel a cool strength emanating from it, and as the quartz touched my skin I felt a jolt of energy shoot through my body. I knew this crystal, and it recognised me. I hung it around my neck, cradling it in my hand as I waved goodbye to Crystal. I felt calm, peaceful, and truly happy for the first time in months.

27

The next day, back at work, doing my normal, human routine, I started to feel awkward again. I knew the truth about myself but it would still take a while to truly accept and embrace it. Along with the quartz pendant, Crystal had given me a pile of books to read, which she said would help me understand the witches a little more. I had one on the desk beside me to read during quiet times in the shop. I sat staring into space, playing with the quartz pendant, all the while aware of the power that trembled through my body. Everything looked different to me now. I could see faint clouds of colour spiralling around people. It was their auras, the natural energy field created by all living creatures. Outside I could see beings flitting in and out among the shoppers in the street. They were elementals, fairies, elves, and even angels. Their bodies were distinct to me, but invisible to the average human. They glowed and shimmered with their own individual powers.

I had told Jack and Danny to be themselves around me, because I didn't want to see them as human when it wasn't natural. Now I would discover just how different they truly were. During the next two weeks, we settled back into a routine of sorts. I ran the shop, I saw Liz and Amy two or three times a week, and I spent my evenings with Jack. We still split our time between the Mason's house and my apartment, though I found once more that I felt comfortable at Jack's house. At first Danny was still tense around me, nervous about another tiger attack. But he soon calmed down, and then he started showing me more of his true self.

Werewolves are naturally playful creatures, just like dogs really. I would watch Danny with Simon and Sally when they spent time at his house, or when we were all at the Ship. Their behaviour wasn't disturbing, but it certainly wasn't normal. They were far more intimate than most humans, especially in public. At first I was surprised to see that Danny was barely alone. Then he explained that he was simply being a pack animal. They preferred company. He spent a lot of time at the lair, but I didn't return after my encounter with the wolf Kimberley. I hadn't the nerve, especially after what had happened with my tiger. Danny agreed that I should leave them for a while, just until we settled down and I was more used to my magical abilities.

One Sunday afternoon I returned from a meeting with Crystal and some of the witches from her coven. We had been at Crystal's house in the suburbs of Plymouth, and I had really enjoyed making new friends and learning more about being a witch. They told me stories about their escapades; making me laugh about the embarrassing situations their magick had put them in at times. Crystal provided a delicious home cooked meal for lunch, and we all participated in a group meditation ritual to invoke our animal familiars. I felt better when I discovered that Crystal's animal was a cheetah, and the other witches had a fox, a coyote, a falcon and even a wolf. Knowing that I wasn't the only one to deal with such an exotic animal was reassuring, and hearing the other experiences was a huge comfort to me. I would eventually learn to coexist with Suri, and I wouldn't always be on tenterhooks around the wolves once we had reached an agreement about our behaviour.

I parked up on Jack's driveway, next to Danny's car. Jack was out somewhere with Marcus. He had been very mysterious, and when I insisted on him telling me his whereabouts, he confessed he was going hunting.

"What do you mean, hunting?" I asked suspiciously.

Jack stared at me with glowing blue eyes and a serious expression.

"Marcus and I like to hunt wild animals together," he said, "We feed, and we kill. It is a way to dissipate some of our excess energy that would only harm the humans in our vicinity otherwise."

My heart sank as I glimpsed Jack and Marcus flying through the forest, chasing a poor innocent prey animal. I couldn't stop them. It was, after all, in their nature. It was no worse than a wolf hunting for food I supposed. I suppressed the image, shivered, and left Jack to his excursion.

Now, feeling happy and relaxed after my meeting with Crystal and her witches, I jumped out of my car and walked to the front door. Checking my phone I saw no messages from Jack, so assumed he was still out. Danny could be home, but then again the presence of his car was not always a guarantee. Reaching for my key, I let myself into the house, calling out as I entered.

"Hello," I called, "Anybody home?"

I heard movement in the living room, and stuck my head round the door. I gasped as I faced the sleeping forms of three large wolves, all curled up together on the rug in front of the fireplace. One lifted its head and blinked large amber eyes. The other two watched but didn't immediately react. With my heart pounding and adrenaline pumping, I walked slowly into the room, approaching them cautiously.

"Um, Danny," I said, "Is that you?"

The wolf stood up, making a strange noise somewhere between a whine and a bark. It approached me slowly, wagging its tail. I was certain it was Danny, because I vaguely remembered the colouring of his brindle fur, and the streaks of gold on his belly. The animal nuzzled my hand, and I laughed nervously, stroking his head, unsure how to react.

"And is that you, Simon?" I asked, looking at the grey wolf now standing behind his master.

"And, Sally?" I asked, directing my attention to the slightly smaller, caramel coloured wolf standing beside him.

They all shook themselves, and I stepped back as the atmosphere in the room suddenly changed. Catching my breath, I realised that Suri had woken and was scenting the air from her position in the rocky mountain cave. I gasped, shaking my head, and the room seemed to shimmer with a white mist. The larger wolf lifted his head, scenting the air, and then he barked and growled as if in warning. Suri threw back her head and howled, and the sound echoed from my human mouth before I had time to think. Clapping a hand to my mouth, I backed off.

"No, Suri," I whispered, "Please, not now."

It was too late. Suri leaped up and bounded forward, and my body jolted as if she had jumped into my skin. It certainly felt like it. My body went rigid, I held my arms out in front of me, expecting to see sparks or lightening bolts shooting from my fingers. I screamed, begging Suri to leave me alone, to calm down, anything. But she wanted the wolves. I leaped forward in a totally inhuman movement, and my target was Danny. He changed form in a flash, and I landed on top of a naked man, my body both burning and freezing at the same time, trying to move away from him, but fighting the tiger that would use my human limbs for her own entertainment.

"No!" I screamed, "Suri, please, stop this!"

"Jessica!" Danny shouted from beneath me. He grabbed my arms, trying to make eye contact with me. I glimpsed his bright blue eyes, his familiar face, and I momentarily regained some control.

"Jessica," Danny said again, loudly, "You can force her back. Be strong."

Shaking my head, I replied with tears streaming down my face.

"She is too strong, Danny," I whimpered, "I can't stop her."

Suri roared again through my mouth, and I bared my teeth, aiming for Danny's neck. He managed to shove me aside onto the floor, sitting astride my body, fighting to pin my arms and not injure me.

"Get Marcus, now!" he said over his shoulder, and I saw Simon and Sally run from the room, still in wolf form.

Suri was angry. She wanted the wolf. She wanted to tussle and play, bite and nip at his body. Then she wanted to use my human body and Danny's human body to mate as only a wild animal should. I screwed my eyes shut as if I could block out the images she was thrusting into my mind. I tried to relax under Danny's grip so he would release me, and I felt the pressure on my arms ease slightly.

"Jessica," Danny said more calmly, "Are you with me?"

Suri was pacing, back in her cave where I had banished her. But she hadn't given up yet. As she felt Danny retreat from my body, she lunged again, and I sprang up and attacked him with a snarl. We rolled around the floor, tussling and fighting, Danny trying desperately not to injure me, and Suri growing more arrogant and trying her hardest to provoke him. I had rolled him onto his back in a submissive stance, and was sitting astride him ready to attack, when we both sensed a change in the atmosphere of the room. We barely had time to react when something flew at me in a blur, strong cold arms wrapped around my body, and Marcus struck, biting my neck. I screamed, struggled to push him away, and we both fell back onto the floor beside Danny. Suri was gone. Marcus had wrenched her power away from me, at least for the time being.

"Let me go." I gasped, and Marcus released his grip.

Panting, sweating, trying desperately to catch my breath, I crawled over to the sofa and heaved myself onto the seat. Danny and Marcus sat on the floor, staring at me. Marcus licked my blood from his lips, wiping his mouth with the back of his hand. Danny's chest was heaving as his breathing slowly calmed, and the energy in the room gradually subsided to something more normal, more human. I clasped a hand to my neck, feeling wetness and the sharp sting of a new wound. My whole body was aching as my muscles contracted and relaxed after my fight with both Suri and Danny.

"You're naked." I said to Danny.

He glanced down, then back at me, and laughed.

"Phew!" he said, "You are back with us, Jess."

He looked across the room, and I saw a very human looking Simon waiting for orders. Without a word he nodded and disappeared into the hallway. Sally walked uncertainly into the living room and sat on the armchair in the bay window, staring at us all in turn. She was dressed, only just, in her underwear. It was a pretty white bra and knickers, a matching set trimmed with embroidered roses. It seemed so out of place and innocent in this scene.

Simon reappeared through the kitchen door, and handed Danny a pair of shorts. Simon was dressed in his customary baggy jeans, and he approached me carefully, wary of my reaction. He was carrying a first aid box.

"May I clean your wound, Jessica?" he asked cautiously.

I nodded and managed a weak smile.

"Yes, Simon," I replied, "Thank you."

Wincing as Simon applied antiseptic lotion and dabbed my neck with cotton wool, I turned my attention back to Marcus.

"I thought you were with Jack." I said.

Marcus nodded, smoothing his clothes and standing up in one fluid movement.

"I was with Jack," he said, "I had just returned home when Danny's wolves appeared and requested my assistance."

"So where's Jack?" I asked in a sharp tone.

Marcus shrugged.

"I have no idea," he said, "He must have been called away."

"Are you back in control, Jessica?" Danny asked me as he stood up and pulled on his shorts.

I hissed in pain, and swore as Simon finished cleaning my wound.

"Nearly done now." he said with a small smile.

He applied a bandage, gathered up the used cotton wool and empty packaging, and stepped back.

"Yes," I said to Danny, "I am back in control. Marcus took Suri away from me."

The wolves all stared questioningly at Marcus. He smiled.

"Jessica is correct," he said confidently, "I have temporarily taken the strength of the witch's familiar. She resides within me until Jessica's blood leaves my system."

Danny frowned.

"How is that possible?" he asked curiously.

"I fed on her energy, my friend," Marcus replied, "The tiger remains within Jessica, but she is weakened and has retreated to her lair."

I nodded in agreement.

"Yes," I said, "She can't do anything for a while. I am so sorry about this Danny."

He shook his head.

"You were not to know this would happen," Danny replied, "At least we know the vampires can subdue her until you get her under control."

Exhausted and in pain, I collapsed back onto the sofa. Marcus left us, and Danny dismissed Simon and Sally, telling them he was confident there would be no more problems with the tiger this evening. When Jack finally returned home an hour later, I was dozing on the sofa with a blanket over me, and Danny was playing *Call of Duty* on his Playstation. We briefly explained the incident to Jack, but I hadn't the energy for conversation, and I still felt mildly annoyed that he hadn't been there, even though I knew it was silly. I managed to eat some food after a while, and eventually went to bed early, leaving Jack and Danny to discuss the events of the day.

28

Sinking gratefully into bed, my mind woke up. It was typical that now I needed to sleep, I was wide-awake. I replayed the events of that day. I had enjoyed a relaxing morning with the witches, we had meditated, and I had even spoken with Suri and believed that she would listen to my pleas and leave the wolves alone. Clearly I was mistaken there, and I felt angry at my animal familiar for disobeying me so blatantly. In fact, the more I thought about it, the angrier I became. Suri was my tiger. She resided within my magick. Therefore she should obey my command, and stop being so impulsive and nasty. As I thought all of this, Suri's voice drifted through my mind.

"*You cannot control me, Jessica,*" she said scornfully, "*I am a thing of magick and mystery. You humans have no idea what you are dealing with.*"

I laughed aloud to the empty room, and spoke my reply.

"Don't be so sure, Suri," I said sternly, "I am learning what to do with you, and you will obey me."

"*Really?*" She asked in a mocking tone, "*and what do you intend to do?*"

I sighed aloud, and then laughed again as a thought crossed my mind.

"You are just a spoiled child, aren't you Suri?" I asked.

She was quiet for a few moments, and I thought she had disappeared. Then her voice came to me, and it wavered as though she weren't so sure of herself suddenly.

"*I simply seek a little entertainment after spending a lifetime trapped in your power*," she said, "*is that so wrong?*"

Sighing again, I shook my head.

"No," I said heavily, "I suppose not. But you really do need to calm down, Suri. We have more important things to worry about than you tormenting the wolves. I need them on my side, and you know how they feel about me right now."

"*Very well,*" Suri replied, "*I will behave for the moment. I will simply arise again at your call, and will aid you in your battles.*"

"Thank you." I said.

The room was silent. It was early evening really, only about 9:00pm. It wasn't surprising that I couldn't sleep. My mind was wandering, remembering all of my recent experiences, and worrying about what was yet to come. I thought about the conversations with my mother, and the impending battle with a vengeful vampire. I wondered if I could defeat Emily Rose on my own, or if I would need help from Danny and his wolves. Then my thoughts turned to Danny. He was clearly wary of me at the moment, and I couldn't blame him. It seemed that recently all I had done was torment him. Even when I wasn't struggling to control Suri, I found it difficult to look on him as a friend. There was a niggling voice in my head, constantly saying, what if. Jack didn't seem concerned about my feelings for his brother. Maybe I should relax my morals and give in to the lust. After all, I had done it with Marcus. This was not much worse in all honesty.

Shaking my head, I chastised myself for thinking such vulgar things. There was a vampire determined to kill me, and a werewolf pack full of mistrust and anger, all determined not to let me close to their master. I was anxious about Emily Rose. My mother had returned in several dreams, and each time she warned me that the old vampire was drawing near, but that she would not attack in the traditional sense. I had no idea what my mother meant, and when I asked her, she also admitted that her senses were weak and she could not quite see what Emily Rose was doing. She only knew that it posed a threat to both me, and my relationship with Jack, and that Emily Rose was drawing close.

I finally confessed to Jack one night when I had a visit from the vampire herself. We were asleep in Jack's bed, and I was tired after a busy day at work. Jack had been out late on business, and I barely woke when he crawled into bed at some point in the early hours. I promptly fell back into a deep sleep, and that was when Emily Rose appeared again. I woke to find her sitting on the bed staring at me, and I sat bolt upright, glancing at Jack for help. He was literally dead to the world, his face glowing white so I knew he had exhausted his energy and would need feeding. When Emily Rose didn't immediately attack, I gathered my senses and spoke.

"What do you want?" I asked, "Why are you here now, in the middle of the night?"

She smiled, her rich red lips pouting and full. Her glossy black hair shone in the moonlight, and I noticed that the curtains were open. I thought I had closed them before bed. I reached to switch the lamp on, but her hand shot out to stop me. I reared back at her icy touch on my bare skin, and my tiger growled as she sensed the enemy. Emily Rose simply laughed.

"Why would he choose a witch," she said scathingly, "When he has me?"

I shook my head slowly.

"Because he doesn't want you," I said, "He loves me, and we are together. You should just leave him alone."

"I made him," she declared, "He is mine whenever I choose. And you shall not stand in my way."

I suddenly realised that this was a dream, or a vision, or something.

"You aren't really here," I said, "Are you?"

Her expression sobered, and her eyes glittered dangerously.

"You are very perceptive," she said icily, "I may not be here in body, but I can still do this."

She lunged at me, her fangs bared, hissing and grabbing at my face. I screamed and woke up, thrashing around in the bedcovers.

"Jessica," Jack said urgently, "Jessica! Wake up!"

He grabbed my shoulders, and I stopped fighting and opened my eyes. His were glowing silver in the darkness. Glancing over his shoulder, I saw that the curtains were drawn as I had left them.

"I'm ok," I said, "You can let go."

Slowly he released my shoulders and sat back, still staring at me. My heart was pounding, I was sweating with fear, and my tiger was still growling from her place deep within my energy. Suri was pacing in tight circles in her wooded clearing, anxious for me to call her forward. I shook my head, rubbed my eyes, and reached for the bedside lamp. The dim lighting of the energy saving bulb soon calmed me as I saw that the bedroom was normal and we were alone.

"What was it Jessica?" Jack asked.

"It was her," I replied quietly, "Emily Rose. She is waiting to attack, and I don't know when or where."

His face paled, and I confessed about the conversations with my mother. Jack was initially angry with me for hiding it from him, but eventually he drew me close to his body, wrapping his arms around me and kissing my head.

"She will not harm you," he said, "I will see to it."

"But you can't do anything to her," I replied, "You said before. You are powerless against her."

"I may be," Jack replied grimly, "But my brother isn't. He is spoiling for a fight with someone. We must call her out, and put an end to it."

His tone of voice made me shiver violently, and he held me tighter. Eventually we lay back down to sleep, but I couldn't settle and spent the next day at work feeling exhausted and very sorry for myself. I could not figure out how to deal with this situation. We didn't even know where Emily Rose was. We told Danny at breakfast the next day, and he promised to stay close to home, in case I needed his help. It was true that he was a better choice to fight against Emily Rose as and when she struck. Because she made Jack, she held control of his senses. If she commanded him, he would obey. In fact, we were probably safer to keep him away from her, and maybe even from me, in case she decided to use him as her weapon of destruction. When the brothers explained this to me, my blood ran cold. But I accepted their words. I knew that we were running out of options. As it was, Emily Rose couldn't wait much longer. She finally made her move a week after our encounter.

29

I was actually enjoying my training with Crystal. She started visiting me twice a week after my latest tiger incident, and she took me for more meetings with her friends. She was a priestess of the coven, and was therefore seen as their leader, although I quickly learned it was nothing like the wolf pack. These witches were not interested in power and control. They were gentle creatures, and they used their powers only for healing and well being, and to offer thanks to the gods and goddesses of nature. The witches enjoyed their ceremonies and festivals, and I was looking forward to celebrating Samhain with them, on the holiday that I had always known as Halloween. There was also something called Mabon, which was a celebration of the changing season. I was still learning about it, but the festival sounded fun.

During Crystal's training sessions we would meditate, and I would visit my tiger friend Suri in her enchanted frozen forest. I grew to love this place very quickly, since I shared Suri's pride and sense of ownership. It was a peaceful, beautiful, magical place, and Suri explained that as my natural abilities manifested, and the more comfortable I became with my true self, the more I would discover about the world around me and its true spiritual inhabitants. In the meantime I spoke to Crystal's witch friends, and listened to their stories and experiences. It was surprising how easy I found it to accept and believe their tales, although when I reflected on what had happened recently, it didn't seem so outrageous to acknowledge the existence of fairies, nymphs, elves and mermaids.

Every day I made time to meditate, knowing now how important it was. I always felt refreshed and energised afterwards, and it was a good way to dissipate the electrical energy that buzzed through my body. I allowed Jack to feed from me again, but I didn't want it to become a regular, normal occurrence. It was such an intense experience, and I still felt that niggling doubt about whether he would be able to stop, and whether I was able to prevent him turning me into a vampire, or even killing me. Jack protested that of course he would never do that, he loved me, but I reasoned that his love alone would not keep me safe with his vengeful maker out to destroy us. There was also the issue of him potentially using Suri's power through my blood. I was determined to be strong, and part of that was to begin my self-defence training, which included a crash course on the use of firearms.

I couldn't learn everything in such a short space of time of course. Jack had barely begun my physical training when Emily Rose attacked me. We had been using Jack and Danny's home gym, which was set up in the fourth bedroom of their home. They both enjoyed weight lifting, and both exercised frequently. This was partly to work off their own excess psychic energy, and partly to keep their physical bodies fit and active. They explained that supernatural creatures would always be agile and nimble, but there was a difference between that and being in top physical shape. The exercise program gave Jack and Danny a focus, and was their favourite hobby, besides playing computer games.

I was reading through some books that Crystal had loaned to me, which explained about the witch festivals and the different forms of witchcraft that were known to exist. The books explained about meditating, about setting up an altar at home, which was basically a sacred space on which to focus our thoughts, and the meanings behind various rituals and the tools that were used. I soon learned that I would be doing quite a bit of supernatural shopping, but the thought excited me, and I set about searching the Internet, browsing the sites that had been recommended. Actually, as the days wore on, I felt more excited about my newfound abilities, and less frightened about the threat of the vengeful vampire. I knew that I would fight Emily Rose. I knew that it would be hard, and I would most likely end up injured again. But I also knew without a doubt that I would survive and she would perish. I would do whatever was necessary to protect myself, and the man I loved.

Liz noticed a change in my attitude, and she questioned me one evening. I was sitting on the sofa cuddling Amy, marvelling at the tiny baby. She had very fine, dark hair, and big blue eyes, which would apparently change colour as she grew. Her skin was soft as velvet, and full of fascinating little wrinkles. I was amazed at her tiny fingers and toes, and the little snuffling noises she would make to express contentment or unease. Even her crying was wonderful to hear, except for when she screamed in sheer frustration.

"Jessica," Liz asked, "Are you feeling better now?"

I looked up, a frown on my face.

"What do you mean?" I replied.

"Well," Liz continued, "Don't take this the wrong way, but you seem different somehow."

My heart leaped, skipped a beat, and jumped into my throat. I stifled a gasp, and fought to keep my expression neutral, frowning a little more to show my confusion at her question.

"What do you mean, different?" I asked.

Liz laughed, and I could hear the unease in her voice. There was a tension in the room that hadn't been there a moment earlier. Perhaps I could sense it with my witch abilities. Whatever, I knew it was there.

"You seem, I don't know, animated," Liz said, struggling to find the words, "I mean, you look great, and I am so glad that you have recovered."

I laughed in reply, and offered Amy my little finger, watching intently as the little girl's tiny fingers curled around mine in a fearsome grip.

"I am recovered Liz," I said, "And you are right. I do feel much better."

"That's great Jess," she replied, "But it seems a bit sudden. I mean, I'm happy for you, but are you sure you aren't hiding anything?"

I stared at her for a minute. She knew. She must have guessed that I was keeping secrets. Maybe she had met one of my new witch friends, or maybe Rob had told her the truth. But then, if he had she wouldn't be so calm. Liz would be furious if she found out what we had been keeping from her. She must simply have sensed a change in me. I should be more careful.

"I'm only hiding the trauma of what happened Liz," I said slowly, choosing my words carefully, "It's nothing to be worried about. I have moved on, I am moving on, and it's all in the past now."

Love Kills

She returned my gaze, and I knew that she wanted to probe more. Liz knew I wasn't telling her the whole story, but she was afraid of upsetting me by bringing the subject up. I watched the emotions and thoughts flicker across her face, and finally she relaxed and laughed again.

"As long as you are happy," she said brightly, "Then I'm happy."

And that was it, at least for now. I knew she wouldn't give up so easily, and that Liz felt she should know my secrets, since we were as close as sisters. But she was also preoccupied with her new baby, and was still adjusting to parenthood, so for now she would leave me alone. I was glad about baby Amy for so many reasons.

30

It was a long, slow, boring day in the shop. I barely had any customers, our Internet orders were up to date, and I sat behind the counter reading one of Crystal's books. My mind began to wander, and I thought about all the events of the past few months. As I thought about the night I discovered Jack and Danny's secrets, the scars on my neck throbbed as if remembering the trauma. Rubbing my neck absentmindedly, I remembered the visions in which the vampire Emily Rose had visited me. Shivering, I swallowed nervously and tried hard to banish the fear that swept through me. Something big was coming, and despite my newfound power, I would still be rendered helpless. My human self was still strong, and sitting here in this average bookshop on an average Friday morning, it was hard to even believe in vampires and werewolves.

I could feel Suri inside me. She was quiet today, but she reminded me of her presence every so often. I would have a random memory of wading through an icy river, or climbing up a mountainside, or being curled up in a cave at dusk. Each time I witnessed these thoughts, I could feel what it was like to be the tiger, and it scared me. What made it worse was that it felt so natural.

"*Of course it feels natural,*" Suri said in my head, "*you and I are kindred spirits. We share the essence of each other.*"

I acknowledged her words, but I was in no fit state to analyse them. My mind wandered to the issue of my relationship with Danny. My feelings were becoming more confused every time I saw him, especially while we were dealing with the supernatural incidents. While I was certain that I didn't love him the way that I loved Jack, I was curious about the kind of love I was feeling for Danny. And I was terrified about my growing lust for his body. I knew that this was partly Suri's influence, but I couldn't ignore it.

When I had awoken that morning, I had found Jack sitting in a chair beside his bed, staring at me with his eerie, unblinking eyes. Forgetting about the en suite, I had stumbled towards the bathroom and ran straight into Danny as he exited, having just taken a shower himself. Stuttering, and feeling a hot flush of embarrassment, I had backed away from him.

"Good morning, Jessica," he had said, "I will leave you and be on my way to work."

I had only managed to nod and mumble a "good morning" in return, before rushing into the bathroom and locking the door securely behind me. All I had done was touch Danny's bare skin when I hit his chest. But my body had instantly reacted, and Suri had jumped up with an excited howl. I had quickly subdued her, forcing her back with a strength I hadn't previously possessed. It terrified me. Jack had barely spoken, but I felt his eyes boring into me as I moved around the bedroom getting dressed and blow-drying my hair. He had insisted on accompanying me home, following me into my kitchen, and he reluctantly left when I said I was opening the shop. I was actually glad to see him go, and my guilt burned deeper and more intense at every conflicting emotion I experienced.

Business picked up during the afternoon, and I forced my best professional smile to my face as customers began to appear. I served a variety of people, until the shop emptied again, except for a woman browsing the crime fiction section. I glanced across at her, and my stomach lurched, although at first I didn't understand why. Alarm bells were ringing in my head. This woman was dangerous, but I didn't know who she was. I choked back the panic, as I remembered the time not so long ago, when Seamus Tully's pack mates had marched in here and given me a message for Danny. The two women had terrified me, and that was before I knew about the werewolves. This woman was definitely not human, and I had a feeling she was a wolf, though I didn't know what made me so sure. Then I reasoned with myself. She had to be one of Danny's wolves, in which case she wouldn't hurt me. I was calm and collected, smiling politely when she approached the counter.

"Hello," I said, "May I help you?"

The woman was tall, and although slim, I could see muscles rippling in her arms through the tight sleeves of her blue fitted sweater. She had long dyed blond hair, and large brown eyes. Her expression was not so polite, and was definitely hostile.

Her painted red lips curled unpleasantly when she spoke. "I am Marianne Wayne, a member of the Redcliffe pack," she said in a strong, clear voice, "and we do not allow humans into our lair."

I blinked, surprised and confused at her words.

"I'm sorry," I replied, "I don't understand."

My heart was pounding, and I fought not to show the fear that was coursing through me in waves. Marianne sniffed the air in a very inhuman gesture, and her grimace became a cruel smile.

"You know perfectly well what I mean," she said, "You have bewitched my pack leader, and I am here to warn you that he will not be yours."

I was shocked, and it was obvious in my voice when I replied.

"Danny?" I exclaimed, "What do you mean? I am with Jack; his brother."

Marianne laughed scornfully.

"I know what you witches do," she said, "You have fixed your desire on both of them, and I will not allow it. If there is to be any alpha female in Redcliffe, it will be me."

Her voice rose shrilly as she spoke, and I shivered at her words.

"Alpha female," I repeated stupidly, "I don't want to be an alpha, let alone for Danny Mason. I think you should leave my shop, now."

Marianne stared at me intently. She was most definitely an intimidating woman, and her words frightened me. But I was defiant. I refused to be scared in my own shop, and I would not have some strange woman telling me who to be friends with. She could take it up with Danny for all I cared. After a minute she turned to walk out of the shop.

"He wants you, witch," she said over her shoulder, "And I am warning you to leave him alone. You are welcome to the vampire. We do not want him."

And she was gone, slamming the door so that the bell above it jangled wildly, almost falling off its bracket with the force. I let out a breath and sat down suddenly on my chair. I willed my heart to beat more slowly, more regularly. My head was spinning. My day had just gotten worse.

31

That evening I was sitting at my kitchen table, nibbling some toast and reading a book when Jack and Danny arrived. I was surprised to see them together, but I got up to let them in. I had started locking all my exterior doors more regularly since my near death experiences. You never knew who was out to get you nowadays. I felt self-conscious about my dishevelled appearance, and the way my mouth felt unclean and mucky after eating the food. Then I shook myself. They had both seen me at death's door, with blood pouring from my neck, and wounds covering my body. They could handle it. I stepped back as they entered my kitchen.

"Hello, Jessica," Jack said, leaning forward for a kiss, "How are you?"

I responded, allowing him a peck on the lips. We were not touching tongues until I could grab some chewing gum or a fresh mint. He didn't seem to mind, and I supposed he was reading my thoughts.

"I'm fine, thanks," I said, turning my head, "Hi, Danny."

Danny responded, and I gestured to the fridge.

"Do you want a drink?" I asked them both.

Danny accepted a can of Coke, but Jack told me had already eaten. His expression told me he had taken blood and was fully sated. I went cold momentarily, but told myself I had to get used to it. My boyfriend was a blood drinker. It was only like being diabetic. There were some things that you could eat safely, and some that you couldn't.

Danny gulped down half of the can in one mouthful as he walked further into the room, heading for my stairs. I guessed we would go up to my living room and watch TV, so first I started clearing my dishes off the table, and rinsing them in the sink ready for washing later.

"What's wrong, Danny?" Jack asked from his position near the back door.

I turned my head to see Danny standing by the door that led

into the storeroom adjoining my shop. His face was tilted up, and I realised he was scenting the air like a dog. Or more accurately, like a wolf. My blood ran cold as I watched, and I turned the tap off and moved to give him my full attention. Danny slowly turned his head to look at me, and I stifled a gasp when I saw his wolf eyes glowing. Suri roused from her sleep, responding to his power. The atmosphere in my kitchen was thick, warm, and dangerous.

"One of my wolves was here today," Danny said in a gruff voice, "Which one, and why?"

I shrugged my shoulders, trying to act casual.

"What do you mean?" I asked.

In a sudden movement, Danny was across the room, gripping my wrists as though to emphasize the importance of his question. I yelped and wriggled, and Jack stepped forward to intervene.

"Danny," he said quietly, "You are hurting Jessica."

Danny looked at my wrists clamped beneath his fingers, and he slowly loosened his grip and stepped back.

"My apologies, Jessica," he said, obviously trying to restrain himself, "Please, tell me who was here. I know it was a female. Was she simply a customer, or was there a purpose for her visit?"

I couldn't lie to him. I wanted to. This would only end badly, and my instincts told me to run and hide. I could not hide from Danny, especially when he was in this mood. Glancing at Jack, I took a deep breath, and told them both about Marianne and her threats. When I had finished there was a dead silence in the room. The only sound was the dripping of my tap, which I hadn't turned off properly. And there was the steady low-level hum from my fridge-freezer. I stared at Danny fearfully. The anger was rolling off him in waves, and I did not need supernatural senses to feel it.

"This ends now." Danny said in a rough, animal voice.

He stepped back and pulled his mobile phone from the pocket of his jeans. The recipient of his call answered almost immediately, and I was betting it was Simon.

"Call a pack meeting," Danny said abruptly into the phone, "I want everyone assembled in 30 minutes."

He shoved the phone back into his pocket and looked from

me to Jack. Then he lunged forward and grabbed my wrist again, pulling me towards the door.

"Danny!" I shouted, "Let go! What are you doing?"

"I am making this right," he replied, still holding onto me, "She will be punished, and you will receive the apology and respect that you deserve."

"Danny," Jack said, stepping forward and stopping his brother. He touched Danny's hand, calmly peeling his fingers from their hold on my wrist. I sagged and clasped my bruised arm, glaring at Danny.

"That was not exactly respectful, Danny," I said, choking back tears, "What the hell is wrong with you?"

Danny stared at me for a moment, and I realised that he wasn't used to being the bad guy. He didn't see that he had hurt me. He had forgotten I was human. His expression changed, his eyes shone blue, and he ducked his head apologetically.

"I am sorry, Jessica," he said, "I forgot myself. Please come to the lair with me. I will take care of this situation."

I stared at him. I did not want to visit the wolves' lair. It terrified me, and I associated it with pain after my recent experiences. I knew that Danny wouldn't back down. He had expected me to follow him automatically, as though I was one of his wolves. He talked about me being respected by them, but I could see that this incident went far beyond that. While my instincts screamed danger, my human curiosity got the better of me.

"Jack," I said, looking at my boyfriend, "Will you come with us?"

Jack looked at his brother, and Danny nodded.

"Yes." He replied.

I managed to turn off the dripping tap, took my handbag from the chair it was hanging on, and shoved my feet into a pair of trainers that were kept near the back door. Grabbing my keys from the glass bowl on my kitchen counter, I followed the men out of the back door, carefully locking up behind me. The evening was cool, and I was wearing only a thin cardigan and a jersey t-shirt. Hugging the soft material around me, I hurried to the waiting car and climbed into the back seat. I had barely fastened my seatbelt when Danny sped off with a squeal of tires. I really hoped my neighbours weren't watching. I thought they were already suspicious about the recent comings and goings at my place. But I had more important things to worry about, like what was about to happen at the wolves' lair.

32

We pulled into the pub car park in less than five minutes. Danny was out of the car and at the back door of the pub before I had even climbed out of my seat. Jack waited for me, and Danny pressed the button on his key fob to lock the vehicle. We followed Danny into the dimly lit hallway, through the door marked 'Staff Only' and down into the cellar. My heart was pounding so hard I thought it might leap from my chest, and I grabbed Jack's hand for support. He squeezed my hand reassuringly, and I glanced up at him. He gave me a small smile, but his expression was serious. He wanted to be here even less than I did. I wondered how it was for him, being hated by so many people simply because he was a different species. And I wondered why exactly vampires and werewolves hated each other specifically. There had to be more than just pride and a territorial attitude involved, surely.

Danny led us into his office, where he paced the room angrily. I sat uneasily on the sofa, with Jack beside me. I looked up as Simon entered the room, and I smiled automatically. He glanced at me, but his attention was solely for his master. I couldn't fault him for that. This is what made him such a good and loyal lieutenant."Master," Simon said respectfully, bowing his head, "May I ask what the meeting is about?"

Danny stopped pacing and stared at him. Again I felt his power rolling around the room, angry and dangerous. I could almost see Danny's wolf, superimposed over him like a ghost. And I could hear it in the rough growl of his voice. Suri stirred deep within me, and I forced her back into the forest. She snarled and disappeared with a swish of her tail. I would pay for my show of dominance. Ignoring the angry tiger, I focused on Danny and Simon, determined to remain strong during the next few hours.

"Marianne Wayne has threatened Jessica," Danny said, "She must be punished, and the pack will be warned not to do anything like this again."

Simon went very still and glanced at me again.

"I see," he said quietly, "They are all assembled now."

Danny nodded and strode to the door, with Simon close on his heels. Sally was in the corridor, and she fell into step on the other side of her master. Jack and I followed behind. I gripped Jack's hand tightly, and stood close to him for protection. "Do not fear, Jessica," he murmured, "You will come to no harm."

We walked into the throne room, and I hesitated as I saw the assembled pack. There must have been about two hundred people crammed into this cave. It was large enough to accommodate everyone, but I felt a wave of nausea as I realised I was the only human. Or at least, I was the only one with human frailties. I silently called on Suri to protect me, and she answered with a growl. She was angry too, and she wanted me to release her. I couldn't, or I wouldn't until I knew exactly what that meant. I was not about to pick a fight with a werewolf, even if I had a tiger for assistance. I walked to the far corner of the room, beside the low platform on which Danny stood with Simon and Sally. Jack stood at my side, holding my hand, monitoring the room. We watched as Danny paced along the platform, surveying the crowd.

"I recently told you all," Danny said loudly in a fearsome growling voice, "that Jessica Stone was a friend of the Redcliffe pack, and that she is under our protection."

His voice rang out through the room, and no one moved.

"One of you disobeyed my order," Danny shouted, "And you will be punished."

Suddenly he leaped from the platform and into the waiting crowd. There was a yelp as he grabbed a woman by her hair. I watched as he dragged Marianne Wayne up onto the platform with him and threw her down at his feet.

"Did you think I would not catch your scent in her shop?" he thundered at the terrified woman, "She would not have told me, had I not been alpha enough to notice your presence."

Danny dragged Marianne to her feet and slapped her hard across the cheek, sending her crashing back into the ceremonial thrones. She screamed, and I cringed at the thud. We all watched as she struggled to her feet, turning a tear stained face to her master. There was blood running down her cheek where the furniture had cut her.

"Please, Master," she begged, "I meant only to protect you. I am yours, and I wish to be your guardian."

Danny threw back his head and laughed, but the sound was evil and I shivered with fear.

"You think yourself good enough to be my mate?" he asked scornfully, "You would never be to my standard."

He leaped forward and grabbed Marianne again, and I shuddered as he pounded her with his fists. I wasn't even sure where he hit her, but she was soon huddled at his feet, crying loudly and begging for his forgiveness. I looked up at Jack. This had to stop. Surely Danny would kill her if he continued. Jack returned my gaze and shook his head slightly. He could not interfere with pack business. We had to remain silent. Danny turned his attention back to the room, addressing the wolves.

"Take this as a lesson," he said loudly, "We protect Jessica Stone. We do not intimidate her, and we ensure no more harm comes to her, whatever the cost. Do you understand?"

They all nodded in unison, muttering "Yes, Master."

"And be warned," Danny continued, "I am your Master. Not one of you is strong enough to overthrow me. If you want to try, then challenge me now."

The room was silent. Nobody moved.

"Good," Danny said, "I am not looking for a mate at this time. But when I do, you can be sure of who my first choice would be."

Here he looked directly at Sally. She kept a straight face, but I could feel her joy and pride at being singled out for this. Danny turned his attention back to Marianne. She was now sitting, cradling her arm, the wounds on her face healing fast but still dripping blood. Gone was the confident, arrogant woman. She was broken and defeated.

"Marianne," Danny said firmly, "No matter the reasons for your behaviour, you must be punished for your disobedience to me."

He looked again at Sally.

"Take her away," he said, "And punish her as you see fit."

Sally's expression twisted into one of cruelty and excitement. I realised that she disliked this woman as much as Danny, if not more. I actually felt sorry for Marianne when I thought about the beating she was going to receive. Then I remembered her words and her threat. She was a wolf. She could handle this, and she would heal. It was none of my business. Danny once again addressed the waiting crowd.

"You are dismissed," he announced, "But heed my warning."

They all nodded, and then turned and began shuffling out of the room. A steady murmur of conversation arose, and all the wolves carefully avoided looking at Jack and me. Sally grabbed Marianne roughly and marched the taller woman out of the room. Marianne didn't speak. She was resigned to her punishment. I decided to wait until the room was empty and then leave. Danny had disappeared, I supposed to his office. Jack was still holding my hand.

I jumped when Jack suddenly vanished. Turning round, scanning the room, I fought the blind panic that rose in my chest. I gasped in shock when I located him. He was holding a middle-aged man by the throat, pinning him to the rough stone wall only a few yards from where we stood.

"Jack!" I cried, "What are you doing?"

Jack ignored me, and I felt his cold power swirling around us. His skin was almost glowing, and his eyes were silver. I saw his fangs as he spoke to the man in a low and dangerous voice.

"Do not disrespect me in my brother's domain," Jack hissed, "I could snap your neck, you weak little dog."

The man struggled as Jack lifted him off his feet. He growled, and I saw that he was trying to summon his wolf energy. He was defiant, even after Danny's display of violence.

"You are not welcome in our lair, vampire," the man spat, struggling to breathe, "This is our business."

Danny appeared at Jack's side.

"What is the meaning of this?" he asked sharply, glaring at the wolf.

"This idiot was complaining to his companion about my presence here," Jack said in a dangerous voice, "I will not stand for it."

Danny pursed his lips. He looked around, and Simon caught his eye and immediately came to attention.

"Simon," Danny said, "Take this beast to Sally. Tell her to punish him along with Marianne. I have no more patience for disobedient wolves."

With that he turned and left. I was shocked. I knew that Jack and Danny were dangerous. But I had not seen this sort of behaviour at such close quarters. It terrified me. What the hell was I involved in? It was like some sort of mafia family. I was probably in too deep to escape them. I didn't want to escape them. My love for Jack would never fade, no matter how he behaved. And as for Danny, well I was still trying to figure him out. I watched silently as Jack released the wolf, and Simon took him by the scruff of his neck and marched him out of the room and down the corridor. Jack turned to face me, and his expression became more human.

"I am sorry you had to witness that, Jessica," he said quietly, "Perhaps we should have a drink in Danny's office, and calm down."

I nodded, unable to speak, and I followed him as he turned and walked away.

33

I sank gratefully onto the comfortable sofa in Danny's office. Danny was seated at his desk, still rigid and angry, but slowly beginning to relax into his usual self. Jack stood beside the sofa, and I wondered if he felt bad about showing me such a rough side to his character. Simon soon returned, carrying a tray containing a bottle of single malt whiskey, and four glasses. He set it on Danny's desk, poured the drinks, and held out a glass to me. I stared at him in surprise. I never drank whiskey. It was too strong for me.

"Take it, Jessica," Simon said quietly, "It will make you feel better."

I hesitated, and then took the glass with a shaking hand. I was surprised to see my body acting in such a way. I suppose I was in a form of shock, having witnessed such inhuman and violent behaviour from people that I loved. I had no idea what to say, or even what to think about the whole situation. I watched Jack, Danny and Simon as they each downed their drinks in one mouthful. Danny reached out to refill his, and Jack moved towards the desk for the same. I licked my lips, and decided to go for it. Steeling myself for the sharp taste, I lifted the glass to my lips and swallowed the amber liquid. It burned my throat, and I coughed and spluttered. But after a few moments it felt good, and I closed my eyes, savouring the very human sensations and the comforting familiarity of alcohol.

After several minutes of silence, I could take it no longer.

"Why did you make me watch that, Danny?" I asked, impressed at how strong my voice sounded despite the tears stinging my eyes.

Danny turned his head towards me. In a smooth, quick movement he was out of his seat and crouching before me. I sat upright on the sofa, leaning forward instinctively to hear his words. He held my gaze with his deep blue eyes, and I saw the flame burning deep within, the same as I saw in Jack. I half-turned to confirm that Jack was still beside me, and then stared back at Danny.

"This is all for you, Jessica," Danny said, "I can no longer deny my feelings for you."

My heart skipped a beat and the room spun around me. It was nothing to do with the whiskey. I swallowed nervously, again glancing from Jack to Danny. My boyfriend was silent at my side, and I was aware of Simon standing just in front of the desk.

"W-what do you mean?" I asked shakily.

Danny placed his hands on my knees, and I sat rigid, unable to move. Suri stirred again within me. I was aware of her lifting her head, surveying the scene with interest. I could hear her thinking how useful this situation could be to her. She pleaded again for me to allow her release.

"Not now, Suri," I whispered, and Danny looked at me sharply.

"Your tiger is here," he said with a faint smile, "I can feel her. She wants me. Do you want me, Jessica?"

I licked my lips nervously. Yes, I wanted Danny, and it terrified me. How could I do this to Jack? Surely I could not be in love with two men. It wasn't possible. Well, maybe it wasn't love. But I certainly felt something for Danny, and I could no longer deny it. He knew. He stared at me with growing comprehension, and his expression grew triumphant.

Before I could reply, Suri took her chance. She surged forward, and I cried out as my body lurched with her impact. I was still conscious, but she was there, fighting for control of me. As I stared at Danny, all I wanted was a kiss. I slowly placed my hands on his, and moved my face so that our lips met. He responded with a gentle kiss, but the moment Suri felt the wolf, she roared with excitement. I leaped forward, pushing Danny back on to the floor. Straddling his body, my kisses grew passionate and excited, as I shoved my tongue into his mouth, nipping at his lips.

"Jessica." I jumped as I heard Jack's voice behind me.

Rearing back, I stared in horror at the man lying beneath me. Then I turned my head to see Jack crouched beside us. His expression was serious but not angry. Simon was positioned on our other side, looking concerned more than anything.

"What did I do?" I whispered.

Suri paced around inside me, excited and wanting more. I forced her back, and she growled at me angrily, trying to swipe me with her huge, sharp claws. I scrambled back off Danny, struggling to my feet. Looking wildly round at the men who were staring at me, I backed away to the door.

"I need some air." I said shakily.

I turned and fled.

34

I ran blindly through the long stone corridor, hurtled through the antechamber where I had almost died, and found myself approaching the huge wooden door that led back into the cellar of the Ship. Suri roared as I ran, her strong voice echoing through my lips, and the wolves replied instinctively. Adrenaline shot through me, my body burning both hot and cold, the need to escape foremost in my mind. I barely registered the weight of the heavy door as I pulled it open, using Suri for strength. She did not argue but simply allowed me to leave, knowing that I was in control of our body.

As I charged up the wooden stairs of the cellar, my feet echoing heavily on the boards, I came to my senses. I flung the door open and almost slammed it against the wall, forgetting that this was a normal interior door and could be opened by a human. A couple of women walking down the hallway jumped in surprise, and stared at me curiously as I appeared so suddenly. I stopped moving, smiled weakly at them, and made a big show of closing the door behind me and walking slowly out of the rear door onto the smoking deck.

The smell of cigarette smoke was a welcome relief. I inhaled deeply, tasting both nicotine and sea salt on my tongue, and immediately I began to calm down. I was safe. Whatever had just happened, I would deal with later. For now I needed some distance and some time away from the Mason brothers and the Redcliffe wolf pack. The cigarette smoke actually reminded me of Simon, which was partly a comfort and partly unsettling given his current situation with Danny Mason. Shaking my head, ignoring the curious stares from pub patrons on the deck, I walked down the steps onto the car park. I slipped a little on the wet flooring, since the air was damp. It wasn't quite raining but there was a definite chill in the air and it was fairly gloomy. Shivering, I pulled my thin cardigan around me and buttoned it up for what good that did. I cursed Danny silently for not giving me time to grab a jacket when we left my house.

Lifting my head, I strode across the smooth black tarmac of the pub car park, and suddenly realised I had no clear destination in mind. My instinct was to return home, but that seemed bleak and unappealing. Besides, I wasn't convinced that one of the men wouldn't follow me home, try to reason with me, or even bring me back to the pub. It seemed like something they would do. No, I needed to be somewhere alone, somewhere safe. I stared along the promenade and my gaze settled on the bright lights of the pier. The fairground was still open, and there were enough people on there to form a decent sized crowd into which I could hopefully slip unnoticed. Smiling, I shook my hair back, running my fingers through it to loosen a few knots. I walked quickly onto the promenade and headed for my destination.

As I walked I could see Suri pacing around a clearing in her forest. She was agitated, angry, and she wanted out. She wanted me to return to the wolves' lair and continue what I started with Danny. I silently told her that wasn't going to happen. No way could I even consider sleeping with my boyfriend's brother, no matter what had happened recently. She refused to accept my protestation.

"*We share the same human body, Jessica,*" Suri coaxed, "*And you want the wolf just as much as I do.*"

I sighed heavily, still walking steadily along the tarmac pavement that formed Redcliffe promenade. It was quiet tonight and I only passed a couple of people, who smiled politely in greeting, which I duly returned.

"*Suri, I am so confused about all of this,*" I said in my head, "*Please don't torment me anymore. We have the issue with Emily Rose to deal with, I don't need you playing with the wolves right now.*"

Suri hissed and swiped the air with her paw, as if she wished it were my body.

"*Enough!*" she snarled, "*I will kill the vampire when she finally arrives before us. She is no match for me, no matter her age and power. I am hungry and you continue to deny me that which we both desire.*"

My heart sank. Not only was I dealing with a vampire boyfriend and his egotistical, amorous werewolf brother, apparently I had an egotistical and demanding animal familiar who refused to be quiet and docile. I was drawing close to

Love Kills

Redcliffe pier now, and I smelt candyfloss and hotdogs on the air, mingling with the pervading sea salt. My stomach growled emptily, and I realised I would need food. Ignoring Suri, I stepped onto the smooth Victorian wooden boards, and approached the ornate wrought iron gates that enclosed the fairground.

"No," Suri snarled, swishing her tail and turning in circles, *"You cannot enter this place. I have no control here."*

That was interesting.

"What do you mean?" I asked, intrigued.

"I do not like these places of human habitation," Suri said bitterly, *"They confuse me. I must leave."*

She turned tail and ran, disappearing into the closely-knit trees of her forest. My heart leaped. Suri couldn't handle the fairground. That meant I could finally have some peace inside my own head, at least for an hour or so. It must be the fluorescent lighting and loud noises that upset her. I would remember this for future reference.

Smiling broadly as I wove through the diminishing crowd, I headed for my favourite fast food outlet, a hotdog stand located behind the dodgems. I ordered a tray of chips with mushy peas, and set to devouring them hungrily, wandering between the fairground rides and watching people enjoying their late summer holidays. The food warmed me, and I began to feel more human, and decidedly happier. I would walk around here for a bit, maybe spend some time in the amusement arcade, and just enjoy some time completely alone while I could.

After I polished off the food, I stopped at another food stall and picked up a large cup of hot chocolate. Cupping my hands around the cardboard container, I walked towards the amusement arcade and stood under the canopy, just outside the entrance doors. Here I was sheltered from the drizzling rain that kept threatening, and I was warmer standing near the heaters that were switched on just inside the building. I hid at the side of a children's ride-on machine, ignoring the blaring music that played on a loop. Instead I watched people coming and going, and savoured the smell and taste of my hot chocolate.

I could not relax completely. After only five minutes my shoulders itched, and I was sure someone was staring at me. Turning round, I scanned the people inside the arcade through the large glass windows. There were no familiar faces, and no one was looking at me curiously, or even giving me the time of day. Facing out onto the pier again, I tried looking ahead, but again found no one of interest. I was certain I was being watched.

"I know you are there," I murmured, sipping my drink, "Show yourself."

35

A figure seemed to swoop down to stand before me, making me jump. I cursed and almost spilt my chocolate, just righting the cup in time and turning an angry gaze up to my new stalker. It was Marcus Scott. My heart sank, and I felt a mixture of irritation and relief flood through me. I was irritated because he had disturbed my alone time. I was relieved because at least this was someone I knew, and not another enemy to add to my growing list.

"Hello, Marcus," I said heavily, "Why were you watching me, and what are you doing here?"

Marcus smiled broadly, showing his fangs. I managed not to react, and I could sense his disappointment. He was clearly looking for some sort of admiration or show of fear for his antics. Instead all I gave him was a weary smile and a forced show of warmth at his appearance.

"I am hunting, Jessica." he said, stepping in close to me and touching a fingertip to my cheek.

I shivered at his caress and forced myself to remain calm. Lifting my cup, I made a great show of sipping the now cooling chocolate drink, forcing some distance between us with my hands. Marcus dropped his hand and stared at me with glowing silver eyes.

"You are upset," he said, "Tell me what has happened."

Ignoring his question, I focused on his first statement instead.

"Who were you hunting, Marcus?" I asked.

He shrugged, and stared past me through the windows of the arcade.

"No-one in particular," he replied, "I am hungry and restless. I was hoping for a diversion here, and now it seems I have found one."

Again he touched my face, and my body reacted forcefully to him. Suri was still hidden in her forest, so I couldn't even blame her for my feelings. The lust was all my own, and I was at the same time ashamed and defiant. I stuck with the irritation, and tried to keep my voice firm as I spoke again.

"Sorry to disappoint you," I said, "But after what's happened to me tonight, I am in no mood for dealing with more supernatural shit."

I pushed past Marcus and walked back towards the pier entrance, intending to head back home as quickly as possible. Tossing my empty cup into a nearby dustbin, I felt him following me even before he darted in front and appeared in my path. He was determined, and I was angry.

"Marcus just leave me alone!" I almost shouted, only just remembering myself in time and not wanting to cause a scene in public.

He ignored my anger, and stood smiling arrogantly. I saw a group of teenage girls walk past, all staring at Marcus in blatant admiration. They giggled and chattered noisily as they passed us, and I overheard a few scattered words from their conversation. So did Marcus. He stared at me with eyes that were now their usual icy blue colour, but his fangs still showed when he spoke.

"I need human blood, Jessica," he said quietly, blocking my path as I tried to push past, "Perhaps those young girls will suffice."

My heart lurched in fear at his tone, and I glanced over my shoulder. The girls were huddled by the railings, pretending to look out to sea but all the while darting coy glances at Marcus and me. I knew they thought we were a couple having an argument, and they were hoping to attract Marcus' attention after I stormed off in a huff. I could not allow him to seduce them and take their innocence in such a way. Taking a deep breath, I forced myself to calm down.

"No, Marcus," I said, "Please leave them alone." I sighed and fixed my gaze on his, "I'm going home. I suppose you can come along if you want."

I knew he wouldn't leave me, and I did not want to risk him hurting some poor innocent girl at my expense. At least I could handle the vampire feeding on me, or so I told myself. I carried on walking back out onto the promenade, and jumped as I felt Marcus slip his jacket over my shoulders. I stopped, turned my head, and smiled weakly at him.

"Thanks," I said, "It has gone a bit cold."

"You are welcome," Marcus replied, "You were shivering, and I am a gentleman after all."

I laughed at his joke. He might well be a gentleman, trained in the Victorian era, but he was still a vampire and a predator. He fell into step beside me, walking at human pace, matching my stride.

"Tell me what happened today." Marcus said after a few minutes.

I opened my mouth to say I didn't want to talk, but then I hesitated. He would know soon enough, because Jack would tell him no doubt. And besides, he would not let me be silent now he had found me in this state. I gave him a shortened version of the events of my day, and was pleased that I didn't cry or even feel tearful towards the end when I recounted Danny almost beating a woman to death, Jack attacking another werewolf, and me kissing the brother of the man I loved. Marcus didn't interrupt, and by the time I finished my story we were almost at my door.

I unlocked the door and stepped inside, switching on the light and making way for Marcus. I gasped as he suddenly rushed past me in a blur, and I saw movement on the stairs. He was standing on the bottom stair, in the shadows away from the intense beam of my spotlights. I shook my head and turned to shut the door, locking it behind me out of habit. Dropping my handbag onto the kitchen table, I spoke as I moved.

"Is that a vampire thing, not liking my kitchen light?" I asked with only a hint of sarcasm.

"Yes," Marcus replied simply, "The light is damaging to our vision. We prefer the shadows and the natural light of the moon."

I nodded.

"Well, go on upstairs," I said, "I'll be up in a minute."

Marcus disappeared in a blur again, and I felt uneasy at his behaviour. This must be Marcus the hunter. I felt very confused. I had basically offered myself as food for the vampire, and I had brought him to my home to do it. So much for some time alone. That reminded me of Suri. As I searched my mind for her presence, I found she was still missing, still hidden deep in her forest. Well, good. That was one less distraction for me to contend with. I walked slowly up the stairs, switching off the kitchen light and switching on the one in the stairwell as I went. I hoped Marcus was waiting in my living room and not my bedroom.

36

I hesitated in the living room doorway. My apartment was silent, and the only light came from behind me. I shivered in anticipation, not sure what to expect. I had to allow Marcus to take my blood, otherwise he might return to the pier and attack some poor innocent girl. I could not have that on my conscience. Besides, I had so many scars on my neck now that it made no difference anymore. I felt a strange sense of calm, accepting of the fate I had allowed for myself.

Entering the room, I looked around for Marcus. As my eyes adjusted to the darkness, aided only by the moonlight shining through my windows, and a faint glow from streetlights, I saw him sitting on a chair. He sat perfectly still, and I wouldn't have noticed him if I wasn't looking. I wondered fleetingly if he had been in here before without my knowledge. That thought sent a shiver of dread trembling through my body, and I quickly quashed it.

I crossed the room and switched on the floor lamp that stood in one corner. It had an energy saving light bulb, and took several minutes to light up properly. I walked over to the windows and slowly drew the curtains in my usual nightly ritual. I liked to shut myself in, and be nice and cosy at home when I was alone. The strange thing was, I did not feel frightened by Marcus. I knew he was a predator, and he was not acting anything like a human at all. But at least I knew him, and I knew what to expect. He wouldn't actually harm me, I was sure of that.

"Ok," I said, turning to face him after closing the curtains, "What now?"

Marcus smiled and stood smoothly, as though he were pulled upright by strings. I marvelled at his grace and elegance, and once again my body reacted to the sight of him. He was wearing black jeans and a lavender coloured sweater with the emblem of an expensive designer embroidered on it. The sweater skimmed over his well-defined muscles just enough to tantalise any hot-blooded female, or indeed, any male of the same persuasion. He smiled broadly, showing his fangs, and his eyes glowed silver. In a flash he was standing before me, his hands cupping my face, his lips moving in for a soft kiss, full of promise and excitement.

I broke the embrace when Marcus' tongue entered my mouth. It took all my effort and self-control, but I stepped back.

"Whoa, Marcus," I said, "I am only your food, remember? I don't need any more complications right now."

He stared at me for a moment.

"Sex is food for a vampire, Jessica," he said quietly, "You must know this by now."

I shivered again. I was aware of this fact, but I was still in denial. I wanted nothing more right now than to be with Marcus in every way possible. I wanted him to fuck me, and the stark realisation of my emotions terrified me. This must be the vampire's seduction. He was doing this to me, and I refused to give in. I swallowed nervously, straightened my back and returned his gaze.

"I cannot give you that, Marcus," I said, "Isn't that why you have Alice?"

Alice was Marcus' personal assistant, both at work and in their private life. Apparently she was about sixty years old, but she looked thirty-five thanks to her ingesting vampire blood at regular intervals. I was still confused about why she wasn't a vampire, but apparently she didn't want that. She and Marcus had an open relationship, they loved each other, but she allowed for the nature of his beast as it were. I jumped as Marcus grabbed me roughly, his fingers in my hair, forcing me to bend backwards under his weight.

"This is about you and me, Jessica," he hissed, "I must have you again or I will go insane."

"Marcus, let go," I cried, "You are hurting me!"

He refused, and my struggle was about as effective as a deer in the jaws of a wolf. I screamed as he bit my neck roughly, all attempts at being a gentleman forgotten. The vampire was hungry and angry, and I had only made things worse. I tried to relax, let him do what he needed, but by instinct I couldn't. His teeth grazed my neck, the pain was sharp and intense, and I felt the pull of his frenzy as he sucked hungrily at my blood. My panic grew when Marcus' hands moved down my body, pulling at my clothes, ripping open my cardigan and tearing at my t-shirt.

"Marcus, please," I whimpered as he fed. "Please stop this."

I cried out silently for Suri but she was still hidden, and refused to answer my call. I called for Lillian, my mother, but our connection was weak and she was powerless to intervene. In desperation, I called out for Jack, hating myself for being weak and powerless. Just as I remembered I had my own power, the faintness grew. Marcus had taken too much blood, and now I was falling into an abyss. He may have killed me, I wasn't sure. My arms fell limp and my head lolled as he pulled away. I just barely saw Jack appear from the shadows and throw Marcus across the room before I slumped into unconsciousness.

37

"Jack." I murmured, trying to lift my head.

"Shush, Jessica," he replied, gently pushing me back.

Opening my eyes slowly, I realised I was lying in bed fully clothed. Jack was kneeling beside the bed, stroking my hair.

"You are weak," Jack said, "You must rest."

"Where is Marcus?" I managed to ask.

"He is gone," Jack said grimly, "I am sorry about what he did."

"Why did he attack me?" I asked, barely noticing the tears that rolled down my cheeks.

"I cannot explain at present," Jack said sadly, "Somehow you angered the vampire, and it seems he lost control."

As my consciousness slowly returned, I opened my eyes more fully to look at Jack. I felt a weight of sadness above all else, and then the throbbing pain began in my neck. I groaned and lifted my heavy hand to feel the wound. I touched yet another bandage, and my heart sank.

"Is it bad?" I whispered.

Jack nodded almost imperceptibly.

"He was rough with you Jessica," he said, "The wound is quite ragged. I am sorry."

I sighed and managed a weak smile.

"I think you should stop being sorry, Jack," I said, "It's not making things any better."

He nodded again and continued to stroke my hair. I closed my eyes, enjoying his gentle caress. I managed to ignore the rough, angry, vampire Jack I had witnessed only a few hours ago. This was the man I loved, the man who would help me recover from my ordeal. I thought back to what happened with Marcus. Despite my predicament, I could not feel angry or even frightened at what he did. I was confused. Somehow I had tipped him over the edge. Marcus would not intentionally have treated me that way, I was certain. But I would give him some distance for a long while now. Emotion flooded through me and I gasped and hiccupped, trying to force back the tears. Jack climbed onto the bed and gathered me into his arms, cradling me to his chest and wrapping his arms around me. I gave in and released the fear, anger and sheer hopelessness of our situation. He held me as I cried, and when I eventually relaxed, he lay down beside me, holding me close.

"What did you do to Marcus?" I asked when I could speak.

Jack's body tensed beside me, and he hesitated before saying.

"I threw him out of the window," he said seriously.

My heart skipped a beat and then thudded in my chest. I struggled to sit up, leaning on one arm to look at Jack. My bedside lamp was switched on so I could at least see him clearly. He stared at me with deep, clear blue eyes.

"You threw him out of my window?" I asked slowly, "Did you break it? Did anyone see?"

"No," Jack replied, "I moved fast and no humans would have witnessed it."

"Oh." I replied.

My arm began to shake under the pressure, and I slowly lay down again beside Jack. I turned on my side to face him, and he shifted his position to make it easier.

"How are you feeling now?" he asked quietly, reaching over to push some stray hair from my face.

I thought for a few moments.

"My neck is throbbing, and I have a headache," I said, "But actually I feel sort of numb really. What happened at the lair when I left?"

Jack reached up an arm and ruffled a hand through his hair. My body reacted instinctively at his familiar gesture of self-comfort. He kept his expression blank, giving away nothing.

"We were confused about the actions of your familiar," Jack said carefully, "And then concerned for your welfare."

"But you didn't follow me." I said.

"No," Jack replied, "One of the wolves was on the smoking deck when you left. He tracked you onto the pier and then reported back. I decided to leave you alone for an hour and then come here. It seems I was too late to intervene with Marcus."

I breathed in and out deeply.

"I wanted you to leave me alone," I said, "I thought you were following me, but then I discovered it was Marcus."

"He was hunting." Jack said.

"Yes," I nodded, wincing as my neck wound protested, "Does he do it often?"

"He has started hunting closer to home in recent months," Jack said, "Before that his favourite haunts were city bars and colleagues at business meetings."

I sighed.

"I wanted to be alone for a while," I said, "But then Marcus threatened to attack some teenage girls we saw. I couldn't let him do that, so I sort of offered myself as food. I thought I could handle him."

"You underestimated his hunger," Jack said, "I am sure he will be deeply sorry in the morning."

I laughed bitterly.

"It's a bit late then," I snorted, "What is it with you two? Is it a vampire thing, just bite now and think about it later?"

Jack looked down, embarrassed. Then he fixed his piercing gaze on me again.

"No," he said quietly, "We should have more control over our hunger. I believe it has something to do with your natural powers. Somehow you draw us in, you intensify our hunger, and we lose control of our senses. Perhaps we need to speak with Crystal about this."

I nodded, my heart sinking. Here were more problems to contend with.

"So I'm a danger to myself around vampires," I said, "Is that it?"

"Something like that," Jack said, "Perhaps we should agree to avoid feeding on you for the time being, at least until we discover the reason for our frenzy."

"Yes," I agreed, "That should help."

Jack reached out to stroke my cheek. I closed my eyes, enjoying the sensations. I was too exhausted for any kind of physical activity, but I welcomed his attentions.

"What about Danny?" Jack asked after a few minutes.

My eyes flew open and my heart pounded hard in my chest. I slowly sat up, wincing with pain as I awkwardly turned to look at Jack.

"What do you mean?" I asked.

"You kissed my brother tonight," Jack said, "While I watched. I know that it was not all your own doing, but I could still feel your excitement at the same time." I flopped onto my back beside him, our tender moment ruined. I turned my face towards him as I spoke.

"I'm confused, Jack," I said, "I mean, it wasn't so long ago that you tried to force me into your brother's bed. Now you seem upset about me kissing him."

Jack set his jaw in a firm, defiant expression.

"I thought I could handle it," he said, "But now I am not convinced. It wasn't you, Jessica. It was your damn tiger. She is out of control."

At his words I felt Suri return from her hideout. She stalked into the woodland clearing, swishing her tail, and looking for all the world like the proverbial Cheshire cat as she heard Jack's statement. I felt a mixture of anger and stubborn denial as I replied.

"She is not out of control, Jack," I said tightly, "But she is getting very excited with the wolves. I told you I didn't want to return to their lair, but you both insisted."

"I admit that I was a little too hasty to follow my brother," Jack said grudgingly, "But we both had your best interests at heart."

I stared at him, lost for words. A wave of exhaustion washed over me and I yawned loudly.

"Look, Jack," I said, "It has been a long day, on top of a very rough few weeks. Right now I need to sleep. Can we talk about this tomorrow?"

"Yes we can." He agreed.

I slowly and painfully made it to the bathroom, refusing Jack's help in my determination to be strong. I stripped off, took care of business, and dressed in warm button through pyjamas for comfort. When I returned to my bedroom Jack was lying in bed wearing only his boxer shorts and looking delicious as always. I ignored the lust that burned through my body, and climbed into bed beside him. I instinctively spooned against his body, and he drew me in close, wrapping his arms around me and kissing my head. Pulling the duvet up to my chin, I reached over and switched off the bedside light, allowing my body to finally relax.

38

The next morning I was awake before my alarm sounded. Jack was already in the shower so I stayed in bed until he finished. I lay staring up at the ceiling, thinking about all the problems I had to deal with. I didn't know where to start, and my head was pounding with the effort of thinking. Even Suri seemed to have run away for now; when I mentally searched for her in the forest and her caves, she was nowhere to be seen. Sighing, I opened my eyes and dragged myself out of bed, stumbling to the bathroom as I heard Jack switch off the shower. He hadn't locked the bathroom door so I walked in and waited as he stepped out of the bath. His body was glowing with good health, tanned and muscular, and my lust exploded so suddenly at the sight of him that I gasped and stepped back.

"Are you well, Jessica?" Jack asked, stepping towards me.

He was totally oblivious to the fact that he was naked, and I watched as he absently grabbed a towel from the rail and began rubbing his skin dry.

"Yes," I stammered, shaking my head, "I'm fine. I need a shower."

I hurriedly stripped off my clothes, switched the shower on, and dived into the bath. The water was cold for a moment, and I jumped back with a shout. I slowly eased back under the powerful jet as the temperature rose to something more comfortable, and then I rubbed my hair and turned my face up to the spray. Feeling the bandage still stuck to my neck, I stood under the water as I peeled it away, reaching round and throwing it into the bin I kept next to the sink.

"How is your wound, Jessica?" Jack asked.

I jumped, startled. I had forgotten he was there because he was so quiet. Tilting my head to splash water on the wound, I hissed as it throbbed sharply, and blood ran into the bath mingled with the water.

"It's sore," I said grumpily, "And it's bleeding again."

Jack was silent for a few moments. I wondered if the blood

was tormenting him, and I actually tensed in preparation for him leaping into the bath. He didn't, and I breathed a sigh of relief when he spoke again.

"I will leave you to your shower," he said.

I felt better after a good wash, and when I returned to my bedroom I peered into the mirror on my dressing table to inspect my latest wound. It was ragged, rough, and very sore. It had stopped bleeding so I didn't bother with another bandage. My neck was a mess of raw, red scar tissue, and bruises around the vampire bites. I opted to wear a scarf with my outfit for the day, fixing it carefully into place and using make-up to disguise the worst of the bruises and redness.

Jack was sitting at the kitchen table when I walked downstairs. He had made me a mug of coffee and it sat steaming on the worktop next to a bowl of cereal. Jack had left the milk beside my bowl, knowing that I wouldn't eat soggy cereal if he had prepared it too soon. Smiling at his simple gesture, I collected my breakfast and sat down opposite him. He sipped his own mug of coffee and stared at me with hypnotic blue eyes. I didn't know what to say. It was too early for a conversation about our recent drama, but the silence was killing me. Jack must have sensed it, because he spoke first.

"I will speak with Marcus today, Jessica," he said, "And try to decipher what triggered his bloodlust. I will be close to home all day if you need me."

I nodded, sipping my drink.

"Ok," I replied, "Do you expect something to happen?"

"No," he said, "I believe Emily Rose is plotting her attack, and I am certain the wolves will no longer pose a threat to you."

My heart thudded but my voice remained calm.

"Alright," I said, "I won't go anywhere alone if it makes you happy."

Jack's lips twitched as if he wanted to smile.

"I will not be happy until she is defeated," he said, "But thank you."

We carefully avoided any mention of Danny and my apparently uncontrollable lust for him. Jack asked me where Suri was. He surprised me, but apparently he sensed she was missing from my energy. I admitted I did not know, and promised to phone Crystal later that day for some advice. A

Love Kills

silence fell between us, broken only by me munching my cereal. Jack was checking messages on his phone, and I reached for a magazine that lay on the table. Finally, Jack left me to go to work. He kissed my lips very tenderly, and I almost refused to let him go, but I shook myself and resolved to be strong. Jack also seemed reluctant to leave, and I was relieved at least that we had each other to face our problems. I admitted to myself that I would have been devastated if he had been angry with me this morning for the events of the previous night.

The shop had been open for only thirty minutes when a courier entered carrying the biggest bouquet of flowers I had ever received. She handed them over to me with a smile.

"Someone's a lucky girl today." she remarked with a wink.

I took the flowers awkwardly and signed for them. When the courier left, I reached for the attached card. It read 'To Jessica, with my deepest apologies, Marcus.' My heart lurched and I choked back tears that rose from nowhere. Despite what he did, I could not be angry or even frightened of Marcus. Somehow I felt a connection with him. It was different to what I felt for Jack or Danny, but it was there and I could not deny my feelings. I was confused about how I provoked him, but was certain that it had to do with my witch powers. I would simply learn to control myself better and not allow Marcus or Jack to feed from me for a while. Or any other vampire for that matter. Shivering, I forced all thoughts of Emily Rose from my mind, and went to find a vase for the flowers.

It was Saturday afternoon, and I was desperate to close up the shop and retire for the weekend. At first it hadn't seemed so bad to work six days a week. I knew that many millions of people do the same thing all the time. But it wasn't working for me. I missed my extra day off in the week, though I wouldn't confess to Liz just yet. She felt bad enough about me working alone, and I didn't want her to feel guilty. I wanted her to enjoy time with her baby, and to embrace motherhood because she had wanted it for so long. We had decided to bring in a manager while Liz took extended maternity leave. We had posted an advertisement locally, and I was collecting CVs from interested applicants. Liz and me planned to draw up a shortlist of candidates, and I would interview and choose a suitable person, with Liz's agreement of course. For now, I struggled along, but tonight I was ready for a rest.

All week I had been plagued by strange dreams. My mother visited twice and spoke in more stilted conversations, and confusing language. I established that she was trying to warn me about some impending danger, but all I knew was that it meant Emily Rose was nearly upon me, and I was on the alert as a result. I had told Jack and Danny, and they were both anxious, keeping close contact with me and not allowing me out alone, not even to the shops. They insisted that I needed a bodyguard at least until the vampire was stopped. The bookshop turned out to be the only place I was alone, and for now at least, I enjoyed the time. Today had been unusually busy, which was great for our business, but not so great for me when I was tired and grumpy. I was glad to lock the front door and turn the sign to say 'closed.'

As was customary at the moment, I sent Jack a text message once I closed up, and then I also sent Danny a message. One or both of the men would arrive at my kitchen door promptly, and we would then either stay at home or travel to the men's house for the evening. I was a little nervous about being so intimate with Danny, but as both men explained, if Jack was caught up in a meeting or some unexpected vampire business, I needed a back up. And Danny was better able to resist Emily Rose's charms when she did finally show herself to me.

This arrangement had only been in place for the past week, since my encounter with the vampire, and I was trying to tell myself that it was fine, and that I should loosen up in Danny's presence. But after last night I didn't dare face him again. I would have to, certainly if I decided to stay at Jack's house, but I felt embarrassed and confused. I was attracted to Danny; I couldn't deny that. He was Jack's identical twin. And apparently Jack was leaving me to decide whether to take my relationship with his brother further or not, although I was certain he wasn't too happy about it. The idea was so crazy that I desperately tried to ignore it, hoping it might go away. I knew I was kidding myself.

These thoughts were whirling around my head as I absently tidied the bookshelves, and prepared to shut down the computer and stash the till drawer in our safe. I had to print off some daily sales reports for our records, and check the figures. They were looking very healthy, and I smiled happily. At least we needn't worry about money for a while. That was one huge consolation.

And since I was working all the time, I wasn't out spending, and could therefore save up for a big shopping spree at Christmas, or in the New Year sales. That turned my attention to more pleasant thoughts, and I was in a daydream as I walked into the storeroom to deposit the till. I returned to switch the shop lights off, checked that the door was locked and everything was secure, and walked back into the storeroom and approached the door that led to my kitchen. And I froze. My senses were alive, and there was someone in my kitchen.

It was a vampire. I knew that much because my enhanced abilities told me so. My skin crawled, and I felt electricity buzzing through my veins, trying to shoot out of my fingers. I stepped back from the door and took a deep breath, letting it out slowly, regulating my breathing to slow my racing thoughts and regain some measure of calm in my body. 'Be calm.' I told myself. 'She knows that you are here, and she is waiting for you.' I realised that I couldn't turn and run now. The vampire was much faster than me, and I could not cause a scene in our street and risk exposing the supernatural community. Plus I didn't want any innocent people to get killed or injured.

Backing away from the door a bit further, I thought about my options. I could wait until Jack or Danny appeared, and hope that they could defeat my enemy. Or I could face her myself, and call upon Suri for help. Taking another deep breath, I nodded. It was time to be strong. I had to stand up for myself, and I was capable of doing this. At the very least I could stall Emily Rose until my back up arrived. Sliding my phone from my pocket again, I quickly sent a warning text message to both Jack and Danny: 'Vampire in my kitchen. Come quickly. I can't hide anymore.' Then I raised my head, shook back my hair, and reached for the door.

I had no weapons to hand. There was nothing in my shop or storeroom that was remotely useful. I needed silver or a wooden stake. I had neither. Even my jewellery was gold, which right now seemed the most stupid thing in the world. I could have prepared myself better. No matter, the time had come, and I had to make the best out of a bad situation. Turning the handle, I slowly opened the door and entered my previously warm and cosy kitchen, which was now enveloped in the cold stench of death and destruction.

39

As I cautiously peeped round the door I was surprised at what I saw. There was a vampire standing in my kitchen. It was not Emily Rose. I gasped, and stepped carefully into the room, closing the door behind me. I would not try to run back through the shop and risk causing a scene in front of the humans. This business had to be kept secret, no matter who got hurt or killed. The woman stood near my back door. The door had been kicked in; I was surprised I hadn't heard the noise since the wood looked badly damaged. I stared at the new vampire. She looked around my age, perhaps a little older, although of course, she might be ancient. Her appearance was nothing spectacular. Her brown hair was cut into a bob, her skin was pale, and her brown eyes shone with power. It was not the same brilliance I saw in Jack or Marcus, or even in Emily Rose.

"Who are you?" I asked steadily, "Why are you here?"

I knew it was a stupid question. Clearly she was here to kill me. But if I could stall her, I had a chance of back-up arriving in the form of Jack and Danny. I stepped slowly into the room, keeping my back to the wall, partly for support, and partly so she couldn't move behind me. I was aiming for the knife block I kept near the cooker. Perhaps I could arm myself before she struck. The vampire stood still as a statue, smiling at me. Her expression was unpleasant, and I felt her power swirling around the room. It was cold and sharp, like needles poking my skin. Instinctively I threw up my own psychic barriers, an easier task since I began my training with Crystal. Without taking my eyes off the vampire I breathed in and out deeply, and silently warned Suri that we were in danger. The tiger stalked out of her forest, swishing her tail. I asked her to hold back for the moment. She was my secret weapon against Emily Rose, and I would keep her hidden for as long as possible.

The vampire spoke suddenly, and I jumped at the unexpected sound.

"Why do you ask such stupid questions?" she asked.

Without any warning she flung out a fist and punched me in the face, covering the distance between us at a lightening speed too fast for me to anticipate. Still walking slowly towards my cupboards, I was taken by surprise. I flew backwards, colliding with the wooden cupboard doors, and I crumpled to the floor, my face burning with pain and my body struggling with the sudden hard impact. Coughing and spluttering, I managed to draw myself up onto my hands and knees while the vampire advanced upon me.

"Wait," I wheezed, holding up a hand, "Please wait. Please tell me who you are, and why you are doing this to me."

The vampire hesitated, her mouth open as though she were about to strike. She cocked her head, as if listening to a voice I couldn't hear. I knew who was behind her attack. I had not expected Emily Rose to use another vampire to do her dirty work. The woman blinked slowly, and nodded once.

"Alright," she said, standing over me where I sat on the floor, "I will answer your questions. I am Detective Angela Gold."

My heart sank as I stared at her.

"You are Jack's partner," I said faintly.

She smiled broadly.

"Yes," she replied, "And what a fine partner he turned out to be."

Adrenaline pulsed through me, along with my power, and I swallowed nervously, trying to hide it from her.

"What do you mean?" I asked, "What did you do to him?"

Angela smiled and licked her lips slowly, although her expression soured when she replied.

"I did nothing I was not instructed to do," she said cryptically, "Although I would have enjoyed so much more of him."

I felt a surge of possessive anger flow through my body, and blood pounded in my ears. I was certain Jack had remained faithful. This woman was trying to upset me. I could not give her the satisfaction.

"Emily Rose sent you," I said, trying to evade her imminent physical attack.

Angela actually laughed, although the sound was bitter and unhappy.

"Emily Rose made me," she said, "And now I must follow her orders."

She launched herself at me again, but this time I was more prepared.

"Wait!" I shouted, holding up my arms to block her.

If I could stall her for a few more minutes I knew that Jack would arrive, and he would take care of her. Or maybe I could use my own power. It was time to embrace my heritage. I called out to Suri. The tiger growled in response to my silent call, but she was reluctant to respond. She smelled the vampire and I felt her distaste. She did not take pleasure in dead things unless they were food. The vampire held no interest for her. I begged her to help save my life, and that I would offer her something more exciting in return. In my dazed state of mind, I did not comprehend what I was offering. Without hesitation Suri agreed, and suddenly I felt her charging through the forest, and diving straight into my body with a jolt of electricity.

Angela stopped her attack, staring at me in surprise as she felt the power, and her eyes were wide with shock.

"What did you do?" she asked in a whisper, backing away from me fearfully.

I stood up slowly and smoothly, my human body moving in a way that no ordinary person could. I smiled, and I knew that it was twisted and frightening. I was glad; no I was ecstatic. The vampire was afraid of me. I could work with that. When I spoke, my voice was smooth and silky; almost feline in the way I formed words and the intonation I used. It did not sound like my own voice.

"I am protecting myself against attack," I said simply, "You did not expect me to roll over and allow you to destroy me, did you?"

I laughed, and it sent shivers down my spine. The electricity that flooded my body was spilling outwards, shooting through my hands and fingertips in slivers of silver fire. I felt my eyes burning, but it was power and not pain. I turned that sharp gaze on Angela, and she staggered backwards as I directed my electric energy at her. She flew back across the room, slamming into the far wall in between my dining table and my splintered back door. She scrambled to her feet, but her young vampire body was quite clumsy. I knew that she had not been turned for long; I sensed her inexperience with my own power. She still felt her human movements and responses.

Love Kills

"I must destroy you Jessica," she said with a sob, her strength dissipated suddenly, "I cannot stop it."

I frowned and lowered my arms, giving her a moment of respite from my energetic psychokinetic attack. All of a sudden she was cowering before me, and I felt a rush of sympathy.

"Why must you?" I asked, and it was sounding more like my voice now.

I could feel Suri just beneath the surface of myself. It was a strange sensation, as though the tiger were superimposed over my body. She could feel my movements and reactions, and I could feel hers. We were both separate and together at the same time. Angela's legs buckled and she dropped to her knees. I could feel her fear and confusion, and I saw the tears that poured down her cheeks.

"I must obey my Master," she sobbed, "Please Jessica, if you can fight back, do it. Kill me if you must."

I stepped back warily, shocked and confused.

"Are you serious?" I asked, but I already knew the answer.

Angela broke down in tears again, and my heart went out to her. She seemed so helpless. I fought the urge to draw close and put my arms around her.

"*Be wise,*" Suri instructed, "*She is not what she seems.*"

I nodded, trusting the tiger's instincts. My own intuition was warning me to stay away, so I stepped back once more, and felt behind me for the knife block that I had originally aimed for. Angela raised her head fearfully, as if listening again to that hidden voice. Her eyes darted from side to side, and she shuddered.

"It is her," Angela said through her tears, "Emily Rose."

Suddenly her tears quieted and she raised her head, scenting the air.

"No," she whispered, "Please leave me alone. I cannot do this for you. Jessica is innocent."

I watched her body tense, her head jerked up, her muscles contracted, and then she relaxed. It all happened so quickly, but at the same time I immediately felt the change in atmosphere. The dank, cold air suddenly grew darker, but now I smelled a musky, heady scent. It warned of danger and destruction. I knew what had happened.

Angela shook back her hair and stood up in a smooth, liquid

motion. It was a movement that I had grown to associate with both Jack and Marcus, and I realised that it distinguished an older vampire from a younger one. I knew that Angela was no longer in control of her body. My heart pounded in my chest, and Suri roared in anger and hatred at the sight of a creature of death. The roar reverberated around my body and erupted from my own mouth, which would have shocked me, had I not already been facing a woman who terrified me beyond reason.

"Well, well, my little witch," Emily Rose said in her heavy French accent, "You have been embracing your powers in my short absence."

She reached out a hand as if to touch me, and I reared back, determined not to let her so close. I remembered when she had first possessed me shortly after my first werewolf attack. She had used magick and power to render me paralysed, and had kissed me on the lips, filling me with her hateful essence. I was not about to let that happen again.

"Stay back!" I said, and I brandished the carving knife that I had grabbed.

In Angela's tall, athletic body I could clearly see the persona of Emily Rose. She was superimposed on Angela in the way that Suri was with me, but poor Angela had been completely possessed. She was no longer in control of her body or her thoughts, but she was witnessing everything that Emily Rose was doing. I was sure I heard her screaming and crying, but the sound was faint, as if she were far away and shouting down a telephone line.

Emily Rose laughed, and then inclined her head, listening to something behind her. I looked up and my heart leaped as I saw Jack in the doorway. He flew into the room and then stopped dead as he took in the scene. My face was still smarting, and I was sure there was a red mark across my cheek, or maybe my nose was broken, I wasn't sure. He saw the knife in my hand, and he saw his police colleague standing before me. His nostrils flared, his eyes glowed silver, and I knew that he understood the real threat in this room.

"Ah, Jack," Emily Rose said over her shoulder, "You are just in time to witness me defending your honour once again."

Suddenly she struck, flying at me with such force that I screamed and reacted instinctively. She stopped dead just in front of me, her expression one of shock and surprise. I looked down and saw the knife handle sticking out of Angela's chest, and a large red stain appearing on her white shirt. My hands dropped to my sides, and I looked back into Angela's face. Her expression quickly changed into a smile, and she slowly shook her head, tutting at me, and saying something in French that I was sure was a rebuff.

"You cannot kill a vampire with a stainless steel blade, little witch." she said.

Slowly, she clamped her hands around the knife handle, and pulled it out of the wound with a loud wet sound. My stomach lurched, and I fought to keep myself from vomiting. Swallowing carefully, I tried to edge away as Suri screamed at me to escape the danger. I glanced at Jack, but he was motionless, apparently rooted to the spot.

"He cannot save you," Emily Rose said as she removed the knife, "I have forbidden him from interfering. This is our battle little witch; you and I."

Without warning, she flipped the knife over and rammed it into my stomach. I screamed again, and looked down to see the blood now blossoming on my own shirt. For a moment I felt no pain, but my body collapsed, and I fell back against the cupboard once more. Then the pain erupted, and I screamed and writhed, trying desperately to fight it.

"Jack!" I cried, "Help me!"

As my vision began to fade, I was aware of him moving closer, and he dropped to his knees.

"I cannot," he said, "I am so sorry, Jessica."

I turned my attention back to Emily Rose, who was watching me with a look of pure satisfaction on her face. She was smiling and radiant, and I knew that she thought the war was over. She had won. I was dying, and Jack would return to her. But I would not give up so easily. Suri rallied around me, offering me her strength, and I took it gratefully. Swallowing painfully, I gripped the handle of the knife and pulled it out of my stomach, in a strange repetition of what had just happened with the vampire.

Emily Rose stopped laughing and stared at me in surprise, as I pulled the knife free. I felt stronger, and the faintness had subsided. My aura was filled with the tiger's energy, and I could feel her warmth and power flood through me, heating my blood and healing my wounds. Both vampires scented the air, and both stared at me with a mixture of confusion and fear in their faces. I turned the knife over in my hand, gripping the blade, ignoring the sharp searing pain in my hand as blood dripped to the floor. Then I lunged forward, forcing the wooden handle into Angela's chest, screaming out my effort and pain as I moved. Using Suri's immense strength, I shoved the knife handle as hard as I could, and it punctured the vampire's body.

"No!" Emily Rose cried, "You cannot do this!"

Angela's body fell backwards, and as she stared at me in shock, I realised with a sinking heart that Emily Rose had retreated. I had just dealt a killing blow to a helpless woman. She looked down at the bloody blade sticking out of her chest, and then her gaze slowly lifted to face my eyes.

"I am sorry, Jessica," she whispered.

Angela collapsed onto the kitchen floor, and I cried out and reached forward in a futile attempt to help her. Jack moved at the same time, but he already knew what to expect.

"She is gone, Jessica," he said, "We cannot save her."

I watched in horror as the vampire's body writhed and convulsed. She cried out once, and I was sure I saw a white mist escape through her mouth. The room was thick with fear, pain and anguish, and my head pounded. I was in the middle of a storm, and yet to the human eye everything would appear normal, apart from the dying woman on my floor. After another minute Angela's body reached a crescendo, and then she turned grey, her body became a skeleton, and finally it crumbled into ash, clothes and everything.

As the storm settled, I turned my gaze on Jack, staring at him in bewilderment. His expression was one of sadness and pain, but he moved quickly to take me in his arms. The adrenaline left my body, and I heard Suri whisper a goodbye as she retreated.

"Our battle is over," she said, *"I will return for payment after a time."*

I barely registered her words, too upset about what I had just witnessed. I had killed a vampire. I had murdered an innocent woman.

"I killed her, Jack," I whispered, "I killed Angela."

"Shush," he said, "You had no choice."

I collapsed into his arms, holding him tightly against me,

forgetting about my injuries for the moment. Jack hugged me, and then slowly began to extricate himself so he could examine my wounds. He took my hands in his, and I winced and cried out as he touched the still bleeding gash on my right hand. Holding my hand palm upwards, I allowed Jack to carefully unfasten my shirt so he could see the knife wound in my stomach. It didn't hurt as much I expected. Maybe Suri had partially healed me. Or maybe I was simply in shock and had not registered the seriousness of my situation.

"Shall we go to the hospital?" Jack asked quietly.

I shook my head.

"No," I said, "I can't go back there again. They won't believe us."

"Then you must drink my blood," he replied, and he bit his wrist until blood welled up, thick and dark against his white skin, "It will heal you."

"No!" I gasped, "I can't!"

Jack nodded.

"If you don't take it," he said calmly, "you will die. It will not turn you into a vampire. Please, drink it."

I knew he was right. I could not return to hospital and risk closing the shop for an indefinite time. For starters I couldn't explain the whole situation to Liz, much less the curious doctors who might report Jack and me to the authorities. I took a deep breath, lowered my face to his wrist, and tasted his blood.

40

My stomach lurched as I tentatively lowered my mouth to the wound. Jack had given me his blood shortly after my werewolf attack, but at the time I had been barely conscious and so I didn't remember the incident. I did remember the aftermath however, when Emily Rose had invaded my dreams and possessed me on several occasions. I did not want that to happen again, but I had no choice. At least now I might be able to defend myself against her.

Swallowing nervously, I reached out my tongue, expecting the blood to taste bitter and repulsive. I was pleasantly surprised. It was rich, warm, and somehow spicy. It reminded me of mulled wine, but a more exotic version. I could not explain it, but I wanted more, and I was suddenly gulping it down greedily. My fingers gripped Jack's wrist as he crouched before me, and all coherent thought left my head. All that mattered was the blood I was drinking, and its amazing restorative effect that I could already feel working its way through my body.

"Jessica," Jack said slowly, "I think you've had enough."

He tried to pull his arm away, but I gripped tighter and made noises of protest.

"Jessica?" A female voice said, "Jessica, what are you doing?"

That brought me to my senses. I reared away from Jack and looked up at the door behind him. Liz was standing in the doorway, her face white and her expression a mixture of horror and confusion. She stood stiffly, and I realised there was someone with her. Was it Robert? Oh god, I hoped they hadn't brought the baby here.

I tensed as Liz moved forward in a jerky motion, and then I relaxed only slightly as I saw that her companion was Danny. He was holding her arm, and he propelled her further into the room and closed the splintered door behind them. His expression was serious, and there was anger bubbling beneath the surface. As I stared at him, I felt movement deep within me, as Suri sensed his presence. She rose from her slumber, and padded forward, and I realised that she wanted out again.

"Please, Suri," I whispered, "Not now."

"*Yes, now,*" she replied, "*I want my reward for assisting you.*"

"Jessica," Liz asked faintly, "Who are you talking to?"

I blinked slowly, and begged Suri to leave me for a while longer. I promised her that she could play later. She grudgingly agreed and retreated into the shadows of the frozen forest. I shivered as her power swept over me in waves of ice-cold snow. Opening my eyes, I stared up into Liz's white face, and Danny's angry one. Jack was still motionless in front of me, almost like a statue, and I glanced at him to see what was happening. His skin was white and his eyes were glowing silver. He needed blood. My heart leaped in panic.

"Liz," I said more urgently, "You must leave. Now, please."

She backed away only slightly, and then jumped as Danny once again gripped her arm. She stared at his fingers as they clamped around her sleeve, and then she gazed slowly up into his face, and saw his glowing amber eyes.

"What are you?" she gasped in horror.

"Danny," I said sharply, "What are you doing? Let her go."

He shook his head.

"No," he said in a cold tone I had never heard before, "She has seen too much. It is time to explain the truth."

Jack startled me by standing up suddenly. One second he was crouched silently before me, and the next he towered above me. I felt his cold power sweeping around us, and I breathed in and out, feeling strangely happy with the sensation. It felt right. It reminded me of home. Then my human responses woke up, and pain shot through my wounds. I struggled and tried to stand, scrabbling ineffectually at the worktop behind me. My legs were weak and refused to cooperate, and I gasped and whimpered in pain as Jack swiftly swept me up into his arms.

"We must take you upstairs," he said brusquely, "Sally will tend to your wounds."

Liz snapped back to attention and spoke out indignantly.

"She needs an ambulance!" she cried, reaching for her mobile phone. Again Danny stopped her, but this time she tried to resist his strength, her concern for me bringing out her anger.

"Keep your hands off me, Danny Mason!" she retorted.

"Danny," I said weakly, "Liz, please, I don't need an ambulance."

Those words resonated with something in my memory. Jack had uttered almost the exact same sentence to me the night I discovered the truth about him and Danny. I shivered violently, and Jack cuddled me close, although his body gave out no heat. He was already approaching the stairs, and we were on the landing almost immediately, with Liz and Danny following behind.

Jack laid me carefully on my bed, eased off my shoes, and pulled back the duvet. Danny appeared with a towel from the bathroom, and a flannel that he had soaked in cold water. He pressed the towel to my stomach, and somewhere in my rational mind I grumbled about ruining it. I was beginning to feel faint as the adrenaline subsided and my body tried desperately to deal with the new trauma. My hand smarted, although the gash had almost healed. My stomach wound was deeper, and would require a little more than the small amount of vampire blood I had ingested. I knew all of this instinctively, but I didn't question it at the time.

Liz came into view, hovering uncertainly at the head of my bed. I turned my face towards her, attempting to smile, though it came out more of a grimace. She deserved an explanation, and a whole load of apologies. Why did she have to discover these secrets under such circumstances?

"Liz," I said, and then swallowed nervously, my mouth unusually dry, "I am so sorry about all of this."

She fell to her knees beside the bed, reaching for my hand. Shaking her head, she choked back tears as she replied.

"I don't know exactly what you are sorry for, Jess," she said with a sob, "But I am so confused and so scared. Why won't you go to hospital? You were stabbed with a knife."

A wave of shock coursed through me. She had witnessed Emily Rose's attack. I would have to explain everything.

"What did you see, Liz?" I asked feebly, fighting the growing nausea and faintness. I was vaguely aware of movement in the room, and Danny disappeared for a few minutes. I heard voices drifting up the stairs, and recognised Sally's in the group. Relaxing slightly, I looked at Liz again.

"I saw that woman attacking you," she said quietly, "I was walking up the path, and I saw that your door was open. Something felt wrong, so I slowed down and crept up. Then I saw her hitting you, and I panicked."

"You saw the whole thing?" I asked.

Liz nodded, tears rolling down her cheeks.

"I should have helped you Jess," she said, "But I didn't know what to do. I have never been in a fight before. And then she changed." Liz hesitated, her voice wavering as she spoke.

Our attention was turned as Sally bustled into my bedroom, carrying a large medical bag slung over one shoulder.

"Hello Jessica," she said in her practical nurse voice, "You are certainly in the wars a lot lately."

She moved Liz away from the bed and set to work, cleaning my stomach wound and applying sutures. I was impressed at her efficient work.

"Shouldn't a doctor be doing this, Sally?" I asked, "I mean, not that you can't or anything."

Sally laughed, concentrating on her task.

"I am a doctor," she replied, "Just not by human standards. I trained with a shape shifter academy, in secret, but I needed a job and the hospital was hiring. I tend to the injured non humans in and around our area, as part of my role in the Redcliffe pack."

My eyes rolled in the direction of where Liz was standing.

"Shape shifter academy?" she asked faintly.

Sally never flinched, and spoke while she attached an IV drip to my arm.

"Yes," she said shortly, "I believe you and Jessica need to talk. You may have to wait until she has slept. I doubt she will be in a coherent frame of mind soon enough."

Almost immediately, I began to feel drowsy. Sally had given me a sedative, or maybe an antibiotic, or most likely a mixture of both. The room began to fade around me, and I gladly fell into the darkness as my body shut down. The last words I heard were Sally's as she ushered everybody out of my bedroom, telling them she would change my clothes and take care of me. I relaxed completely.

41

"Jessica," my mother said, "Jessica, can you hear me?"

"Yes," I replied, but it came out in a whisper as my voice refused to work. I coughed to clear my throat, and tried again, "Yes," I said more firmly, "I can hear you, Mum."

"That is good," she said with obvious relief, "I was afraid the tiger had become too strong for you."

I opened my eyes and panicked when I saw blackness, not a chink of light anywhere. I tried to sit up, crying out in alarm.

"I can't see!" I shouted wildly, "Lillian, I can't see!"

"Shush, child," she replied calmly, "You are dreaming. There is nothing to see."

I relaxed only slightly. This was a new experience, and I did not like being in darkness. I felt claustrophobic, and I tried to calm the fear that rose in my chest.

"Why aren't we on the beach?" I asked, breathing in and out slowly, forcing myself to remain still.

"I need only to speak with you," Lillian replied, "We need not waste our energy creating a mirage for our exchange."

I frowned.

"Why are you talking like that?" I asked, confused, "You sound strange."

Lillian laughed.

"You have so much to learn about our kind, Jessica," she said fondly, "We have no use for the spoken word in the place I exist. I speak only to converse with you in your human consciousness."

I shook my head. This whole conversation was bizarre. I remembered my fight with Angela, and my heart sank as I thought about how I had killed her. Glancing down, I couldn't even see my body in the darkness, but I could still feel. My wounds were not hurting. In fact, I felt strangely numb, but not in a frightening way. It was some form of suspended dream state, but I knew instinctively that I was safe. My mother was with me, and she would not harm me.

"So what do you want to say?" I asked, "Is it about what happened?"

"Yes," she said, and I heard a note of sadness in her voice, "Do not dwell on what you did. It was unfair that the innocent vampire suffered, but you were not the true cause of her demise. Emily Rose is a dangerous enemy, and she is not finished with you yet."

"I guessed as much," I said, "Mum, I killed somebody. Of course I'm going to think about it. And I will feel guilty."

"I understand," she replied sadly, "But you have work to do. You must learn your magic, and harness your power. The tiger can be both your greatest asset and your greatest problem."

"You know about Suri," I said, "How?"

"Yes I know about her," my mother said, "Every witch has a power animal. Humans refer to them as our familiars, but Crystal already explained that to you."

"How did you know she was a tiger?" I asked.

"I saw her in visions when I was pregnant with you," Lillian replied, "And then again as you were growing up. She waited for you, until you were able to truly open your eyes and acknowledge her presence."

I thought about her words. When I was living with foster families, my favourite and most precious toy had been a stuffed tiger. I couldn't remember where it came from, or how I acquired it, but I insisted on carrying it everywhere with me. When I grew too old for toys, the tiger spent some time shoved in the back of wardrobes and cupboards. Now it sat on the chest of drawers in my bedroom, facing my bed. A jolt of realisation shot through me. I had known all along. Tigers always fascinated me when I saw them on the TV, or on rare visits to the zoo. And I distinctly remembered once telling a schoolteacher that my tiger was silver and white, and that she lived in a frozen forest. This had been after a discussion about safari animals, where I had objected to the traditional human view of tigers. My schoolteacher had very gently humoured me, and eventually we had moved on from the subject. Now the whole incident sprung to mind as if it had only happened yesterday.

"She was always there," I said in wonder, "How did I not see this?"

My mother's voice was gentle and patient.

"You had no need of your protector before," she said, "And when Seamus Tully attacked you, it was not the right time for her to come forward. You had to acknowledge her existence, and to truly believe in her, before she could intercept in your activities."

"Why now?" I asked, "Why is all of this happening so suddenly?"

"It has always been there, Jessica," Lillian replied, "You never believed in yourself. You were raised as a human, and now you think and act like one. But you are a witch, and Suri is your power animal. She is strong, and you must learn to handle her efficiently or she will overpower you and you will shift."

"What do you mean, 'shift?'" I asked slowly.

"Suri offered you her protection against Emily Rose this evening," Lillian said, "But she insisted that you promise to repay her. Do you know what she meant?"

I was quiet for a few minutes as I thought about the situation. I had promised Suri anything if she would save my life. I had no idea what exactly she wanted.

"No," I said, "I don't know what she wants."

"She wants to use your human body," Lillian said, "She wishes to interact with other shape shifters. And she has developed an attraction to Danny Mason."

"But he's a wolf!" I said, "Surely that's wrong?"

"It means nothing to an animal of spirit," Lillian replied, "Suri is attracted to his power and strength. She wishes to control him, to feel him bow down to her. She will use you in whatever way she sees fit."

"But why?" I asked again, "I am so confused!"

"You must understand, Jessica, " Lillian replied patiently, "There are no straightforward explanations for any of this. Please accept that you hold great power within you, and that Emily Rose will attack you directly if only to destroy you. Your tiger will protect you, but please be wary of what you offer in exchange. It will all become clear as you progress in your magickal training. Now you must rest, and heal your wounds."

I woke slowly, blinking my eyes and flexing my fingers. As I opened my eyes I was relieved to see the familiar white painted walls of my bedroom, and when I turned my head to the side, there was my stuffed toy tiger sitting on the chest of drawers. I tried to sit up, and groaned as I felt a dull ache in my stomach, punctuated with sharper pains as the knife wound protested.

"Jessica," Jack was suddenly standing beside the bed, reaching out to restrain me, "How are you feeling?"

I swallowed, and tilted my head from side to side, feeling the scar tissue on my neck stretch and relax with my movements. It was strangely comforting, to know that I was back in my body, back in the real world. I looked up at Jack and tried to smile, but the drugs that Sally had given me were still in my system. I felt a little groggy and my limbs were heavy.

"I feel rough," I replied, "And I'm starving."

Jack smiled, and I saw the blue flame fade in his eyes. He looked almost human, apart from his marble white skin. I frowned, or at least, I tried to.

"Have you eaten?" I asked, "You are white."

"No," he replied, "I have not left your side."

I scoffed and shook my head, then moaned as a wave of dizziness flooded my senses.

"Go and feed," I instructed, "You are no use to me like that."

"I am fine," Jack said shortly, "You need care."

"I need rest, and food," I said, "And surely the smell of my blood must be driving you crazy."

Jack's expression was one of surprise and curiosity as he stared at me.

"Yes, your blood is tempting," he replied, "But I can control my hunger. I have been in worse situations before."

My lips twitched.

"Yes," I said, "And look what happened last time. You attacked me."

He stepped back, and I felt instantly guilty when I saw the look of pain cross his face.

"Jack," I said, "I'm sorry. I shouldn't have said that. I didn't mean it to sound horrible."

He closed his eyes and stood very still. I felt a change in his energy, a distinct cool breeze flowing across the room. When Jack opened his eyes again after a few seconds, they were glowing bright blue, and his features had the clear signs of vampire. I couldn't explain it in words. It was a subtle hue to his skin, the glow in his eyes, and the fangs that protruded very slightly when he opened his mouth.

Before either of us could speak, Jack turned his head towards the door. It opened quietly, and Danny stepped into the room. At the scent of his wolf energy, I felt Suri stirring somewhere deep within me. She couldn't surface because of my medication, but she was aware of the werewolf, and she wanted out. Thankfully I could ignore her for now. Danny looked from me to Jack, and back again.

"What's happening in here?" he asked, shivering, "It's as cold as the grave out there in the living room."

I looked at Jack again. He spoke quietly.

"Jessica is aware that I need to feed," he said, "I will return in one hour."

He stared at me, stepped forward and hesitated. I saw the confusion in his eyes. He wanted to kiss me, but he was afraid. I didn't know if he was afraid of me, or of what he might do if he came too close. I nodded slowly; to show him I didn't mind if he left. Then he was gone, and all that remained was that cool breeze, which quickly died down in his wake. I returned my attention to Danny.

"Are you hungry, Jess?" he asked, "I've got pizza in the other room."

Lifting my face, I sniffed the air and sure enough, I could smell the familiar, comforting scent of tomatoes and cheese. My stomach rumbled loudly, and Danny laughed.

"I take it that's a yes," he said, "Shall I bring it in here?"

"No," I said, "I need to get up."

I tried to swing my legs round and climb out of bed, but my body refused to cooperate. Danny appeared at my side.

"Let me help," he said gently, "Sally gave you some powerful drugs. They will make you weak for a while."

I grudgingly allowed him to lift me from the bed, but I insisted he set me on my feet. Clinging to his arms, I concentrated on holding my own weight, and managed a few tentative steps out of the room. Sally had found a pair of loose pyjamas with a button-through top, and had dressed me in them while I was unconscious. I felt a little queasy about being so vulnerable, but then, I was in the same situation when I was in hospital. And Sally was a nurse. There were more important things to worry about.

Danny helped me to the bathroom and waited outside while I

did the necessary human activities. I had to grip the toilet and sink as I moved about, but I managed and I didn't faint or collapse, which was impressive considering how I had been after the werewolf attack. At that time I had fainted in the bathroom after pulling the bandage off my neck. Both Jack and Danny had come to my aid, and I had been both embarrassed and terrified at their mercy. Perhaps I had more strength than I thought after all. Right now I just felt human, and that was both a blessing and a curse.

    Half an hour late I was snuggled on my sofa, a knitted blanket tucked around my legs, and a slice of cheese pizza in my hands. Danny lay with his legs draped over the arm of the adjacent chair, eating his own meat feast pizza. We watched a drama program on TV, and I began to relax again. I decided not to think about my conversation with Lillian, or the fact that I had killed a vampire. Those were issues to be dealt with later, when my body had healed better. Jack returned after an hour looking much better. His skin glowed, his eyes were bright, and I could feel the energy rolling off him in waves. He was protective and watchful all night, and I knew it was because he feared Emily Rose might possess me again, as she had done previously when I had Jack's blood. Tonight however, she was unsuccessful. It was partly due to the medication Sally had given me, and partly my own enhanced psychic protection abilities after my recent training.

42

The next morning I woke feeling a little groggy, but amazingly without too much pain or discomfort. Jack was sleeping beside me in bed, lying on his back with a space between us. Usually we slept in a spooning position, with me lying against him, our bodies curving together naturally, but this time we had allowed for my injuries. I slid carefully out of bed, and he woke immediately when I moved.

"How are you feeling, Jessica?" he asked, sitting up in bed.

"Alright I think," I replied, "I'm going to the bathroom."

"I will assist you," Jack said, and he was suddenly out of bed and standing by the bedroom door, looking irresistibly gorgeous wearing nothing but a pair of black boxer shorts. My body reacted at the sight of him, and as I shuffled forward I winced as a stab of pain shot through my stomach wound.

"You are not well," Jack said, catching me in his arms, "You must rest."

"I'm fine," I replied, straightening up and smiling bravely, "Honestly, Jack. It was just a sudden pain, that's all. It took me by surprise, but I'll manage."

Jack grudgingly followed me to the bathroom, staying close in case I felt faint. Luckily, I felt better after a brief shower. I carefully avoided the wound on my stomach, and Jack helped me to wash my hair without getting shampoo near the bandage. The wound on my right hand was now merely a long, thin scratch, and I barely noticed it except for when I gripped anything. There were a few awkward moments, and some laughing and embarrassment on my part as I lost my balance and staggered a few times. Jack was serious throughout, always catching me before I could do more damage to myself. He tried again to put me back in bed, but I insisted on getting dressed.

"No, Jack," I said, "I must go and see Liz. She deserves an explanation for what happened, and I have to face up to her. I've kept too many secrets recently, and now she needs answers."

My stomach lurched at the thought of what Liz had seen last

night. I felt very sad that she had to witness such an event, and I felt a terrible guilt at my deception of my best friend. She did not deserve that, especially now when she was dealing with a new baby. I wondered why she had come round to my house at that time. She hadn't left the baby with anyone yet. Perhaps it had been a trial, leaving Amy with Rob and seeing how they coped. I had ruined that particular event.

Then my mind wandered back to the subject of what I had done. I had killed a vampire. I essentially drove a wooden stake through Angela's heart, and she did not deserve it. How had I even managed such a feat? I had never been in a fight before. Even when Seamus Tully and his wolves had ambushed me only months before, I hadn't fought because I didn't know how. At that time I had relied on Jack, Danny, Sally and Simon to defend me, and I had struggled in vain when Seamus captured me. I was determined to amend that particular problem, and do some more self-defence training with Jack and Danny, but it would have to wait until I was healed, again.

As I walked slowly down the stairs, I felt sick with nerves at what sight might await me in the kitchen. Jack had informed me that some wolves had been called in to clean up the mess, but I would still be there at the scene of the crime, so to speak. My warm, cosy kitchen would now always be tainted with death and deceit. Jack followed me down the stairs, walking at a human pace. He seemed to know that I needed him to be human today, and his movements were deliberately slow and careful. Of course, he would know, since he could sense my thoughts. Hesitating on the bottom stair, I took a deep breath, then moved forward into the kitchen.

It was spotless. The furniture had been straightened and cleaned up, the cabinet doors had been repaired, and as I glanced at the back door, I saw that it too had been replaced. The previous wooden one had been destroyed when Angela forced the lock, so a new door was the only option. It was identical to my previous one, but it was shiny and clean, gleaming white, and the panes of frosted glass in the top half were crystal clear. My gaze swept around the room, and settled on the spot where my knife block used to stand. Jack saw where I was looking.

"We took away the knives," he said quietly, "Someone will bring a replacement set later today."

I nodded and turned to face him, ignoring the niggling pain in my stomach.

"Did you need the carving knife for evidence?" I asked, my voice shaking with a sudden rush of emotion, "I mean, will I be arrested for Angela's disappearance?"

Jack shook his head, smiling softly.

"No," he said gently, "There will be no police investigation. I will arrange it so her disappearance is not questioned."

I nodded again, feeling so guilty for what I had done that tears sprang to my eyes. Forgetting his human facade, Jack was suddenly gathering me in his arms, and I welcomed his warm embrace. I relaxed against his body and cried, my tears falling hot and heavy on his shoulder. He wrapped his arms around me, and held me until my tears subsided. When I had calmed down sufficiently, I drew away from Jack, and he led me over to the table, sitting me down.

"I will make you some breakfast," he said, "You need to rest."

I watched as he filled the kettle and switched it on, spooned some coffee granules into a mug, added milk, and prepared a bowl of my favourite cereal. When he set the meal in front of me I realised that I was actually starving, and I ate hungrily while Jack sat opposite me at the table. I was munching through two slices of hot buttered toast when Danny appeared at the door. He bounced into the kitchen full of life and energy, closely followed by Simon and Sally.

"Good morning, Jessica," Danny said, "How are you feeling?"

I finished a mouthful of food before I replied.

"Not bad," I said, "Considering that I killed a vampire, got stabbed in the stomach, and now have to explain to my best friend that vampires and werewolves are actually real."

Danny sat down beside Jack and reached over for a piece of toast. Normally I would shout at him for stealing, and maybe smack his hand as a joke, but today I hadn't the energy. Sally was carrying a medical bag, and she stood before me, while Simon walked over to the kettle and began making more drinks and toast.

"May I check your wounds, Jessica?" Sally asked, "I will need to change the dressing on your stomach."

I nodded, and Sally and me walked upstairs where she could tend to my injuries in the bedroom. Truthfully I sort of hobbled up the stairs, taking each step one at a time, as if I was an invalid. I felt clumsy and humiliated, but I choked back my pride and pretended to ignore our differences in agility. Sally quietly followed behind me, saying nothing about my awkward, shuffling gait. With much effort on my part as I approached my bedroom door, I finally entered the room. I lay obediently on my bed and pulled my t-shirt up. Sally perched beside me, pulled on a pair of medical gloves, and set to work, carefully peeling off the dressing she had previously applied. I winced again as pains shot through me, but they weren't as bad as before.

"She is safe, Jack," Sally said softly, turning her head slightly toward the door, "I will simply change the bandage and leave you alone."

I frowned, lifted my head, and looked at the empty doorway. Jack stepped into the room, and I was surprised to see him there so suddenly.

"How did you creep upstairs so quietly?" I asked, and then I went hot with embarrassment as I realised what a stupid question that was.

"I mean, oh crap," I added, "Ask a stupid question Jessica."

I tried again, "Why did you say that, Sally?" I asked curiously.

Sally smiled and glanced at Jack, never faltering in her task. She had removed the old bandage, cleaned the edges of my wound where it had bled slightly, checked the sutures, and now she was applying a new dressing. I looked down with interest, and saw a neatly stitched line, about three inches long, where the knife had penetrated. Sally had done an excellent job patching me up.

"Jack is protecting you, Jessica," Sally replied, "He distrusts me instinctively because I am a wolf."

I frowned, and looked up at Jack. He stood silently at the foot of the bed, not moving a muscle. Even his expression didn't change. I saw his eyes glowing as he watching Sally's movements, and he glanced at my face a few times.

"Jack," I said, "Why don't you trust Sally?"

"I trust that she will not disobey her alpha," Jack replied in a serious tone, "But I must watch her to be certain. I have left you alone too often recently, and this is the second time you have been injured in such a way. I cannot let it happen again."

Sally finished her task and sat back, but I noticed that her movements were slow and deliberate. She moved like a wary prey animal, watching out for attack from the predator. It was impossible to explain, because I was watching two people who looked like humans, but who were displaying very animal-like qualities. She very slowly removed her gloves, picked up the discarded bandages and her medical bag, and moved towards the door. Jack stepped aside to let her through, and when she left the room I shivered as a cold sensation swept down my spine. Shaking my head, I straightened my clothes, slid off the bed, and walked stiffly out of the room and back downstairs. Jack stopped me in the doorway, gripping my arms, and I gasped at his forcefulness.

"I will protect you, Jessica," he said seriously, staring into my eyes, "Emily Rose may return at any moment, and we must be prepared. I cannot lose you to her. I love you."

43

My heart lurched at his words, and I swallowed nervously. His energy wrapped around us, like a cloud that was both hot and cold. I shivered and felt the electricity sparking through my body, tingling at my fingertips once again. My tiger awoke as the magick called to her. I saw her in my mind's eye. She lifted her head, yawned, stretched, and looked straight at me, her bright, clear eyes filled with intelligence and cunning.

"*You are better now,*" she said silently, "*It is time for my payment.*"

I closed my eyes, breathing slowly and deeply to calm my nerves.

"*What payment?*" I replied in the same way, "*Surely you need no payment for saving my life.*"

I heard her laughter inside my head, and it was strangely human.

"*You are such a simple creature,*" she said cheerfully, "*I may have saved your life, but everything comes at a cost. Do not worry; I ask of nothing too difficult.*"

"Jessica," Jack said, and his voice sounded far away, "Jessica, come back to me."

"*Ignore the vampire,*" Suri said with a snarl, "*It is not him that I am interested in.*"

"*What do you want?*" I asked, but I already knew her answer, and the fear was coursing through my body.

Suri laughed. The human sounds were eerie when I knew where they came from. They seemed to echo through my skeleton, causing me to shudder as though I were cold.

"*I want his brother,*" she said simply, "*I need another beast to play with, and since there are precious few tigers in your world, the wolf will have to suffice.*"

I shook my head, and Jack gripped my arms more tightly.

"Jessica," he said loudly, "Jessica, speak to me."

"I am fine," I murmured, but I kept my eyes closed. The tiger had my full attention.

"Jack?" Danny said from somewhere behind me, "What is wrong?"

Suri turned her head, as if she too heard his voice. She roared and stood upright, and I knew what was coming.

"*Please Suri,*" I begged, "*Please just let me heal first.*"

But she wouldn't wait. She leaped, and my body went rigid, and then relaxed in Jack's arms. Breathing out slowly, I opened my eyes. Jack was staring at me, his own eyes glowing silver in his agitated state. He was of no interest to me. I did not want the dead, cold body of the vampire. I turned slowly, but he wouldn't release me.

"Jessica," he said, turning my chin towards him, "What happened?"

I smiled, feeling dreamy and disjointed. I was in a strange kind of dream world, not quite anchored in reality.

"Nothing happened Jack," I said softly, "Release me. It is not your mistress."

Danny moved slowly round to stand beside Jack. His eyes were also glowing, but they were amber, and his wolf was present in every tense muscle of his body. When he spoke, his voice was deeper, almost a growl, and I shivered with delight in response to it.

"She speaks the truth, brother," he said, "This is not the vampire. This is the tiger."

Suri used my body to step forward, reaching my hand up to touch Danny's face. I stroked his cheek and he went still beneath my fingers. He wanted to attack, but he would not injure me. I felt his confusion, and my smile widened.

"Relax, wolf," I said, "I do not mean you harm. You intrigue me. It has been many years since I encountered one of your kind."

"Jessica," Danny said firmly, "Jessica, push her away. Send her back to the forest. She cannot control you like this."

I heard his words but they meant nothing to me. I was in control of my body, but Suri was whispering to me that we could play and have some fun. A part of me wanted to listen to her, wanted to believe her words. We would play with the wolf. He would give us what we needed. I rocked forward on my toes, putting my face right in front of Danny's, and then I brushed my lips against his. He stiffened at my touch, desperate to respond but terrified of what possessed me. My kiss became more insistent, and as he slowly began to return the caress, I came to my senses. Suddenly, I woke up kissing my boyfriend's brother. I gasped and jumped back, hands to my mouth.

"Oh shit," I whispered, staring at Danny, "What did I do?"

He stared at me with those strange, amber eyes, and then he blinked and stepped back. I looked at Jack, who was staring at me with a mixture of horror and confusion on his face. Shaking my head, I stepped back, and half turned to see Simon and Sally staring at me from their position at the top of the stairs. Both were serious and I could feel their unease.

"The tiger," Jack said quietly, "She wants Danny. She wants his power, and his energy. She misses the contact of other beasts. And you are to be her vessel."

"No," I said, "No. I can't handle this! I need some air."

And I bolted. I ran down the stairs, shoved on a pair of trainers that had been discarded near the back door, and I ran out of the house. I didn't stop until I was on the promenade, and I turned round, expecting to see Jack or Danny, or both, following me. They weren't, and I was relieved. I needed to be away from them for a while. I needed to think. But first, I needed to see Liz, and I hoped that she would speak to me.

44

I had calmed down a little after the short walk to Liz and Rob's house. Breathing in the fresh sea air, and feeling the sun on my skin made me feel slightly more human. My stomach was also hurting a little, but I actually welcomed the pain. At least that was something I could make sense of. And it was only temporary. I wondered where Lillian was in all of this. She answered almost like an echo in my head, telling me she was here but was helpless to intervene. Apparently this was another part of my life lesson in being a witch. I laughed out loud as I walked, amused at the totally insane turn of events I was experiencing. An elderly couple glanced sharply at me as they hurried past. I simply smiled and ignored them. They were of no importance to me.

Suri paced around the forest somewhere deep in my psyche. She was pleased with her efforts, and in no hurry to continue. Now she had found a way to manipulate me, she would play again later, when she felt like it. I only hoped that before that time I could speak to Crystal and find a way to subdue the tiger. Crystal had already explained that witches did not control their animal familiars, but worked with them. I had to reach an understanding with Suri, find a middle ground where we could live together and both be happy. I had no idea where to start with that one. But I might at least be able to save my human friendship.

Turning into the quiet, suburban street, I approached Liz and Rob's house. Theirs was a quaint little cottage with a surprising amount of space behind its old red brick walls. The house suited them perfectly, being a mixture of period charm and contemporary order. Rob answered the door. His face was pale and tired, and I could see the stress clearly in his features. Amy was crying from somewhere in the house, and I sensed immediately that this place was full of anger and confusion. I could almost hear the echo of an argument that had been raging all night between the new parents. My guilt deepened, and I

Love Kills

choked back tears of self-pity. I smiled weakly at Rob, and then stepped into the hallway as he made way for me.

"How is she?" I asked.

He shook his head, and I saw moisture in his eyes. I tried to ignore it. I did not know how to handle a crying man. I could barely even deal with an emotional woman. Rob blinked away his tears, removing his glasses and wiping them methodically on the hem of his t-shirt. After a pause he answered in a strained voice.

"She is angry, Jessica," he said, "She came home terrified and confused, and I had to tell her the truth. Now she won't speak to me."

I nodded.

"Where is she?" I asked, "This is my mess, and I need to clear it up."

He gestured to the stairs.

"She's upstairs, packing," he said, "She says she needs a break."

My heart skipped a beat, and I walked slowly up the stairs, stumbling a little as my wounds stung. I resisted the urge to clutch my stomach, knowing that it would only aggravate Liz more. I was healing, and I was determined to be strong. Steeling myself to be strong and face the music, I cautiously opened the bedroom door. Amy was lying in her wicker crib, her tiny face red and her eyes screwed tight shut as she screamed. Her fists waved in the air, and her little legs kicked furiously. She was obviously aware of her mother's mood. Liz was shoving clothes into a suitcase, her hair dishevelled, her face red and puffy from crying. She glanced at me as I entered the room, but she didn't speak. I watched her for a moment as she flew around the small space, pulling things out of cupboards and drawers, fetching toiletries from the en suite bathroom. It had been several years since I had since Liz in such a state, and that had been after a rough break up with an ex boyfriend. Now I actually felt fear as I sensed the pain and anger that emanated from her. My guilt increased tenfold when I thought about what this was doing to the baby.

Liz," I said tentatively, but she ignored me. I tried again. "Elizabeth!" I said loudly, "Please stop. We need to talk."

Liz hesitated and looked at me, sniffing as she fought her tears.

"I have nothing to say to you, Jessica," she said, "Rob told me the truth. He lied to me. You lied to me. I will not be made a fool of."

"Please Liz," I begged, "Please, just listen to me."

She stopped packing and stared at me.

"Why?" she asked bitterly, "What are you going to say? You are sorry for keeping such a huge secret from me? Or that you didn't know how to explain the truth about your 'accident' and what your boyfriend really is." She spat the words out in a stinging torrent, and my heart sank.

I shook my head, grimacing and putting a hand to my stomach as I felt the wound stinging again. I held my other hand rigid because it too was hurting, though not as badly. Liz saw my pain, and her eyes flicked down momentarily. I watched her take a few deep breaths while she considered her response to my predicament. She was determined to be strong and not give sympathy however, and I didn't want her to. I didn't deserve it.

"I only found out just before my attack," I said quietly, "And then I didn't know how to tell you. Would you have believed me Liz, really?" I implored.

She shrugged, squashed her clothes fiercely into her suitcase, and flipped the lid over; zipping it so ferociously I was surprised the zip didn't burst.

"You could have tried," she said angrily, "I know that you aren't crazy, Jessica. I would at least have listened. It all makes sense now. Jack and Danny were always weird, and I knew there was something different about them. And that pub! The staff are so strange. I'm just amazed that nobody else has discovered their secret."

Liz swung the suitcase off the bed and plonked it on the floor near the door with a thud. She carefully avoided any close contact with me, and I instinctively moved out of her way as she approached. She then grabbed a bag and began shovelling baby clothes and paraphernalia into it. Her movements were angry and forceful, and I watched silently as I thought of a reply.

"Why did you come round last night, Liz?" I asked, "And what exactly did you see?"

She stopped, looked at me, and then sank onto the bed, deflated. All of a sudden her energy had dissipated. Her emotions had clearly exhausted her. I slowly moved over and sat on the opposite side. Amy was calming down, and Rob cautiously stepped into the room, gathered his baby daughter up into his arms, and retreated, shushing the baby as he went. I watched them go, and then turned my attention back to Liz. She swallowed, thinking about my questions. We both listened to Rob as he walked slowly down the stairs, singing quietly to Amy. She seemed to respond, and I heard a huge sigh escape from her tiny body as she relaxed in her father's arms.

"I wanted a word about the shop," Liz said after a minute, "Rob said he would watch Amy, and I thought maybe I could try an hour away from her. She was asleep, it seemed the perfect opportunity."

I nodded and waited for her to continue.

"When I got to the garden gate," Liz said, "I saw the door open, and something felt wrong. So I crept up the path, and then I saw…"

Her words trailed off and her eyes watered as she remembered the events. I waited quietly. Liz looked up at me, and the tears ran down her cheeks.

"I saw that woman standing in front of you," she said, "Then I saw the knife in your hand, and you…" she hiccupped, "you stabbed her."

Her voice broke and she cried. Huge, heartfelt sobs wracked her body and I was completely helpless. I wanted so much to take her in my arms and comfort her as I used to. But I couldn't. Liz was afraid of me, and I could feel it. She still cared, but she wasn't sure she knew me anymore. Indeed, I wasn't even sure I knew myself.

"I had to kill her Liz," I said softly, "She would have killed me otherwise. That was my first time, and I feel horrible. I can't describe it."

"But she did injure you," Liz said, wiping her cheeks with the back of her hand, "I saw you fall to the floor, covered in blood."

She looked at my stomach, and then my face.

"And Jack," she said, "He… you…" she couldn't bring herself to say the words.

I nodded.

"Jack gave me his vampire blood to save my life," I said gently, "And you saw the exchange."

Liz nodded. She shifted and stood up again, and I mirrored her actions.

"I can't handle this," she said, shaking her head, holding her hands out defensively, "Not with a new baby and everything. My hormones are crazy; I still hurt from the birth. I need a break."

"You don't have to deal with this, Liz," I said, "Please, just focus on Amy and yourself. The rest can wait."

"You know that's a lie Jessica," she replied, staring straight at me, "I'm going to stay with my parents. I don't know how I feel about Rob at the moment. He betrayed me, and I need some space. I'm taking Amy with me. You can manage the shop."

I nodded and backed away to the door. I couldn't argue with Liz. She would deal with the revelations in her own way, and all I could do was let her go.

"Alright," I said, "Phone me if you want to talk. I am sorry, Liz."

I walked slowly downstairs, and into the living room where Rob was sitting on the sofa, cradling Amy in his arms. His head was bent low over her face, and I felt his pain and torment. He couldn't bear the thought of being parted from his new baby and his wife, but now it was happening because he had kept the secrets about his friends. There was nothing I could say or do to help.

"I'm going, Rob," I said quietly. "You know where I am if you need anything."

He raised his head to look at me.

"Thanks Jessica," he said, "I brought this on myself. I have to make it better with Liz. You deal with the vampire problem."

Nodding, I took a deep breath.

"I will," I said grimly, "We will sort this out once and for all."

45

I walked slowly out of the house, down the driveway, and onto the quiet suburban street. The houses scattered around were silent, their occupants either still in bed, or more likely enjoying a family daytrip while it was the weekend. I felt a pang of longing to be part of one of those families, just an ordinary mother and wife, with everyday issues to deal with. That would never be my life now. Jack was never going to be a normal husband, if indeed he even wanted to marry me. Our family would always be closely entwined with Danny and the werewolves. My shoulders heaved as I let out a huge, heavy sigh which rumbled from my stomach and out through my lips. The bright, late summer sunshine seemed totally at odds with my black, depressive mood. At least the air was chilly today, although it was more refreshing than oppressive, and that irritated me. It was if the elements themselves were taunting me.

Sighing again, so heavily that my body shuddered, I walked listlessly down the street. As I aimlessly wandered back in the direction of home, I was hit with another shooting pain at the wound in my stomach. Doubling over with the force of it, I gasped, trying not to cry out, hoping desperately that I didn't attract attention. Squeezing my eyes shut tight, I gritted my teeth and tried to breathe through the pain. It would subside if I just let it go. I was aware of a shadow approaching, and I cautiously opened my eyes, squinting in the bright light. A huge, black vehicle slowed to a stop at the kerbside, and I turned my head and recognized Jack's car. Smiling with relief, I tried to stand up straight and move towards it. Jack was there to hold me, carefully assisting me as I scrambled awkwardly into the passenger seat, gasping with pains that seemed to have erupted from nowhere. Grimly, Jack fastened my seatbelt, and then appeared in the driver's seat beside me. I leaned my head back against the cool leather upholstery as he pulled off and drove back in the direction of my home.

"How did you know I was there?" I asked weakly, rolling my head to the side so I could see him.

"I phoned the house and Robert answered." Jack replied.

"Oh," was all I could manage in response.

When Jack parked up in his usual space behind my car, I unclipped my seatbelt and made a feeble attempt to open the door. My body simply refused to function. All of my limbs were like lead weights, and I had a fleeting memory of being drugged up in the Intensive Care Unit shortly after my werewolf attack from Seamus Tully. This was worse, because I didn't know why I felt this way. I most certainly did not want a return visit to the hospital. Grimacing and tensing my body, I forced myself to slide clumsily out of the car. Jack was in front of me, as I stood uncertainly on the pavement, reluctant to let go of the car door in case I fell. He tried to pick me up but I protested.

"Jack, no," I said, "Someone might see us."

I looked around, focusing on the terraced houses across the road. They were the sort where the inhabitants might be watching me from a window, and might decide to call the police, or even an ambulance. I did not want to draw their attention right now. Jack followed my gaze, narrowed his eyes, and then relaxed slightly.

"I see what you mean," he said, "You have some very observant neighbours. At least let me hold your hand, that shouldn't raise their suspicions."

I agreed, and moved my hand from the car door, to Jack's open palm. He shut the door and clicked the button on his key fob to lock the car. We made a slow, painful walk through my garden gate and up the narrow pathway made of concrete paving slabs. At least it was smooth so I didn't stumble. I panicked when I remembered I hadn't picked up my keys, but the back door opened, and I saw Danny staring at me grimly. I smiled with relief.

"Oh, phew," I stammered, "I thought we were locked out."

"No," Danny replied, glancing at Jack, "I waited for your return."

He gave his brother a meaningful look, but I was in too much pain to take any notice. It was just another problem that could wait until later. Along with the tiger issue, my angry best friend, oh and the vengeful vampire that seemed bent on my destruction. Once we stepped inside the kitchen, I didn't complain when Jack picked me up and carried me upstairs. He laid me carefully on my bed, slipped off my shoes, and pulled the duvet over my now shivering body.

"You are in shock," he said quietly, checking my pulse with cool fingers, "It has been delayed because of your adrenaline rush. Sleep now, and allow your body to rest. I will wait here and keep you safe."

My eyes fluttered as I fought to keep them open just a moment longer.

"Where's Danny?" I said faintly, struggling to form words.

"I am here, Jessica," Danny said, and I could vaguely see him standing in the doorway, "I will stay with Jack until you wake."

"Good." I murmured.

The blackness swallowed me, and I fell into a welcome sleep, my body finally relaxing. I had no dreams, and I never even woke for food. My body was exhausted, beaten and defeated. I didn't even have the energy to dream or visit my mother on the beach, and Suri could not break through the haze of oblivion that I wrapped around me. She retreated back into her icy forest.

46

The shop was filled with fresh, floral scents. Staring at Marcus' bouquet I felt only sadness and pain reflected in the beautiful blooms. I had no idea what the flowers were, apart from the pink and white roses I recognized. There were some lovely purple flowers that looked a little like tulips, though I couldn't be certain, and lots of other green, red and yellow sprays. I had ended up splitting the bouquet because I didn't have a vase large enough. I now had one vase on the shop counter and two in my kitchen. I would take one upstairs to the living room later. Miraculously, they had survived the weekend after I had forgotten about them.

Despite everything, the flowers began to cheer me up. My body was in pain and my mind was in turmoil, but now I was at work and everything was supposed to be normal again. Ignoring the pains in my stomach and neck, and my aching head, I swallowed some paracetemol with my coffee and admired my gift as I worked on the computer.

I was roused from my paperwork duties by the ringing of the shop phone. Picking it up, I answered automatically.

"Good morning, Redcliffe Books, Jessica speaking." I chimed in my best professional voice.

There was a moment of silence, and then a familiar voice spoke hesitantly.

"Hi, Jessica," Liz said in a shaking tone.

My heart leaped, thudding in my chest, and I fought the surge of emotion that ran through me. Sitting bolt upright, my grip tightened on the phone receiver.

"Liz," I said, trying to sound normal, "How are you? How is Amy?"

"I'm ok Jess," Liz replied slowly, "I need to speak to you."

"Why?" I asked, "What's up?" That was the stupidest question I had ever asked, "I mean, I, oh dammit, Liz, I don't know what to say!" I finished in exasperation.

Liz laughed weakly, and I smiled with relief.

"There isn't much you can say, Jess," she said, "I am still angry with you, but I'm in shock more than anything. And then I started worrying."

"Worrying about what?" I asked, "You are not in danger, I promise you that."

"Not me, silly," Liz said, and her voice was warmer, "I'm worried about you. There is obviously something big going on with you, Jack and Danny, and I was hoping you might share with me, you know, to lighten the load."

It was my turn for silence. Tears streamed down my cheeks, and I couldn't speak round the lump in my throat. Gasping a couple of times, I tried to form a sentence. Eventually I managed it.

"Thanks, Liz," I said shakily, "I do need to speak to you, but only when you come home. There is too much for one phone conversation."

"I guessed as much," she replied. She took a deep breath, "Well, I will come home at the weekend. Rob is breaking his heart being away from Amy, and I can't be so cruel to him. No matter what he did to me, he deserves to be with his daughter."

I nodded, and remembered that Liz couldn't see me.

"He was only protecting you, Liz," I said, "You know that."

"Yes I do," she replied, "But it still hurts. Anyway, I'll be home at the weekend, and we can talk then. But we are still friends, and you won't lose me over this."

The relief that flooded through me was intense. I hadn't acknowledged the pain I had been feeling about my betrayal to Liz. Now it engulfed me, and the tears ran hot down my cheeks. Luckily the shop remained empty and I was glad. Liz ended our conversation on a light note, telling me about Amy and her doting grandparents. I felt reassured, full of hope, and strangely happy when we said goodbye and I put the phone down. I sat staring into space for several minutes, just being thankful for my best friend and her support. Eventually the jangling of the shop bell roused me, signalling the entrance of some much needed customers. I greeted them cheerfully, and even made a couple of extra sales through my own enthusiasm for their interests. The day was looking up. I would survive my problems. Life goes on.